WHIM TO KILL

Dell Shannon *Whim to Kill*

1971 William Morrow and Company, Inc.
New York

WHIM TO KILL

. . . For I have seen violence and strife
in the city. Day and night they go about
it upon the walls thereof; mischief also
and sorrow are in the midst of it.
Wickedness is in the midst thereof; deceit
and guile depart not from her streets.

———Psalm 55:9–11

I

MENDOZA was reading the autopsy report on the latest unidentified body when Hackett came back from the first call of the
day. It was Wednesday, so Landers was off. Palliser and
Grace were out on something, and both had inquests to attend
later; Higgins was typing a report on yesterday's suicide, and
Piggott and Glasser were out wandering around looking for
possible X's, culled from Records, on the robbery-homicide
of last week. At least the weather was nice, as usual in South-
ern California in April.

"So what's the new one look like?" asked Mendoza as
Hackett came in. The unidentified corpse wasn't anything
interesting: an elderly drifter, probably, dead of a coronary.

Hackett settled his bulk in the chair beside the desk. "At the
Biltmore Hotel," he said. "One of the guests registered there.
Albert Spaulding, home town Pittsburgh, presumably on a
business trip. In the forties somewhere. Some sort of executive
with an oil company, the hotel people think. Anyway,
money. Looks like. I left the lab men poking around the
room. But there's a funny twist to it, Luis—"

"¡Dios me libre!" said Mendoza.

Hackett grinned. "Yeah, come to think we've had our share
lately." He got out a cigarette and lit it thoughtfully. Central
Homicide, L.A.P.D., so seldom did get the exotic or mysterious cases; but just lately they had had a little spate of cases

9

that were—surprising. Not, when unraveled, very complex or even queer, but just surprising. There'd been that witchcraft thing last month, and the girl in the green lace evening gown, and that Holly business—other things.

"So what's the twist?"

"Well, it looks as if he was just knocked over the head with the usual blunt instrument, for what he had. Interns say somewhere around eleven to midnight. He'd left a call for eight o'clock, and when he didn't answer, one of the clerks went up and found him. The hotel people say he had three expensive suitcases with, probably, a lot of expensive clothes, and they're gone. No watch or billfold or jewelry around. But the funny thing is that by all the signs X hung around afterward to take a shower and shave, before he got away with the loot. There's blood on Spaulding's electric razor—"

"*Extraño*," agreed Mendoza. "Funny you can say. Door forced?"

"Nope. I suppose he could have said he was Western Union, or the hotel was on fire, or something. Room on one side unoccupied, and the couple in the one on the other side didn't get back to the hotel until after two, they were at a party. And the man in the room across the hall wears a hearing aid—"

"And takes it off when he goes to bed. We do get them," said Mendoza.

"But on the plus side," said Hackett, "X obligingly left his clothes for us. After showering and shaving he put on some of Spaulding's nice expensive clothes. And the ones he left—pants, jacket, tan shirt, cotton shorts—just might be regulation Army issue."

"Oh, really," said Mendoza. "But what idiots they will be, Art, *¿cómo no?*"

Hackett stubbed out his cigarette. "I'd better get out an initial report on it." Mendoza came out to the anteroom with him just as Higgins appeared at the door of the sergeants' office. Sergeant Lake was on the phone; he swiveled around and said, "Got it. Sit on it—somebody'll be there. New body, Lieutenant. In an alley off Figueroa. There's a black-and-white there now."

"Always something," said Mendoza. "So you can come help look at it, George." He went back for his hat. "And you'd better get onto the Army, Art—if that's so, it could turn up X overnight."

"Will do," said Hackett.

The new body, at first glance, looked like posing a few small mysteries. The alley was in the middle of a business block on Figueroa; the black-and-white squad car sitting at the entrance to mark it, and a badly shaken middle-aged man was still talking compulsively to the uniformed men.

"—Couldn't believe my eyes—a *corpse*, right there at the back door! A dead woman! I couldn't believe my—see, I always come in the back way because the parking lot's in back, for store personnel that is, and I—"

"Mr. Shotwell," said one of the patrolmen, "these are detectives from Homicide. If you'd—"

"Oh, my goodness," said Shotwell. "Homicide. I just couldn't— What? Oh, well, you see, I'm the bookkeeper here —at Pattons'. Pattons' Books and Stationers. I usually get here shortly after nine—we open at nine-thirty—actually I'm alone here this week except for Milly, Mr. Patton's on a trip —oh, my goodness, here *comes* Milly, she oughtn't to see this terrible—"

A plump young dark woman was walking up the alley, just dropping a bunch of keys into her purse. At Mendoza's nod the uniformed men went to intercept her.

"Any use to ask the lab to look around?" said Mendoza.

"Six of one, half dozen of another." Higgins shrugged his massive shoulders. Shotwell retreated to join the group up the alley, to tell Milly all about it.

The body was sprawled across the single shallow step from the rough blacktop of the alley up to the rear door of the bookstore. These old buildings along here were shabby, and the alley had collected a good deal of refuse of this and that sort. The body was that of a slight young woman, and in life she had been a good-looker. Dark hair in a short gamin cut, pert features: a triangular kitten face, big dark eyes. And a very good figure indeed, which was immediately apparent because she hadn't a stitch of clothes on. And at first glance there were no marks on the body of any sort. Nothing to say how she had died, no blood, not even—pending a closer look —any surgical scars or birthmarks.

"*¡Qué lindo!*" said Mendoza under his breath. "She can't have been more than twenty-five, George. A looker, wasn't she? It must be a sign of age, me going sentimental over a corpse, but—" Suddenly he squatted down and carefully moved the corpse's left arm a little. The hand had been hanging down palm up, fingers crooked; he turned it over. "So. A wedding ring," he said interestedly, and reached for the other hand. On that was a larger ring, a big cocktail ring, gold, but only costume jewelry, he thought.

"Here's the ambulance," said Higgins. "You want the whole works according to the rules?"

"I think so," said Mendoza slowly, and Higgins went up to the patrol car to call up the lab truck. "Don't move her," said Mendoza, "but can you give us a rough idea of when?"

One of the interns squatted over the body and uttered an absent wolf-whistle. "Say, this one was really something. Poor damn girl. Damn shame. Doesn't seem to be a mark on her, I can't see she was choked or—" He felt the body, lifted it slightly. "No *rigor* yet, but that doesn't say much—it can vary. From the temperature I'd say very roughly between eight and eleven hours."

"Between ten last night and one this morning," said Mendoza. He lit a cigarette and went on staring thoughtfully at the body.

"And it does happen, young people can have heart attacks," offered the other intern.

"But so seldom when they're stark naked in an alley in downtown L.A.," said Mendoza. Higgins came back and said a lab truck was on the way. He and Mendoza started to search the alley in opposite directions, but nothing showed that might connect with the body—no purse, clothes, anything.

The lab truck arrived and Scarne got out of it and began to take photographs. "You know, George," said Mendoza, "I have a small hunch that this is going to be one of those tough ones."

"And let's hope you're wrong," said Higgins. "After the spate of funny ones we've been getting, I wouldn't complain about some nice plain routine. Did I tell you we've definitely decided on the names? Steve and Laura—those kids, my God, they came up with some wild ones, but we sort of put the collective foot down, you know—" He laughed. Higgins the confirmed bachelor had been pleased and happy enough with his secondhand family, Bert Dwyer's two kids, and he was still feeling a little incredulous that he and Mary would have a firsthand family in October. "Margaret Emily for my mother, or David George. Mary said—"

"Yes," said Mendoza absently. He wondered if those clothes left in the unfortunate Spaulding's hotel room were G.I. issue. A long step further on if they were.

"Can we take her?"

"Take her." Nothing in the alley that was immediately connected to the body. But she looked like a young woman who'd be missed, and reported. If she were living with her husband, and the wedding ring made that probable, he'd miss her right away: maybe already had.

"So suppose we go ask Carey," said Higgins, having arrived

13

at the same conclusion. They walked back to the street, got into Mendoza's long black Ferrari, drove back to headquarters and went up to Missing Persons.

Lieutenant Carey listened to a description of the body and said, "That might ring a bell all right," and rummaged in his current files. "This just got called down from Wilcox Street about an hour ago. A Mrs. Jean Everett, twenty-three, five-one, a hundred and five, dark hair, brown eyes. Address on Berendo in Hollywood. She didn't come home from work yesterday—husband's been out hunting for her all over, asking friends and so on. He called Wilcox Street first thing this morning."

"What's the address? We'd better check it. Maybe I had a dud hunch after all," said Mendoza.

Higgins drove up to Hollywood and found John Everett at the Berendo Street address, a rather handsome young man now wearing a ravaged look. "Jean's *dead*?" he said wildly. "Oh, my God, you're telling me Jean's—but, my God, how could—"

"Take it easy, Mr. Everett. We don't know that this is your wife at all. That's what we want to find out."

"It can't be. It just can't be, I don't see how—but where *is* she, for God's sake? I don't— What? Yes, yes, I understand that, I'll—" He sat beside Higgins in numb silence all the way downtown.

At the morgue, when the attendant slid out the tray, Everett visibly braced himself. He stared at the corpse for twenty seconds and let out a long breath. "Thank God, no, that's not Jean. It's not Jean. Oh, thank God. But—"

"Easy, Mr. Everett," said Higgins. "We have to be sure. *Are* you sure? Naturally you don't want it to be your wife, but by the description—"

Everett straightened. "Of course I'm sure," he said in a steadier voice. "Yes, this—this woman's the same general type as Jean, but you see, Jean—Jean had to have a Caesarean when the baby—And there's no scar on this woman at all. Is there?"

There certainly wasn't.

"But where *is* she? I just can't—"

That wasn't Homicide's business. Higgins sent him home in a patrol car and went back to the office to tell Mendoza it was no dice. They were still going over it for any possible ideas—of course the autopsy would give them something—when Palliser came in from the Fox inquest.

"Short and sweet," he said. "Open verdict. If you ask me, we ought to throw it in Pending now. We'll never get anywhere on it." Isabel Fox, last Wednesday night, had stayed to do some overtime work at her boss's office; she was a legal secretary. She was found next morning, raped and choked to death, beside her car in the building's parking lot. There were absolutely no leads on it; any known rapist from Records might have done it—and there were a lot of those, in a place the size of L.A.—or it might have been somebody's first time round. Being a professional typist, Miss Fox had kept her nails short and there weren't even any scrapings to be had there.

"Well, we have to look as if we're trying, John," said Mendoza.

Palliser said resignedly he knew that, and how long did Mendoza estimate it might take to find and question every rapist out of Records. "And what good would it do? There was nothing to tie anybody in at all." Moodily he went off to write a follow-up report.

Hackett looked in and said, "We'd better go through the motions at the Biltmore. The lab says definitely those clothes are G.I. issue, and they picked up some good latents. Maybe a couple of X's, if we're lucky. I've asked the Army if it has any current AWOLs in this area. Place to start, anyway. Like to come back me up, George?"

"Sure," said Higgins. He stood up, he and Hackett together

suddenly dwarfing Mendoza's office. As they went out, Hackett was asking how Mary was and Higgins telling him about the names; Mendoza grinned after him. The older they were, the harder they fell, all right; and he just hoped Bert Dwyer's widow appreciated George.

Jason Grace came in five minutes later, and he was chuckling to himself. "Joke?" asked Mendoza.

"Oh, my," said Grace. His narrow moustache was as dapper as Mendoza's, his charcoal suit as neat, his dark tie as discreet; the smile widened on his chocolate-brown face. "Join the force and see life, all right. I had to go over to the facility on Alameda to see that Richter again—I think he knows something about the heist shooting, but he's making like the Tar Baby—and just as I came out, up comes a clutch of boys in blue with six nuts. I tell you. They'd had to radio in for blankets—"

"Blankets?"

"I am telling you," said Grace. "Assorted sexes, three of each. They climbed out of a car and started wandering around MacArthur Park naked as jaybirds. They're preaching some new religion, instant utopia—"

"Naked as jaybirds," said Mendoza. "What's that got to do—"

"Oh, the general idea, I gathered, is that clothes represent hypocrisy," said Grace. Mendoza burst out laughing. "There is a kind of point there, I guess. But when not everybody's got a perfect figure—"

"Oh, that reminds me," said Mendoza. "We've got a new one. Another funny one, I think, Jase."

"With a perfect figure?" asked Grace amusedly.

"*¡Seguramente que sí!*" said Mendoza. "Or in the vernacular, wow. And that was absolutely the sole thing there. No clothes, purse, birthmarks, nothing. And I have a small hunch—"

Sergeant Lake came in with a teletype. "New A.P.B. from

Oregon. Sounds like bad medicine—I hope they're not heading for our neck of the woods."

"*¿Qué ocurre?*" Mendoza took the teletype. As he read it, his eyebrows climbed. "*Conforme*, Jimmy. As if we hadn't enough to cope with as it is." The teletype was an all-points bulletin from the warden of the state prison directed to ten western states. It detailed the records, descriptions, and known habits of three unsavory characters who had made a trio for some time and had currently just got loose from the pen, over the wall. Rodney Trasker, six feet, one hundred eighty, thirty-two, dark hair and eyes, assorted tattoos: in for manslaughter; an experienced heist man with a long pedigree from age thirteen; this was his second term for manslaughter. Roger Starr, five-ten, a hundred and sixty, thirty-three, sandy, blue eyes, scar on forehead from knife fight: in for murder second; also a longtime heist man, but had other records of bodily assault, rape, mugging; serving his third count on a felony. Donald Killeen, six-two, two hundred, thirty-one, dark hair, blue eyes: in for murder first; he'd beaten his wife to death during an argument. He had served time for heist jobs and one count of manslaughter. Starr and Trasker had been doing time for the same job, a heist with the clerk shot. None of the three were users but had been known to deal in dope picked up on jobs; all three were hard drinkers and unpredictable in liquor. It was not known whether they'd had outside help on breaking out; it was presumed they had picked up a car, but no make on that. Starr and Trasker hailed originally from L.A., Killeen from San Diego. It was considered probable that they'd stay together. They might be heading south for home territory. All three were to be considered probably armed and dangerous.

"How very nice," said Mendoza, and passed it on to Grace. "I do hope they'll give the big town the go-by and head for San Diego." Piggott looked in the door, his long dark thin face wearing a more morose expression than usual.

"I've picked up one of the possibilities on that heist job. Somebody like to sit in on the questioning?"

"Happy to oblige," said Grace.

At the Biltmore, Mr. Brian Hartnett was saying to Hackett and Higgins, "A soldier? You think a soldier did that—murdered Mr. Spaulding? A G.I.?"

"Well, it's just speculation at the moment, Mr. Hartnett. We're just asking," said Hackett. "Did you notice a soldier at any time in the lobby yesterday?"

Hartnett said apologetically, "Well—I can't see all of the lobby from the desk, of course. I don't recall noticing a soldier, but of course I might not have taken much notice—so many people coming and going, you know— But I can tell you that nobody in uniform checked in. No. But you can ask the bellhops—and in the dining room—"

"Yes, we will," said Higgins.

Hartnett shook his head. "A murder. Here. I can't get over it. And not as if Mr. Spaulding would have had much cash on him, you know. He always carried travelers' checks. What? Oh, yes, he'd stayed here before—he was usually out here at least twice a year. On business, I suppose. He never carried much cash, it was always the travelers' checks, mostly for twenty dollars each."

Which said nothing, of course. These days, with the sea of paper floating around, nobody scrutinized signatures with a magnifying glass. Whoever had Spaulding's travelers' checks might cash quite a few of them without any trouble.

"I wonder," said Hartnett suddenly, "what the family will do about the car. I suppose it could be shipped back—"

"The car?" said Hackett and Higgins simultaneously.

Hartnett looked surprised. "Mr. Spaulding's automobile. He—"

"He was *driving*?" said Hackett.

"Why, yes. He generally did. He told me once that he found cross-country driving very relaxing. The car is, of course, in our underground garage. It—"

"How do we get there?" asked Higgins.

In the cavernous garage, a scrawny young man in a white jump-suit with *Biltmore Hotel* embroidered across the pocket stared at them. "The guy's murdered?" he said. "That guy? In the *hotel*, he's murdered? Well, for gosh sakes! No, I dint hear a word, but I just come on duty—I did some overtime last night to oblige Mike."

"Is the car here?" asked Hackett. "Spaulding's car?"

"I can't get over it. Right in the hotel he's murdered. That guy. Well, I'll be damned," said the attendant suddenly. "Spaulding. That guy. We just don't get too many people with cars, you know. Mostly when we do they're rented wheels, local. People come to town, they gotta have wheels —especially this town. So that's what we get. Mostly. But that guy, it was his own car—"

"Is it *here*?" asked Higgins loudly.

"—Pennsylvania plates, see? So it was his own. I noticed. And he's been here before, last year. Well, I mean, you'd notice it anyways. Would you notice it! See, it's a Rolls. A Rolls-Royce Phantom Five, big four-door baby—dark blue. Not new, but a Rolls, well, I mean, they go on forever, you know? And—"

"Is it still here?" asked Hackett.

"No, it ain't. This young guy picked it up about midnight last night—I was just goin' off duty. Said Mr. Spaulding'd hired him to be a chauffeur. I don't think nothing about it, why should I? He knew who owned it, knew his name O.K., and acourse the keys was in it."

"What did he look like? This young fellow?"

"Oh, well, I dunno as I could say much—I dint look at him to memorize his face, why should I? He was kinda tall and thin—I couldn't say about coloring, well, he was a white man but that's about all I could—"

"It's what we usually get, Arturo," said Mendoza resignedly. "The Army may provide a short-cut." Hackett and Higgins had found him just sitting down at a table at Federico's, along with Palliser. It was just twelve-thirty.

"The muddleheaded citizens," said Hackett. "To think that damn fool never thought to mention Spaulding's car before— No, of course they didn't have a record of the plate-number. But a Rolls Phantom isn't just so common— We can put it on the hot list by make alone. In fact, of course, I did. Just in case. I'll have a Scotch and water and the steak sandwich, Adam."

"Calories," said Palliser, and Hackett growled.

"Ditto for me," said Higgins.

"And you had all better see this," said Mendoza, fishing out the teletype from Oregon.

Hackett was just saying, "What a trio—I hope to God they haven't got a yen for L.A.," when Lieutenant Carey wandered up to the table.

"I see that turned out a dud make on your new corpse."

"Very," said Mendoza. "And I still have the hunch that that's going to be a tough one. Just something—" He shook his head.

"I've got a hunch too," said Carey seriously. He swung a chair around from the next table and sat down alongside Mendoza. "I've got the hell of a hunch that you boys are going to get this handed to you, maybe very shortly, and I think you'd better hear about it from the start. This funny thing—"

"Oh, no," said Mendoza.

"—that happened just after you left my office. The hell of a funny thing," said Carey. His square pugnosed face wore a serious look. "Over on Lafayette Park Place. Quiet neighborhood, older homes—decent neighborhood, you know. This Mrs. Stiffley noticed a little boy from down the block on the street—knows his mother, knows she keeps a strict eye on the kids. Two older kids in school. Normally, the five-year-old wouldn't be that far from home alone. So she went out to talk to him, and what does he tell her? A big man came in and hit Mommy and took her away in a car. Mrs. Stiffley used the common sense and called us. Squad-car called me—well, who else? Technically it's a missing person. I went out and looked. It's funny."

"Mommy gone?" asked Hackett.

"Very much so. By what it looked like, unexpectedly and violently. She'd been ironing in the kitchen—the squad-car boys got there just as the iron burned through the board. There was a struggle of some sort—dishes knocked off the table, basket of clothes upset. The boy says this man walked in the back door and hit Mommy and she fell down and he picked her up and took her out to a car and drove away. What does it look like?" Carey shrugged. "Who does it get passed to? But us? The woman's gone. We contacted the father. One Dave Warthol. The woman's Brenda Warthol, thirty-two, medium height, dark hair, not a very big woman. Warthol is just wild—why don't we *do* something? Well, what can we? Put out her description and wait. But I've got a strong hunch, Mendoza, that if and when she's found, she'll be dead—raped or not."

"Neighbors close around in that area," said Hackett. "Nobody but the boy saw or heard anything?"

"Nary a thing. It's a single house. Single houses either side. One of 'em is for rent, the other occupied by a couple who both work."

"Awkward," said Mendoza. "I have a small hunch that your hunch is valid, Carey. But sufficient is the evil unto the day—at the moment we have quite enough to think about."

"I just thought I'd warn you," said Carey, standing up.

"Thanks so much. Did the boy tell you anything about the strange man's car?"

Carey grinned. "He did indeed. He told us it was painted bright purple."

"*¡Santa María!*" said Mendoza.

2

THEY WENT back to the routine the rest of the day; but at the back of the mind of every man who'd seen that teletype, the thought of that unholy threesome stayed. They had all been cops awhile; they were aware that of the whole list of pro criminals, always the most dangerous is the armed bandit. The pro burglars, con artists, kiteflyers, bunco men, always tended to be shy and wary of violence: the ones like Trasker, Starr and Killeen were the worst medicine there was. They just hoped Trasker, Starr and Killeen had taken a notion to visit Denver or Dallas, Cheyenne or Chicago, instead of L.A.

The teletype hadn't gone out, of course, until Oregon was pretty sure they'd got out of the state. They'd gone over the wall last Sunday night; the alarm wouldn't have been delayed, and all the routine things would have been done: the road-blocks set up, the helicopters out, the look at known associates if any, the search-parties out in rural areas. When all that didn't turn up a smell, the A.P.B. was sent out. Trasker, Starr and Killeen had been loose for nearly three full days. That said for almost sure that they'd had some outside help; and by now they could have pulled off a few new heists for travel money. Anybody's guess what they were driving, but that was practically certain too: a car they'd have.

Mendoza went home at six-thirty, to Rayo Grande Avenue in Hollywood, and found Mrs. MacTaggart peacefully busy over dinner in the kitchen, and redhaired Alison reading *Just-So Stories* to the twins in the nursery. Their recently acquired shaggy dog Cedric sat by apparently listening raptly, with a cat curled on either side: Sheba and Bast. Nefertite was on Alison's lap, and of El Señor there was no sign. Mendoza suffered the twins' usual boisterous and bilingual welcome and kissed Alison.

"Tough day, *hermoso*?"

"So-so," said Mendoza, taking off his jacket. "A couple of new funny ones."

"Daddy read *el cuento*," said Terry insistently, her brown eyes melting.

"Read about *el elefante pequeño!*" said Johnny excitedly.

"Really, you know, we'll have to do something about it, Luis," said Alison worriedly. "They'll be ready for school before we can turn around, and they haven't the slightest notion about any difference between English and Spanish—"

"*Mamacíta* mad?" Terry turned her wide brown gaze on Alison. "Mama *cailin deas*," she added coaxingly, and both her parents burst out laughing.

"Or the occasional Gaelic they pick up from Máiri," said Mendoza. "I admit there is a language problem, but whose fault is it?" He stripped off his tie.

"Ultimately, my father's," admitted Alison, "taking all those engineering jobs in Mexico so I picked up Spanish before English. But honestly, Luis, we'll have to take a solemn oath to use English only for the next year, or something, to get them straightened out."

Mendoza massaged the back of his neck absently. "I think, with all these hunches floating around—and that precious trio on the loose—I need a drink before dinner. *Pues sí*, Terry, I'll come back and read about *el elefante pequeño*—"

"No *elefante*," said Terry. "*El Leopardo*, how his spots come!"

"*Really*, Luis," said Alison, "if you'd just pay attention to what you're saying—"

Mendoza went out to the kitchen and poured himself a jigger of rye, and their alcoholic cat El Señor appeared magically on the counter-top loudly demanding his half-ounce. Mendoza poured it for him. "That cat," said Mrs. Mac-Taggart.

At least, reflected Mendoza, that damned mockingbird that had adopted them last month had apparently finished nesting and departed.

Hackett went home to his Angel busy over various pots and pans on the stove, to nearly-four-year-old Mark imitating a jet bomber in the living room, and his darling Sheila, tottering toward him a bit less drunkenly at sixteen months now.

"Tough day, darling?"

"So-so," said Hackett. "Still the funny ones coming along. And maybe—fingers crossed not—some real bad medicine."

"Oh?"

"Never mind. Don't borrow trouble. As Luis says, 'To morrow is also a day.'"

Higgins went home, to the house on Silver Lake Boulevard, and asked Mary how she felt. Even after this while, he didn't quite believe Mary was his, that he had a family. Her gray eyes smiled at him. "Well, it's not my first attempt, George. I'm fine. Don't fuss. Tough day?"

"The usual." He patted Brucie the Scottie and went to find the kids—Stevie and Laura busy over homework in the living room. The brace off Steve's leg now, and he'd be fine, the doctors said; it had been a long siege since the hit-run accident.

It being Wednesday night, Matt Piggott the earnest Free Methodist went to choir practise. He was still wondering if it was too soon to ask that nice girl Prudence Russell to marry him.

John Palliser, turning up the drive of the forty-thousand-dollar house on Hillside Avenue, thought rather glumly about the payments. He didn't really approve of Roberta going back to teaching again, even for a year; but they hadn't figured on starting a family for a year or so anyway, and there was all the furniture and appliances they'd had to buy. No trouble about the loan; the bank took city employees as good risks. Out of their minds, he thought, a cop nowadays. . . . And that trio of armed bandits—well, hope they were headed somewhere else, that was all.

Thursday was Higgins' day off. Hackett got in early and found a teletype from Army Intelligence awaiting him. Currently AWOL in or from the L.A. area, three men, all buck privates: Jesse Knapp, Roman Coppola, John Patterson. Fingerprints on the way. He called the lab and got Duke.

"You get anything useful in that hotel room?"

"Your guess is as good as mine," said Duke. "It's a class hotel, the rooms get cleaned, but not all that polished to get rid of every latent print everybody ever left there. We picked up quite a lot of those, and a good many belonged to the corpse, of course. Others, no. It's early to say about anything else. Somebody had a drink of Scotch and water out of the bathroom glass—Spaulding had his own bottle there maybe—and we got some good latents off that, not Spaulding's."

That looked promising. "I'll have some possible prints for you to compare eventually," said Hackett. He told Lake that if those photostats came from the Army while he was out, to shoot them up to the lab.

Jesse Knapp had a family living in La Crescenta in the valley. It was just worth a trip out there to ask if they'd heard from him. Hackett got up with a sigh.

Mendoza was late to the office. Palliser and Grace had gone out on a new call, and he was just about to call Dr. Bainbridge to ask if there was anything new on that girl in the alley yesterday when Lake rang him and said, "Captain Fletcher." Mendoza picked up the inside phone.

"So what can I do for Traffic?"

"All these V.I.P.'s," said Fletcher. "Complaints I'm getting. Police harassment. Why, Luis? You putting out the call to check all these Rolls-Royces. Naturally nobody driving a Rolls is just an ordinary citizen. We've had complaints from the vice-president of Magna-World Films, a retired official of Standard Oil, the latest female star, and the new international tennis champ. Why, Luis?"

Mendoza laughed. "It's a hot car tied into a murder and we don't have the plate-number, just the make. Sorry, *amigo*. They all looked kosher, those the traffic detail's checked?"

"I would guess. They're trained men. But the V.I.P.'s always such a nuisance, Luis. They annoy me. All right, I see how it is, but it's just another damn nuisance." Fletcher sighed.

"*Paciencia*," said Mendoza amusedly and put the phone down. Almost at once the outside line buzzed at him and he picked it up. "Mendoza."

"Carey," said a terse voice. "I did say I had the hunch. She's turned up. Brenda Warthol. Dead."

"When and how? Identified?"

"Oh, yes. It got handed around a little. Some P. and R. men found her up past the entrance to the Hollywood Bowl, about an hour ago. They called Wilcox Street. It dawned on them that she answered the description, after they'd chased a crew up there, so they called me. I got hold of Warthol and he's just made the identification—it's her all right. So, the crime having got started in your territory, it's all yours. We thought we'd better leave everything as is, you'll want the lab treatment on it. There's a car sitting on it and I'm just taking the husband home."

"*Gracias*," said Mendoza. "There's not another soul in the office at the—*¡media vuelta!* I take it back," as Palliser and Grace came into the anteroom. "All right, I'm on it. I'll want to see you—and the husband—and the boy."

"Naturally," said Carey. "Have fun."

"—never *saw* such a thing," Palliser was saying. "My God. And it wasn't as if his throat was cut or—I can't figure it." He turned to Mendoza. "This new one—"

"Later, later. Carey's hunch has come true. You want to toss a coin to see who comes with me?"

"I expect the doctors'll tell us something," said Grace, "eventually." He grimaced. "I have seen enough gore for one day, I'll write the report." He turned into the sergeants' office.

"Jimmy, call the lab and shoot a truck up to meet me at the entrance to the Hollywood Bowl." Mendoza got his hat and took Palliser's arm. "You can tell me about the new one on the way."

"Well, gore you can say," said Palliser as they started for the elevator. "My God. This empty house over on Carondelet. It's just been sold, just got through escrow. This William Grubb bought it. He invests in low-rental property, he's a carpenter, handy man, fixes the places up himself. So this morning, the house now being his clear, he goes there to start some repairs and painting and so on. And in the living room is a body and all this blood. Looked like gallons of it, I swear. Body been there some time, probably—Grubb hadn't been there for about ten days and it could be that long. And we couldn't see that the man had any serious injury—couple of stab wounds in one arm, one shoulder. But—"

"Any I.D. on him?"

"Sure. Empty billfold. He was a Robert Ardlow, had a Sears credit card, Social Security, belonged to the Moose—

address on Grand View. Damn it, if you hadn't sidetracked me I ought to have contacted Carey—he must have been missed, there were snapshots of a family in the billfold—"

"Sometimes they come at us a little hot and heavy," said Mendoza. "Jase has been a cop awhile too, John."

"Another funny thing," said Palliser gloomily. "The interns couldn't make it out either. Where are we going and why?"— as they got into the Ferrari.

Mendoza told him.

When the Ferrari turned up into the entrance to the Hollywood Bowl off Cahuenga, two uniformed men lounging beside a squad-car hailed them. Mendoza leaned out the window. "Passing the buck to Central," he said amiably. "And I'll bet you're not half as busy as we are."

"That I wouldn't know, sir," said one of them. "They keep the uniform branch busy enough. I understand this one got started down in your territory. She's up the hill there—we'll show you."

"Lead on."

"You can only drive another hundred yards or so." Beyond that, of course, were all the modern improvements instituted at the Bowl in the past years. Where once music-lovers had toiled on foot up the steep canyon sides left more or less in a natural state, there was now a paved and graded mall, with gradated ramps and steps and even an elevator. But the planners had left as much greenery and trees as possible at both sides of the great natural amphitheatre. There were several young pepper trees, low undergrowth, along the left side of the steps leading up to the rows of benches, and the body was lying under one of those, not far up the hillside.

The mobile lab had pulled up just behind the Ferrari; the men climbed the little slope in silence, and in silence for a moment looked at the body.

Brenda Warthol, if you discounted the dried blood and bruises and disarranged clothing, had probably looked very much like any other middle-class wife and mother occupied with the daily housework, meals, laundry, and bringing up kids on a somewhat inadequate income. She'd been middling nice-looking: a round fair-complexioned face, dark hair rumpled and untidy now: a goodish figure, a trifle plump: blue eyes. Her pink lipstick was all smeared now. She'd been wearing an ordinary pink cotton housedress, and it was pulled up in a tangle above her waist, and her white nylon panties and garter-belt had been ripped off and lay a few feet away with her nylon stockings. Her toenails were manicured and painted pink.

"I do get a little tired," said Mendoza. "The mixture as before. Anybody take any bets?"

"Raped," said Palliser. "Either strangled or beaten. The autopsy will say. But—why here? From—where did Carey say? —Lafayette Park Place?"

"Why indeed. The men who found her?" Mendoza looked at the patrolmen.

"Sergeant Barth told them to stick around for you." Three green-uniformed men a little way down the hill, watching the detectives interestedly. "The Bowl's not open yet, you know. The Parks and Recreation men won't be here every day, but they come a couple of times a week, I guess, landscaping or whatever. Those three came this morning, spotted her right off."

"But," said Mendoza, "no gates or whatever to keep anybody out down there. No." Absently he brushed his moustache the wrong way, brushed it back. "Why, John? Well, Lafayette Park Place. Middle of downtown. Crowded. No decent privacy to commit the rape. With the woman knocked unconscious, he could drive up Temple and get on the Hollywood Freeway in five minutes. Call it another twenty in the fast lane up to the turnoff at Highland and another five to— right here. It wouldn't have taken him much longer to get up into Griffith Park. And it wouldn't have taken him half the time, of course, to get up into Elysian Park right downtown."

"Just like—" Palliser stopped.

"Yes," said Mendoza. Just like that child-killer they'd had a while ago, who had left them in Elysian Park.

"It's a funny place to think of all the same," said Palliser. "Because—"

"Oh, yes," said Mendoza. "Yes, it was done right here." Funny you could say. The woman attacked and knocked unconscious in her own kitchen down there, but brought here for the rape-kill. Intentional kill? That was anybody's guess; so often the rapist didn't intend homicide but was just a little too violent. By the amount of blood around the body, the scuffle-marks in the dirt and low undergrowth, she'd regained consciousness and fought him. Probably done some screaming. To no avail, the silent empty hills around—and all that rush of incessant noisy traffic on the freeway down there. "Well— we have to work it as we can." He looked to see who had turned up from the lab: Scarne and Fisher. "O.K., boys, take some pictures and poke around, see what shows."

"What do you think?" asked Palliser. "Why here?"

"I'd say offhand," said Mendoza, eyeing the P. and R. men waiting silently, "somebody who works for, or once worked for, Parks and Recreation. But anybody like that—wouldn't he think of Elysian first? That much nearer?"

"So?"

"So, who works at the Hollywood Bowl besides P. and R. men?"

"Oh, don't be silly," said Palliser. "All those V.I.P.'s on the board—ticket-sellers—what else?—agents, I suppose—"

"Ushers," said Mendoza. "Hired off the street, I think. But on the other hand, John, anybody in the county would know the Bowl isn't open and won't be for some time—nobody apt to be around up here. Anybody of the millions who've ever been here would know there aren't any fences or gates to shut the public out."

"Which is also a thought," said Palliser, watching the lab men.

"What, has *he* turned up?" Carey sounded surprised. "Where? I'd really put that one down to either suicide or—well, who was it who said that most men live lives of quiet desperation?"

"Emerson," said Grace. "No, Thoreau. Ardlow? You've got him listed?"

"As of last Wednesday. I mean, a week ago this morning."

"Make up your mind," said Grace. "He might have been dead that long."

"Oh? Well, it got reported a week ago today. By the wife and family. They were just struggling along on the pittance he made as a salesman at a men's store—third-class place on Grand. Three kids, twelve down to seven. The place stays open three nights a week, including Wednesday—he should have got home about nine-thirty and didn't. When nothing showed on him—accident or whatever—I was inclined to think he'd just got fed up with the daily grind and walked out. With or without the other female. He's dead?"

"But very. In an empty house on Carondelet," said Grace. "Mysteriously dead. With empty billfold."

"Well, I'll be damned," said Carey. "He couldn't have had much more than ten bucks on him, if that."

"I suppose we'd better let the family know. Get the formal identification."

"Oh, that poor damn woman," said Carey. "A nice woman —I was sorry for her. Doing her best—and the kids seemed like good kids. I'll be damned. What the hell happened to him?"

"We'll hope to find out," said Grace seriously.

Mendoza and Palliser landed back at headquarters just as Hackett came in. Palliser went off to write the initial report on Brenda Warthol, and Hackett brought Mendoza up to date on the Army info.

"I went up to LaCrescenta to see Knapp's family—mother, father, two brothers. They look kosher. Parents pretty upset about his going over the hill. They swear they haven't seen or heard from him and I'll buy that. Have those photostats come from the Army—the prints?"

"I sent 'em up to the lab," said Lake.

Hackett said, "Fine," and followed Mendoza into his office. "What've you got new?"

"What else but Carey's hunch?" Mendoza started to tell him about that, lighting a cigarette with a flick of the gold desk-lighter, and passed on his immediate conclusions.

"Yes, but that gives us nothing to follow up," said Hackett. "All I see on that, Luis—well, why Brenda Warthol? The ordinary housewife. Not specially beautiful or—or exotic, or anything. Little back street. If he picked her, why did he? Or did he pick her? Did he just take a chance on finding some female available to attack and carry off? Nine out of ten women would be alone, at home, or just with the pre-school kids, at that hour in the morning. Was it just at random, was she just unlucky? That could be, I suppose. But if he picked her—"

"Mmh, yes. If he did. Former resident of the neighborhood, who knew her, had a yen for her? A very slim chance, but it could be. We can ask if any other woman around there was bothered, that day or any time— Yes. The strange man came in and hit Mommy and took her away, and *Dios*, what to get out of a five-year-old? But we have to try. I'll see Warthol— it's possible X had approached her before and she'd said something." Mendoza brushed his moustache back and forth, and the inside phone rang. He picked it up. "Mendoza."

"Sometimes," said Duke, "we scientific fellows make it easy for you. On this Spaulding. The X who left the G.I. issue clothes."

33

"What've you got?"

"Your office sent up some photostats of prints—Army records. One set matches some nice latents we got in the hotel room—off the drinking glass and the bureau."

"*Bueno*. How nice. And who is X?"

"One Roman Coppola. By the Army records, a native of Newark, New Jersey. AWOL a couple of weeks. I suppose they gave you a description."

"Well, that's a step further on," said Hackett pleasedly, on hearing that. "But damn it, he might be anywhere by now. In that damn Rolls Phantom. Hell and damnation!" he added suddenly, "call myself a *detective*—Jimmy, get me a long-distance line! Damn it, I called the Pittsburgh chief to break the news to the widow, but that was before that idiot Hartnett told us about the car—somebody back there'll know the plate-number, damn—"

"Which will relieve Captain Fletcher," said Mendoza, lighting a new cigarette. And Art Hackett was a reasonably shrewd detective, but they couldn't always think of everything at once. . . . Yes, just how and why had Brenda Warthol ended up at, of all places, the Hollywood Bowl? Without volition Mendoza opened the top drawer of the desk and took out the pack of cards and began to shuffle it. His surrender to the domesticities had ruined his poker game but he still thought better with the cards in his hands. . . . Methodically he stacked the deck to deal himself a royal flush, contemplated it meditatively, and laid it down and stood up. "I'll be down in Carey's office," he told Lake. "Where's Jase?"

"Well, he went down there awhile back, but he's probably gone to lunch now. Lunch!" said Sergeant Lake bitterly. "Cottage cheese and rye krisp!" After a number of years on the inside desk, he was reduced to counting calories, and eyed Mendoza, who never had to think about such crass matters, bitterly. Mendoza grinned at him.

"I'll check back. If he comes in tell him to stay put—I want him. Our sweet-talker." Which was, in a way, a funny thing too: Grace and his Virginia so anxious to start a family, and no luck yet, but Grace the soft-talker, always so good at questioning the kids, when that had to be done. Higgins good with kids, fond of his secondhand family: Hackett with the kids of his own: and Mendoza, if very belatedly, acquiring the hostages to fortune. But of all of them, Mendoza would like to hear what Jason Grace might get out of the five-year-old who had seen Mommy taken away by the strange man.

He took up his hat: make an appointment to see Dave Warthol, then lunch. But Lake was beckoning him to the phone. "Bainbridge."

"Yes, doctor. What've you got?"

"Well, this body," said Bainbridge. "This girl you sent up yesterday. Wow. She was a beauty, wasn't she?"

"We noticed it," said Mendoza. "You've done the—"

"No, damn it, I'm just getting to her. You're always in such a damn hurry," said Bainbridge. "But I just noticed this, and I thought you'd like to hear—it might say something to you. Somebody tried to wash the body. There's quite a lot of grease on it, here and there, and somebody tried to wash it off."

"Grease?" said Mendoza. "Grease?"

Dave Warthol had worked off the most of his grief and outrage and naked shock. Things like this just didn't happen to the ordinary good citizen—the honest man who earned his living at an honest job and supported his family the best way he could and tried to raise his kids right. Only sometimes it did. He worked for Sears Roebuck, at the big warehouse downtown; he had told Mendoza and Grace what his salary was, how Brenda had been so smart at the budgeting and all, and so good about going without things for herself. Pretty strict with the kids she was, he said dully, and he went along with that. His sister had come to help with the kids: Alec, twelve, Ruth, eight, the baby Douglas, five. Only just turned five: he wasn't in kindergarten yet.

"Why did it have to be Brenda?" asked Warthol. They couldn't tell him. He'd told them he couldn't think of anybody who'd ever—well, made the unwelcome advances to her; there'd never been anything like that. Anybody around the neighborhood like that. She'd never said, about any such thing happening. The sister confirmed that. They'd been a close family, she'd been a good friend of Brenda's, and if anything like that had happened, Brenda'd have told.

And Grace was talking to the boy, gentle and easy. The five-year-old Douglas looked like an average bright boy of that age; he was answering Grace readily, a sandy-haired freckled little boy, blue eyes wide on Grace's regular-featured milk-chocolate face.

"Was he a colored man like me, Douglas?"

"Nope. He weren't. He—he—he hit Mommy with his fist and I—and I—was scared and I ran—and then—Mommy hit him and he let her go but then he hit her again and he yelled and I was scared and he picked Mommy up and took her out to his car—"

"Where was his car, Douglas?"

"I tole the other man. Inna driveway. Right by the garage. It almost hit the garage door. And then he drove away with Mommy—I tole the other man, it was a funny car, a purple car—"

"Douglas, you like to color pictures? In coloring books?" The boy nodded seriously. The five-year-old not really taking it in, understanding the import of all this. Realizing what had happened to Mommy. "Do you have some crayons? You like to show them to me?"

Warthol's sister said listlessly, "He knows his colors pretty well, he's not color blind or anything."

The boy came back with a cardboard box of crayons. "You just show me," said Grace, "what color the man's car was."

"It was *this* color," said the boy emphatically, handing Grace a crayon. "Only it was awful shiny."

And Grace said, looking at it later as they sat in the Ferrari, "Can we take it as gospel? He sounds sure."

"Average bright boy. He seems to have color sense. And damn it," said Mendoza, "what else have we got? And what do we do with it?"

3

I⊤ was the only thing they had at all, unless and until the lab and autopsy reports turned up something else. They had to use it as they could. It was then getting on for three o'clock; Mendoza used the telephone in the Ferrari to call the office, fetch some more hands down to Lafayette Park Place. Piggott and Glasser came down, and they all started ringing doorbells, asking if anybody else on that block had noticed the bright purple car. It was, of course, a block of working people: most of the men would be away all day, some of the women.

Mendoza got the first confirmation, from a Mrs. Hale in the corner house on the opposite side of the street. She had seen a car that color on her way to the market yesterday. Yes, she was sure it was yesterday, she always did her main marketing Wednesdays. Well, it had just been there—parked in the street. On this side of the street. She couldn't hardly help noticing the color, it was so loud. She couldn't say if there was anybody in it then. She'd thought it probably belonged to a kid, they went in for the loud colors. That was about eleven-thirty, on her way to the market, and it had been gone when she came back. She couldn't say what brand it was, she didn't know anything about cars.

They got just one more confirmation, from a fourteen-year-old girl four doors down from the Warthol house; she was home with the 'flu, had been sitting up on the couch in the living room reading, sitting by the window, and she'd happened to look up and see a car like that come by, she'd thought it was her mother coming home from the store. A purple car, yes. "What they call, like, iridescent paint, you know?" That had been sometime between eleven-thirty and noon. Which tied in with the approximate time Mrs. Stiffley had noticed Douglas Warthol.

It was something; a funny something. "¡Por vida!" said Mendoza. "Now if it had been a fourteen-year-old boy, we'd know the make and model and year, damn it. As it is—" As it was, all the girl could say, vaguely, was that it had been a sedan of some kind, not very big, whether two or four door, and "kind of old, I guess." Which might mean almost anything.

"Well, you know what we do with it," said Mendoza when they shut down the neighborhood legwork. "And the good God knows I disapprove heartily of all the damn meddling the bureaucrats do now, I'm not advocating any more, but I will say it would sometimes make the job easier if—let it go, let it go." They went back to headquarters and he called Captain Fletcher. The meddling bureaucrats of the D.M.V. only meddled so far, up to now. The registration form for any vehicle in the state bore its plate-number, its make and model and year, and the owner's name and address: not a word as to what color the vehicle was painted. "I'm sorry, you see how it is," he said to Fletcher. "It's the first and last lead we've got. The lab may turn up something else tomorrow, but meanwhile—"

"Um, yes," said Fletcher.

"We could hardly take just the boy's word, but two other people noticed the purple car along that block at about the right time. It is a lead."

"Sure," said Fletcher. "At least it's not another Rolls Phantom with a V.I.P. inside. You know, Luis, the teen-age kids do go for those far-out colors. A lot of times, an amateur paint job."

"*Así*. And—"

"And I get a faint hint that it might be an oldie. Did you?"

"*Tal vez*. Maybe. And anyway, Hackett got the plate-number on that Rolls for you."

"So he did. I put it out to eight states," said Fletcher, "seeing it's a homicide. I tell you what, Luis. Just playing it by ear—I'm not a smart homicide dick, but being a cop at all, people I know something about. This guy's got no idea you've got any leads on him at all, I suppose. Even the color of his car. Do you think he's a real nut? Knows what he's doing?"

"You are asking me if I'm a mind-reader? To explain a rapist? I don't know. Rapists come all sorts. There's not much M.O. on this, though I will say it's the first time I've ever come across one just like it—woman taken away from her own home. What's in your mind?"

"Something simple. The night shift's about to be briefed. The point is, this joker probably hasn't run—he'll still be around. In his purple car, maybe. So all right. We start it countywide, to begin with, tell all units to keep an eye out for purple cars. Of any make and model. If they've got time, stop 'em and say they're making a random check on brakes, or registration, or drivers' licenses. We do that sometimes, you know. Get the owner's name, the plate-number. Even if they're on a call, haven't time to stop, get the plate number. O.K.? It'll turn up some names for you anyway."

"Well, it's the only way to use the lead. Thanks very much. It's a damned haphazard way of investigating," said Mendoza, annoyed. "But what else can we do?" He was still annoyed when he passed that on to Hackett.

"The trouble with you is," said Hackett, "that you've got too damned orderly a mind, Luis. I don't know how Alison puts up with you. Same as your grandmother used to say, you'd get up off your deathbed to straighten a picture crooked on the wall."

Mendoza admitted it. There were men in the Homicide office who said he counted the hairs in his moustache every morning and trimmed the sides to come out even. And that inborn quality, of course, was one of the things that made Luis Rodolfo Vicente Mendoza a very smart detective. But however necessary, sloppy and random investigative methods irritated him, and the amorphous lead of the purple car irritated him a good deal. He went home and blew off steam to Alison about it.

Grace and Palliser had got deflected off the Ardlow thing by the rape case. On Friday morning they got back on it. There hadn't been an autopsy yet—Dr. Bainbridge was short-handed and in L.A. the bodies did tend to pile up, it being mandatory to perform autopsies on all unidentified or violently dead ones. Palliser and Grace had broken the news yesterday to Mrs. Ardlow that her husband's body had been found, that he was dead. Apparently in the course of robbery. She had broken down. Her sister had been there; they had got the name and address of Ardlow's brother, William, in Redondo Beach; and there it had been left.

On Friday morning, with Hackett off, Grace went down to Redondo Beach to fetch the brother back to make the formal identification, having set up the appointment by phone; and Palliser went to see Mrs. Marian Ardlow at the Grand View Avenue address. A run-down shabby street, old houses, brown lawns.

She looked at Palliser with dull eyes, a shabby, respectable, not very attractive woman in her late thirties: thin, brown hair sprinkled with gray, unfashionable glasses. The children would be at school. Her sister was still there, an older woman with a bad-tempered mouth, dyed black hair. "It just don't seem fair," said Marian Ardlow. "Bob tried so hard. He just never was a money-maker, but he tried. He always supported us, but it's hard—everything so high, and he only went to eighth grade, you know. But he was a good man—a good father. I don't know why this had to happen. He never did anybody any harm."

"Well, we're trying to find out just what did happen, Mrs. Ardlow. The people at the store where he worked say he left at the usual time, a week ago Wednesday night. Started home about five past nine. I understand he took the bus?"

She nodded. "Along Wilshire. He'd get off at Alvarado and walk down to Sixth and on home."

Palliser considered. Sixth was pretty much a main drag, as was Alvarado. Ardlow would have had only one long block to walk down Sixth to the little dark pocket that Grand View would be after dark. If a mugger on foot had jumped him along any dark street, he'd strip him and leave him there. But if the attacker had a car, or say there'd been two attackers— just jumping anybody at random for what was on them?— it'd have been safer, of course, to drag him into a car, take him somewhere handy to strip him.

"The other man said," said the sister, "you thought he was robbed. That that's why whoever it was—that's silly, he wouldn't have had but a few dollars on him."

"Well, sometimes that doesn't make any difference to these characters," said Palliser, still thinking. Carondelet was only a couple of blocks away. Characters from the general neighborhood knowing that house was empty? A handy private place. But—

"I don't know why they had to *kill* him," said Mrs. Ardlow dully. "Just for five or six bucks." She wiped her eyes. "You —nobody told me how he—he did get killed. Did they shoot him, or—"

"No," said Palliser. "Well, we don't quite know yet." He saw again that gory room, the really astonishing extent of the

dark bloodstains, long dried. "There'll be a report in soon."
They were staring at him.

"You don't *know*?" said the sister sharply. "Well, I should
think even the dumb cops—"

"He had a couple of superficial cuts," said Palliser, "but it
didn't—"

Mrs. Ardlow uttered a faint moan and sank back on the
couch. "S-stabbed?" she said. "A knife? Oh, but—he had to
be so careful, you know—about that—I never asked him to
do anything where he might—the doctors told him a long
time back, told his mother, him just a baby—he was always so
careful, had to be! Why, the time he had to have that wisdom
tooth out, he was in the hospital a week and they give him I
don't know how many transfusions—"

Palliser stared at her. "What are you talking about, Mrs.
Ardlow? What do you mean?"

"He was what they call a—a bleeder. Hemo—some long
name. I don't know. Every time he got just a little cut, even a
nosebleed, anything—it wouldn't stop. It didn't—you know
—get thick, and stop. He had to be awful careful."

"My God," said Palliser softly. "My God." A hemophiliac.
They were rare, but not so rare as all that. The poor devil
Ardlow, a bleeder. The casual mugger jumping him, no intent
to kill, and—as he'd pieced it together just now—carting him
off the main drag all in a hurry to that handy empty house, to
strip him. Threatening him with the knife—cutting him just a
little with the knife. And making off, X or a couple of X's,
with no idea that they'd sealed his death-warrant. Ardlow,
minus the life-saving coagulant in his blood, dying slowly
there as his life pumped out onto the floor.

"I will be damned," said Palliser to himself.

"I will be damned," said tubby little Dr. Bainbridge. Grace
had been so interested in what Ardlow's brother had told him,
on the way up from Redondo Beach, that when the formal

identification had been made he interrupted Bainbridge in the midst of an autopsy and passed on the news to him. Bainbridge was squatting over Ardlow's body in its cold tray interestedly. "I will be damned. A bleeder. They do come along here and there. We don't really know the hell of a lot about it yet."

"The brother has it too, he said. Has to be careful."

"Um," said Bainbridge. "That much we do know. Like color-blindness. Funny. Very damn funny."

"Color-blindness?"

"It skips the females," said Bainbridge. "They pass it on, but they're not affected. Just us poor damn males. Look at that." He touched the wounds on the body: a very naked-looking, gray, thin body. "Superficial as all hell. Little cut on the shoulder—two little nicks on the arm. You or me or most people, wear a bandage a couple of days and it wouldn't even leave a scar. But this poor devil, once he started to bleed he couldn't stop. Blood won't coagulate, you see. Just his luck the mugger picked him."

And, thought Grace, that he wasn't left on the street where he'd have been spotted and helped. And another little surprise. . . . If they ever, by chance, caught up with the knife-wielder, it was going to be a big surprise to him too.

Before Mendoza looked at the report left by Schenke and Galeano overnight, Lake handed him another teletype. This one was from Sacramento. In the terse officialese it followed up the A.P.B. on Trasker, Starr and Killeen. Mendoza swore, reading it.

They had got loose last Sunday night. On Tuesday night there had been a heist pulled at a liquor store in Sacramento. One clerk sustained a skull-fracture from a pistol-whipping, the other was shot in the leg. The first clerk was still out, but the other one had now positively identified a mug-shot of Trasker and said there had been three men on the job. So they were probably still together, and had headed that far south at least. Estimated amount of loot from that job, about seven centuries.

"*¡Mil rayos!*" said Mendoza to himself. He had quite enough to think about without a threesome like that in his territory. Tuesday night. They could be here now. He put the teletype down. They ought to get an autopsy report on that girl sometime today; and it was very odd that she hadn't, apparently, yet been missed. Reported missing. She'd looked like somebody who'd be missed at once. . . . He was just about to ask Lake where everybody was—he was supposed to keep tabs on what was going on—when the inside phone rang and he picked it up. "Mendoza."

"It's not at all a common color for a car," said Fletcher. "And every car, whatever color, in the county is not out of its garage twenty-four hours a day, after all."

"I'll concede that. Have you got anything?"

"Three names. Just overnight, I don't think that's at all bad, Luis. All three cars stopped and checked. According to reports, none of the drivers alarmed or nervous at being stopped, just surprised. The first one got spotted in Boyle Heights. Driver's license all in order. Richard Pope, age twenty-one, white, six-one, one-eighty, brown and blue, plate-number JHL590. A 1957 Chevy, amateur paint job. The second one was spotted down in Venice. Girl driving, a Della Boyd, but the car's registered to her brother, Michael Boyd. Her license all kosher. Plate-number FGT444. A 1950 Rambler sedan. You getting this?"

"I'm getting it. For overnight, I'll agree, good. And?"

"Third spotted out in Van Nuys. Edward Goeltz, twenty-nine, six-three, two hundred, white, black and brown, plate-number TJO234. A 1963 T-bird, two-door. License O.K."

"Oh," said Mendoza. "Well, thanks very much. It's a start, at least. Very sloppy way of going at it, but we've got no choice. We'll get on this."

"Happy to cooperate," said Fletcher.

Mendoza went out to the anteroom to see who was in, if anybody. Tom Landers was typing a report and Piggott and Glasser just coming in. Mendoza passed on the information. Landers said gloomily he supposed the report could wait over. "Just another suicide. Damn depressing—the old pensioner with no family, tired of it all." He felt his shoulder, standing up. "A damn weather prophet you can call me, since I got shot up. We're due for more rain. I suppose we go look at these people harder? It'd be the fluke of the century if X was one of these."

"Do I need telling?" said Mendoza. "But we have to start somewhere. I think of these three, the fellow with the T-bird is almost certainly clear—that's a distinctive enough car, damn the year or model, that nearly anybody'd recognize it. But take a look at him anyway."

"Sure," said Landers.

Piggott said they were never going to get anywhere on that heist job of last week. Just no leads. Not a word on it out of any of the pigeons, either.

"Well, keep at it today anyway," said Mendoza. "Depending what turns up tomorrow, maybe throw it in Pending then."

Glasser said, "Oh, hell." Piggott was not a swearing man, but his expression echoed that.

"Where's George, by the way?"

"He went out on—" The switchboard buzzed and Lake plugged in a line. "Central Homicide, Sergeant Lake. . . . He was just asking about you. What's up? Sure." He lifted a finger at Mendoza, handed over the phone.

"George?"

"Luis, I think you'd better come look at this." Higgins sounded harassed. "I tell you, I am fed up to here with all the funny ones. I don't like this."

"Where are you?"

"I'm in Echo Park," said Higgins. "By the Oriental bridge. I mean, I'm calling from the hamburger stand, but that's where—I don't know but what we'd better check the hotel first, but anyway I want you to see this."

"I'm on the way. Not another cut-up corpse?" asked Mendoza, with vivid memories of their last corpse in Echo Park.

"No, no," said Higgins. "It's just—funny."

"I'll be there."

Grace and Palliser landed back at the office together a little after ten, missing Mendoza who'd just taken off for the park. They were comparing interested notes on Ardlow when a new call came in, and they went out on that. "Damn it, we've got to get a follow-up report written on Ardlow some time," said Palliser.

"It'll have to wait—the patrol-car boys say this is a real homicide," said Lake. "Laveta Terrace."

They took Grace's little car—the normally conservative Grace had been smitten with love at first sight of the little blue racing Elva. It was ten-thirty when they pulled up in front of the shabby old four-family apartment house on one of the old narrow streets just up from Echo Park. There was a squad-car ahead of them. They went up steep narrow steps to an open front door: inside the narrow lobby the two uniformed men were listening to a monologue from a stout elderly woman huddled into a man's old gray bathrobe, with dirty terry-cloth mules on bare feet. Her hair was in curlers, a faded blue terry turban partially concealing that.

"Never saw such a terrible thing—just terrible! Poor Mis' Deforrest and Miss Parker—awful it is, I only went up when I see her car was still in the garage, I told you that before—Mis' Deforrest always up and away by eight-thirty, and I thought maybe she's took sick—all this 'flu around—that's why I went up—and when I saw her door open, right away I figure something's wrong because she never—I never thought

about Miss Parker then, why should I—but no sign of Mis'
Deforrest at all, and it wasn't till I come down the back stair
again—I told you that—I seen her door wasn't shut all the
way, and my good Lord, when I— Such nice ladies the both
of 'em, and Mis' Deforrest like a mother to Miss Parker she
was ever since Miss Parker moved here which is nearly five
years back—nine years Mis' Deforrest been here and—"

The taller patrolman stepped away to jerk his head at the
two plainclothesmen. "At the back, sir. The rear left-side
apartment. That's the landlady, Mrs. Lowther. She just found
them."

Palliser and Grace went down the hall and looked, without
touching anything. Two women dead on the floor. They
called in for a mobile lab; on this one they'd want the full
treatment. They sent the uniformed men back on patrol.
They talked, waiting for the lab, and while the lab men were
starting work back there, to Mrs. Lowther.

"Just inseparable they was ever since Miss Parker moved
here and they got acquainted. Just like mother 'n' daughter
they were. They both worked, acourse—Mis' Deforrest at
some laboratory somewhere, and Miss Parker she was a ste-
nographer downtown somewheres. See, about that much difference in age, and Mis' Deforrest bein' all alone, not married,
I guess she just felt like that for Miss Parker." Anne Parker,
Wanda Deforrest, by the nameplates on the apartment doors.
It had not been a very messy kill; they had been able to see this
and that. Wanda Deforrest probably in the forties, a handsome woman rather than pretty, strong regular features, a
hard jaw, black hair streaked with gray. Anne Parker maybe
twenty years younger, a pretty, slight blonde.

And there had been a gun on the floor there, about two feet
from the Deforrest woman's body.

"It's a kind of no man's land, isn't it, Jase?" said Palliser.

"So it is. The head-doctors spouting off reams of stuff
about the fags," said Grace, "but on the female of the species,

no. I don't think anybody can generalize about that. But by what we hear about those two, I might have an educated guess."

"It looked like a .22," said Palliser. "Wouldn't make much noise. These older places are well-built."

"That's a point too," agreed Grace. "Just at first glance, that's what it could be. Lovers' quarrel." He brushed his moustache unconsciously.

"I don't know the hell of a lot about that—well, who does? —the fags, I do know, can work up some hot jealousy. Could be the same with the female of the species. Maybe some other butch laying siege to Parker—"

"Anyway," said Grace, "I think the Lieutenant ought to see this one in person."

"So do I," said Palliser. "I'll call in, see if he's there."

Mendoza was not there. Mendoza was standing just below the Oriental bridge in Echo Park, at the shore of Echo Park Lake, and saying, "What?"

"Damn it," said Higgins, hunching his wide shoulders, "do I remember when we had to drag this damn lake before? All the weeds. Ten to one we'd never get her out. You can see for yourself. We'd better check the hotel."

Mendoza lit a cigarette and squatted over the neat little pile of clothes stacked at the lake's edge. An exquisitely embroidered silk kimono, sky-blue. A pair of black thong sandals. Expensive nylon lingerie: brassiere, white panties, a white slip. On top of the pile a handbag, expensive black crocodile. He opened that; the catch was not fastened. Just two items in it: a receipt from the Hotel Grant in the sum of nine-fifty for a single room, and a cheap I.D. card tucked in a pocket. In precise shaded lettering it was filled out: *Miss Ita-San Lee, 18 Butterfly Road, Kyoto, Japan.*

"Another funny one," said Higgins. "Suicide apparently. In the lake. I suppose it could be she left a note in the hotel room

—we'll look. And when I think of dragging this damn lake again—"

Mendoza straightened up. *"De veras,"* he said absently, stroking his moustache. "Funny—"

"If I hear that word once more— Some poor damned Jap girl," said Higgins, "maybe seduced by a G.I. over there or something—we'd better check the hotel before we start dragging the lake, I suppose."

"You are so damned right," said Mendoza. "This kind of thing annoys me, George. Come on." He started back for the street and the Ferrari, leaving the uniformed men mounting guard over the clothes.

"Annoys you?"

"Like hell," said Mendoza. "We are quite busy enough in the general way." And he said nothing more at all until he'd parked the Ferrari illegally in the red zone outside the front entrance of the Hotel Grant downtown. He marched in and asked the desk-clerk if they had a Miss Ita-San Lee of Kyoto, Japan, registered. They had? He displayed the badge and aroused alarm; he got the clerk to produce a passkey.

"I'll bet she left a note," said Higgins. "They don't figure suicide exactly the way we do, do they, it's kind of tied up to their honor—"

"I would take a bet," said Mendoza, "that she left a note." It was a clean, pleasant, anonymous hotel room. On the bed was one modest suitcase, containing three more silk kimonos, a little underwear, another pair of sandals.

"And there's the note," said Higgins. "Propped up against the Gideon Bible on the desk. My God, that lake. All the weeds. Why she had to pick Echo Park Lake—" He unfolded the single page of hotel stationery. "The poor damned girl. What did I say? American soldier promising to marry her, and—"

"Es hermoso sin duda," said Mendoza. "Oh, beautiful with no buts. I absolve you, George, because smart as you are, I

don't suppose you've ever taken any passionate interest in the opera. This annoys me like hell. Using us—"

"What?" said Higgins. "Opera?"

"Yes, it cost him maybe twenty bucks," said Mendoza. "And he fully expected to see it spread all over the daily press —all the nice publicity—I never did like practical jokes."

"What the hell?" said Higgins. Mendoza swung to the desk-clerk, who had come up with them, twittering excitedly.

"Did the lady register for this room herself?"

"Oh, no, sir—I do remember that. No, it was a gentleman who reserved the room for her—"

"Did you, in fact, ever see the Japanese lady at all?"

"Well, not that I recall, sir, but this is a large hotel, and—"

"And," said Mendoza, "a fairly good hotel, centrally located. You supply the information service for your guests, what theatres are open, what's playing, what night-clubs are featuring, and so on?"

"Why, yes, sir—"

"So you can tell me," said Mendoza gently, "what company is currently about to open with a production of *Madame Butterfly?*"

The desk-clerk gaped at him. "*M-Madame Butterfly?* The opera? Why, yes, sir, I can. The Little Theatre group of Westwood is putting on a production of that beginning next Monday, sir, at the Centre Theatre on—"

"So I think," said Mendoza, "I'd like to talk to their amateur public-relations officer. This annoys me like the very devil. As if we weren't busy enough—"

4

HIGGINS was still feeling like an idiot when he came into Federico's and spotted Palliser and Grace just sitting down. If he hadn't gone to college, he had attended high school when the schools were a good deal more concerned with dispensing education then they seemed to be now, and he had, for God's sake, heard of *Madame Butterfly*. "But I ask you," he said, "why the hell should a fool opera come into my head when I was thinking we'd have to drag that damn lake again? The minute Luis said it, I saw it was just like that fool opera—but I ask you—and I feel like an idiot, falling for—"

"Well, I don't know," said Palliser, "you were thinking like a cop, and all you saw— Yes, I suppose it'd have been good publicity, if we'd all swallowed it and gone to dragging the lake and getting it spread all over the papers."

"Damn practical jokes," said Higgins, swallowing Scotch and water. "Luis' gone to take him down a notch, whoever dreamed it up. I'd like to be there." Palliser laughed. "Come to think, Jase, you've never seen our Luis when he's really riled. In spades."

"How does it take him?" asked Grace interestedly.

"Just the opposite of liquor. He takes more than two drinks at once, he's ready to pick a fight with anybody comes along. When he's really riled, he gets—what's the word I want?— suave," said Higgins. "More and more polished and so deadly damn sarcastic." Grace laughed. "Anyway, that thing's off our minds. Is there anything else new?"

Palliser told him about Deforrest and Parker. "We looked around after the lab was finished. One shot fired out of the gun there—a Hi-Standard .22, so Duke said. One shot in the Parker girl's head. There'd been one hell of a fight, by the looks of that living room. And what the landlady said—what the whole set-up looked like, we just thought there might be a Lesbian angle."

"Could be," agreed Higgins. "Lovers' spat. Where are you going on it?"

"See people who knew them. Feel around," said Grace. "Deforrest worked as a receptionist at a medical lab on Beverly. Parker was a steno at a brokerage house on Spring. First place to start."

"Find any address books there?" asked Higgins.

"Sure. They each had one, why? Whatever happened," said Palliser, "it started in the Parker apartment. Deforrest lived upstairs, Parker in the one just under that. The Deforrest woman's door open, and nothing wrong there—place as neat as sin. And in a way, the apartment sort of bore out that angle. Neat, no knick-knacks standing around—all her clothes the tailored things, suits and shirtmaker dresses. Why address books?"

"The fags," said Higgins, leaning back and lighting a cigarette, "don't bother to cover up so very much. They run openly with the same kind. The girls, no. I doubt very much that if they were that type, anybody where they worked suspected it. If you can locate some closer friends, and they look the same general type, well, it's still only circumstantial evidence."

"Yes, I see that," said Palliser. "Maybe we'd better start with the address books, Jase."

"Start with both," said Grace. "The employers ought to know why they didn't come to work."

"And Luis is still wondering, and so am I," said Higgins, "why the hell that Jane Doe hasn't been missed. Reported missing. She didn't look like just anybody. Did either of you see that follow-up teletype on Trasker and Company?"

"No—what now?"

Higgins passed that on. "Tuesday night. They could be here now."

"God forbid," said Grace seriously.

Trasker, Starr and Killeen were not in L.A. They'd taken the loot from the Sacramento job over to Reno, to the roulette wheels, the poker tables. The games never shut down in Nevada; and they were all ready to live it up a little after a long time in. There were women as well as the tables in Reno: and the one just as expensive as the other.

By early Friday morning the seven C's were gone; Killeen was nursing one hell of a hangover; and Trasker and Starr were feeling surly and cheated. Reno harbored a bunch of damn crooks, they told each other. Let's make tracks.

They had an almost new Pontiac they'd picked up in Sacramento, but they'd had it since Tuesday and it was red hot now. They left it in Sparks, just outside Reno, picking up a two-year-old Caddy in its place. They drove back into California and hit Stockton about two that afternoon, where Trasker and Starr pulled a heist at a liquor store on the outskirts of town; Killeen was still asleep in the back seat. It was a smooth job, no trouble, but all they got was ninety bucks, which was annoying. Trasker at the wheel, they continued to head south. At close on midnight they heisted another liquor store in Bakersfield, but the store-owner pulled a gun, shots were exchanged, and they had to run from a squad-car.

At four that morning they ditched the Caddy in Santa Barbara, in case the fuzz had got the plate-number, and picked up a new Ford Galaxie.

They passed the Los Angeles City Limits sign at nine o'clock on Saturday morning.

"I'm sure," said Mendoza, "you understand me, Mr. Warren. Any unwarranted consumption of our time as public servants is reprehensible. And such—er—childish attempts to deceive the authorities—" his suave half-smile was fixed—"is certainly unwarranted. In short, we just can't have this sort of thing, Mr. Warren." He sat easily in the chair across from the broad mahogany desk, the perennial broad-brimmed black Homburg on his knees, every hair in place, the heavy gold seal ring gleaming as he lifted cigarette to mouth, his hairline moustache neat; and young Mr. Geoffrey Warren at the desk regarded him with the fascinated gaze of rabbit on snake.

Mr. Warren, professionally a very new member of Warren, Cody, Harvey and Billings, Investment Counselors, and extra-curricularly the co-director of the Little Theatre Group of Westwood, was normally a brashly confident young man. He had started out bluffly with Mendoza, regretful that his little brainwave to achieve publicity had been seen through. "But it was a great idea, wasn't it? I thought it was the greatest, and so did all the company—you see, Mr. what-did-you-say—"

"Mendoza. Lieutenant Mendoza," said Mendoza icily.

"Oh, yes. Well, we're really all but professional, we've got some good trained voices, it's no amateur production, and we hope to get our money back anyway, renting a theatre right downtown, and I really did think—a great gag, if the press fell for it—"

Mendoza delivered a precise little lecture to him about the nature of professional police work: protecting the citizenry, and anything that deflected them from that duty was an affront to the taxpayers and a waste of public assets. He never used a one-syllable word where he could find a three-syllable one to substitute; the contemptuous half-smile never changed, and midway through he lit a new cigarette with the solid gold lighter. Mr. Warren began to look younger and younger and less and less brash.

"Practical jokes," said Mendoza, standing up leisurely and dropping his cigarette into the large brass ashtray on the desk, "are always so immature, Mr. Warren. I would have to look up the statute covering this—er—silly little escapade of yours —it is, of course, a misdemeanor, not, unfortunately, a felony —but we are really entirely too much occupied at the moment for me to take the necessary time. However, Mr. Warren— however—" and the smile turned faintly sinister—"I trust that if you are ever inspired to such—mmh—flights of fancy again, you'll curb the impulse."

Warren uttered an indistinct mumble.

"Beverly Hills," said Mendoza, looking around this dignified Beverly Hills office, "Beverly Hills police officers may be accustomed to dealing with such irresponsible idiocies, Mr. Warren, and indulgent. In my territory we have less compunction. Is that clearly understood?"

Warren muttered. He was now reduced to about five years of age; his gaze remained hypnotized on the dapper slender figure in tailored charcoal dacron, the immaculate shirt and Sulka tie and heavy gold cuff-links. Mendoza regarded him amiably from the superior viewpoint of forty-five years, twenty-four of them as a cop on the top force anywhere, and said, "Just keep it in mind, little boy," and went out unhurriedly.

Eso ya es llover sobre mojado, he thought, talk about adding insult to injury. Things like this annoyed him; and he was starving. Unprecedentedly, he stopped at the most expensive restaurant in Beverly Hills and had a martini before lunch.

Landers and Piggott started out on the list of purple cars spotted so far. They had a quick sandwich at a drugstore counter first, and Piggott said again they ought to put that heist-killing in Pending. "It's a pity—the man dead, and only thirty or so, but I figure the Lord has some reason. Well, it stands *to* reason, Tom."

"I suppose so," said Landers.

"Satan going up and down," said Piggott gloomily. "All these women getting killed. The rapists."

"That Fox thing should go in Pending too. I did some work on that with John. We'll never get anything on it. Well, who shall we go see first?" Landers looked at the list.

For pretty sure, the purple T-bird not their baby. But clear him out of the way, if possible. Edward Goeltz, an address in Van Nuys. They took Landers' Corvair.

The address turned out to be an old California bungalow, on a big lot, at the edge of town. The purple T-bird was parked in the drive, and it was a blinding iridescent purple. They rang the doorbell, got no response, and walked down the drive. A man was just coming out of the old one-car garage; he halted in his tracks. "Who the hell are you?"

Landers got out the badge. "Mr. Goeltz? Police. We'd like to ask you a few questions if you don't mind, sir."

"Police? What the hell," said Goeltz blankly. He was a young man, and build like Tarzan. He was naked to the waist, a blue shirt in one hand. "Hey, I got stopped by some cops last night—check my license, they said—what gives? I never been in no cop trouble—why pick on me?" He sounded nervous.

"Just routine, sir," said Landers vaguely. "If—"

"You don't look old enough to be a cop," said Goeltz. "Not in plain clothes anyways." The usual rage filled Landers' heart at this ingenuous comment; he sometimes wished he'd start going bald or something so that people would believe he was over twenty-one. Just his cross to bear.

"Would you mind telling us where you were between eleven A.M. and noon on Wednesday?" he asked evenly.

"What? Why? Wednesday—" Goeltz stared at them. He wasn't bad looking, obviously no genius, but at least average bright. He began to put the shirt on slowly. He said, "Ordinary you wouldn't've found me here. I just come home to get some tools I needed. Wednesday. I got to think. Now where —oh, yeah, I was in Hollywood Wednesday. At Mrs. Gunn's place. Why the hell? Why're cops asking? I never been in no—"

"Actually," said Landers, "to clear you out of the way, Mr. Goeltz. You just showed on the edge of something—"

"Me? On cops' business? You're kidding. I wasn't doing nothing but working." He started to button the shirt.

"At what?"

"I said, at old lady Gunn's place. She lives here but she owns a house there—on Romaine Street. Rents it out. And it needed some things done—leaky faucets fixed and like that. That's what I do, see. I can't keep up with all the business I got, fixing things. Regular plumbers, electricians, they charge like crazy now, people can't afford it. I can fix most anything, paint, do carpenter work, like that. I get kept busy. I was at Mrs. Gunn's place that day, fixing things in the house."

"Could you give us the address?"

"Sure." He did.

"How'd you hurt yourself, Mr. Goeltz?" asked Piggott.

Goeltz looked down at his chest; there was a bandage on it. "Oh, that. Damn fool thing. I got to get a new ladder. Old one give way on me yesterday and I got a nasty cut where I landed on a fence, damn it." His eyes were anxious. "Look, you guys don't think I—did anything? I was just there, working."

"That's all, thanks, Mr. Goeltz," said Landers with a smile. When they got into the Corvair Goeltz was still staring after them. "It'd be about a million to one fluke if the boy we want was in the first three Traffic turned up. I don't think—"

"Oh, neither do I," said Piggott. "But we have to check everything."

Landers agreed; they drove back to Hollywood, found the

address on Romaine, found the neighbor home next door, a vague middle-aged woman who said, oh, yes, she recalled a man working around next door last Wednesday. The house was for rent. So then they drove down to Boyle Heights; and here their joint pessimism received a slight jolt. Richard Pope wasn't at home; they finally found him at a pool-hall on Soto Street, watching a game in progress. He was a big lout of a kid, looking younger than twenty-one, and the second he was pointed out to them Landers and Piggott pricked up their ears.

He reacted to the badge with dismay; the game stopped cold; every eye in the place was on them, and there were mutters. Fuzz. After Dicky. What the hell the fuzz want—

He followed them out to the street unwillingly. "So what the hell the fuzz want with me?"

"We understand you own a 1957 Chevy, painted purple." He nodded once. "Could we see your driver's license, please?" It was in order. But he was wary and nervous, and— what they had first noticed—he bore some deep scratches down both cheeks. Scratches from a female's nails, a female fighting him? "Could you tell us where you were between eleven A.M. and noon on Wednesday?"

"Wednesday. I dunno. Around. Why?"

"Let's have something more definite." He muttered. "Do you have a job?"

He shrugged. "Part-time. At a gas station. I haven't done anything. Why the hell you picking on—"

"Well, Wednesday morning, Mr. Pope. Where were you, doing what?"

"I don't remember. Oh, I guess I was here part of the time. In there." He nodded at the pool-hall. Landers and Piggott exchanged mute glances. Anybody there saying, Sure, Dick was here then.

"Where'd you get the scratches on your face?" asked Piggott casually.

Pope flushed. "Oh, well, a girl," he muttered. "You know."

"Which girl? When? We'd like to hear her name," said Landers.

"What the hell does it matter? Just a girl. Why you got to—"

It went on like that, and after a while they let him go. What with the drive out to the valley, and the interlude in Hollywood, it was getting on for five o'clock then, and instead of going down to Venice after Michael Boyd they went back to the office.

"You know that type, Matt," said Landers. "They'll never give the fuzz the time of day. It can't be him, on the Warthol woman. Out of the first three names we get, just on this purple car bit? It'd be a miracle, and miracles just don't happen for us."

"I know how it looks," said Piggott. "But it's *possible*."

"So it's possible. Too late to go down to the beach and back anyway, now," said Landers. "Just for fun, we'd better see if Pope's in our records."

Mendoza came back to the office at two-thirty to find the autopsy report on their latest Jane Doe waiting on his desk. He read it with interest. As usual, Bainbridge had been thorough. The girl was probably somewhere between twenty-five and thirty. Not *virgo intacta* but she had never had a child. No history of any chronic diseases, V.D., T.B.: everything normal. By the measurements, a small, slight woman; well, they'd known that. The only items on her, two rings, sent to the lab. The best estimate Bainbridge could offer on the time of death was between nine P.M. Tuesday night and one A.M. Wednesday morning. She had eaten a light meal of eggs and toast about two hours before death. There was a very small amount of alcohol in the stomach, equivalent to one scant drink. No drugs present. "Cause of death, immediate: present at back of throat, a quantity of wadded paper toweling amounting to five full-size sections from roll, obviously intended as gag but forced sufficiently far down throat to cut off air in windpipe and deprive victim of oxygen. Primary cause of death suffocation."

"*Así, así,*" said Mendoza and lit a cigarette.

The body had been in contact, over much of its surface, with some type of heavy grease, undoubtedly while in a nude state as areas normally covered by clothing were involved. An attempt had been made to wash the body. Victim had had sexual intercourse within a very short period of time before death, almost certainly by forcible rape since some tearing and bruising was present. Material from under fingernails analyzed, sent to lab for further processing: preliminary study showed black-brown hairs, short, a small amount of tissue, human.

"Helpful," said Mendoza. He got through to Carey's office; Carey wasn't there but he talked to one Sergeant Klein. "That Jane Doe on Figueroa—hasn't anybody asked about her? In three days? But that's damned odd—she's married by that wedding ring, you'd think—"

"Maybe," said Klein, "she left hubby back in Philly and came out here to go into the movies. Maybe he thinks she's visiting her mother so he isn't worried."

"Yes," said Mendoza, "but it's funny. Well, thanks." He sat there thinking about that girl: the very good-looker. The manicure, the pedicure: she'd taken care of herself. She looked like a woman who'd be missed. Of course, that kind of thing was always possible: that whatever family she had thought she was safely elsewhere and weren't worried. But—

He picked up the inside phone. "Get me the lab, Jimmy. . . . Who's this? Scarne. Bainbridge sent a couple of rings up to you. You had a chance to look at them?"

"Those. Sure. One fourteen-karat wedding ring, plain, no engraving. Kind of thing anybody could buy anywhere, just a gold band. The other ring won't be much more use to you —not a custom piece either, twenty-carat acquamarine, worth something all right but set in a plain gold mounting—the stone's emerald cut. It'd be recognized by anyone who knew it, knew who owned it, but that's about all."

"Well, thanks," said Mendoza. So, not costume jewelry. And in a way Brenda Warthol was more immediate; but Jane Doe intrigued him. She wasn't just the usual anonymous unidentified body. After a while, against his own common sense, he went out, went down to the morgue and asked to see the body. The attendant pulled out the cold tray indifferently.

"*No hay más remedio,*" muttered Mendoza. "But, damn it, she's not just anybody. You'd turn to look at her in a crowd. Wouldn't you?"

"What?" said the attendant.

"Well, look at her," said Mendoza. "Doesn't she look like somebody who'd be missed right off the bat?"

"Not like she is now, Lieutenant," said the attendant. "I ain't a ghoul."

"*Estúpido.*" Suddenly it was borne in on Mendoza, looking at her face again, that she looked oddly familiar. *Familiar?* He racked his brains, adding up her features: short straight nose, delicately modeled chin, high forehead—dark hair, short— even white teeth, he remembered (Bainbridge would have made up a dental chart); a rather small but full mouth— Familiar? He didn't have the feeling that he'd ever met her personally, but—somewhere—he had seen her. Or a photograph of her?

He never went to movies, rarely looked at T.V. Was she somebody from that world? Possibly? But surely if she was, that would make it all the likelier that she'd have been missed by now.

On the other hand, that world was quite often one of intrigues, illicit romance, the secret jealousies and affairs and hatreds and thwarted ambitions. If she belonged in that world, something like that just could be the answer. And if she did, and everybody around her—husband, servants, agent, etcetera—believed she was on some director's yacht or playing the tables in Monaco—well, sooner or later she'd be missed.

He shook his head at the lovely cold anonymous face and turned away.

When Higgins and Palliser drifted in at ten minutes to six, he was sitting at the desk dealing himself crooked poker hands. He listened to the gist of the Deforrest-Parker thing and said, "Leaps to the eye. Pure and simple. The lovers' quarrel. New butch luring Parker away. Bang."

"Well, I don't know, Luis." Higgins sat down in the chair beside the desk. "Could be, with all the dirt we see, we get too cynical sometimes?"

"Could we?" asked Mendoza cynically. He shuffled the pack, cut it and turned up the ace of spades.

"Well, we've been out talking to some people who knew them," said Palliser. "I guess Jase still is. And it all looks aboveboard—ordinary people, where they worked—people they knew from other places. If they were that kind, it certainly wasn't suspected anywhere. Apparently they went around together sometimes—shows, restaurants, and so on—but with other people too. The Deforrest woman had been married—she was a widow. Husband was a realtor, he died about ten years ago. She was forty-nine. No children. Parker evidently had a couple of boy-friends—"

"Cover," said Mendoza. "Sometimes they do." He shuffled, cut the deck and turned up the ace of spades. "So you ask the boy-friends—mmh—a few delicate questions, I'll bet you'd find they had the platonic good-night kiss and, *acabamiento*, finish."

"I don't know," said Palliser doubtfully.

"It could be," said Mendoza, "that nobody but themselves did know, John. That's sometimes the case—in fact, rather often—with the Lesbians. They're a hell of a lot more secretive than the fags. I take it you didn't come across any of the—mmh—physical accoutrements of Sapphic love in either place. Well, that says nothing at all—they don't always go in for that."

"There was one bullet fired from the gun. One woman shot, the other beaten, it looked like."

"Which one was shot?"

"Parker."

"So, wait for what Ballistics says. If the slug was out of the gun on the scene, it's open and shut. Any lead on who owns the gun?"

Higgins and Palliser exchanged a glance. "It belonged to Deforrest. She had a permit for it."

"So," said Mendoza. He shuffled and cut the deck and looked at the ace of spades.

"It's a damn good thing you're an honest man, Luis," said Higgins.

"Just keeping my hand in."

Lake came in and handed him a teletype. "Keep your fingers crossed."

"*¡Demonios!*" said Mendoza, reading it. Another follow-up on that first A.P.B. Heist in Stockton, early yesterday afternoon: two men: and the clerk had just identified a mug-shot of Starr as one of them. "Stockton," said Mendoza, handing it to Higgins. "That much farther south. . . ."

He went home, to Alison and the twins and the cats and their shaggy dog, and announced that he needed a drink before dinner, and he didn't know why he stayed at the dirty thankless job. "Will you tell me why I went on riding that squad-car? Twenty-one long years back, when the old man finally died and we found all those safe-deposit boxes and the gilt-edged stock and the land deeds and the cash the old miser took at his crooked gambling? I am a fool. *¡Te lo digo!*"

"*Todo lo cual no es verdad*," said Alison. "You wouldn't know what to do with yourself, *hermoso*. The bad ones come along and somehow you weather through. Calm down. I've got these brochures from the private schools I want you to see—take your mind off—"

"And why I ever got into this domestic scene I'll never know—"

"I know," said Alison sympathetically. "I've ruined your poker game. Not to mention your reputation with females. The man about town Mendoza."

Mendoza finished his rye. "*No importa—¡me gusta!* And who but a redhaired Scots-Irishwoman could have accomplished it?"

"*¡Egoísto!*" said Alison just before his arms came round her.

The night team at Homicide got their first call at just on midnight. Schenke went out on it. Nick Galeano was lackadaisically working a crossword puzzle, twenty minutes later, when the outside phone buzzed and he picked it up. "Central Homicide, Sergeant Galeano."

"Sergeant Gentry, Anaheim headquarters," said a businesslike baritone. "You put out a call on a Rolls Phantom, Pennsy plate UR-5540, yesterday. We've got it. Just now."

"Oh, you don't say?" said Galeano. "How nice. Plus driver?"

"Oh, yes. He doesn't seem to be too sure who he is. Had a lot of travelers' checks on him made out to one Spaulding, and a driver's license ditto, but the license says Spaulding's forty-eight and this guy can't be twenty-two. We're holding him. Do you want him? You do. O.K. What? Well, you can thank Disneyland—the parking attendant there alerted us. He was asleep in the car."

"Somebody'll be down to get him in the morning," said Galeano. Hackett would be pleased, he reflected.

5

"WELL, THAT'S a step in the right direction, for a change," said Hackett, coming in on Saturday morning to hear that Coppola had been picked up. "I suppose I'd better go and fetch him up for questioning—if we can get him to talk about it. Though seeing as we've got the nice solid evidence on him, maybe not, at that. I'll go get him."

"The question is," said Mendoza, "will we have time to question him, Art? *Por Dios*, another one overnight—"he was reading Schenke's report—"and it looks like one that'll consume a little time to look at." They usually had a full load to work, but it was getting a little hot and heavy: and another female. At least everybody was in; it was Lake's day off and Rory Farrell was sitting on the desk.

Overnight Fletcher had got more names, Traffic detail all over the county keeping the eye out for purple cars. Talk about random investigation: you could hardly get more random; but there it was. Mendoza handed the new list—four names—to Landers when he came in and said, "Take Piggott and Glasser. Clean these up as fast as you can—we've got a new one."

"Oh, Lord," said Landers and added, "But I did tell you, didn't I? Rain." It was raining, just a fine thin drizzle, probably the last of the season. "The weather prophet, me. O.K., we're on our way."

Mendoza lit a cigarette. Higgins, Grace and Palliser still on the Deforrest-Parker thing. It wouldn't do any harm to look and ask around the Warthol neighborhood whether any female had been bothered by the amorous peddler or whatever. He went on reading Schenke's report.

The baby-sitter, this time. One Linda Ulner, fifteen, sitting with three kids on Leeward Avenue; mother reported finding her dead when she came home at midnight—a Mrs. Ruthena Kling. Looked like rape-assault, said Schenke; the lab had been on it. The three kids—ten, eight and four—had been asleep and didn't know anything. Back door forced. The father worked the swing shift at a local plant, or the baby-sitter (who had lived in the house next door with her parents) wouldn't have been there.

"*¡Condenación!*" said Mendoza. And nobody reporting Jane Doe missing yet. And these other cases all up in the air. He supposed somebody ought to follow up the new one, and with everybody else busy it looked like being him. It was a little early, however, to drop in on the citizens. It was also early to call the lab and demand results on any of this. The lab liked to take its time. Sighing, he lit another cigarette and went down the hall for a cup of coffee.

"It is just impossible," said Landers, "that it could have been Pope, on Warthol. Miracles like that don't happen, Matt. The only smell of a lead we've got, the purple cars, so we ask Traffic to watch, and they give us three names to start with— just at random, cars spotted—and boom, X is one of them? I don't buy it."

"Well, I don't know that I do," said Piggott, "but it's suggestive. In a way. That little pedigree we turned up on Pope —one count of mugging. Assault, technically speaking."

"Hardly in the same category as rape. And what gets me, you know," said Landers, shooting a glance behind and changing lanes in the freeway hurriedly, "whoever it was, why the hell did he cart her all the way up to the Hollywood Bowl?"

"Maybe we'll find out when we catch him. If we ever do," said Piggott with his usual pessimism.

Before starting out on the new batch Traffic had turned up for them, they wanted to clear away Michael Boyd, so they were making for Venice first, having handed the new names over to Glasser. It was a tedious drive in traffic, and they had to get out the County Guide to locate the address, a back street, short and narrow. It was a four-apartment building, two up, two down; the Boyds lived upstairs on the right-hand side. Arrived at the tiny square cement landing, Landers pushed the doorbell and took off his hat. He rang the bell three times before the door opened to reveal a girl about nineteen or twenty. She had on a cotton housecoat over her nightdress, still zipping it up as she opened the door, her bare feet thrust into gold mules. She was a pretty girl, a natural blonde, peaches-and-cream complexion, but the hair was tousled and her blue eyes bleary. She was yawning. Behind her the expectable modern living room was neat and rather bare.

"Who're you?"

Landers showed her the badge. "We'd like to ask you a few questions if you don't mind—Miss Boyd?"

"Lord," she said through another yawn, "you cops get up early. 'Scuse me. It's O.K. with me only don't expect any brainy answers. At this hour. Lord. Come in, sit down." She sat down in an armchair and shut her eyes.

"Miss Boyd—"

"I s'pose Mother left the coffee on. 'S a terrible thing," she said sleepily, "way a person's made. Read something about it in a magazine once. Night people, day people. Me, I'm night people. I don't think right up to noon. I'll go see. You like some coffee?"

"No, thanks, miss. If you'd—"

She went out, came back in a moment with a cup of black

69

coffee, sat sipping it. "So what do the cops want from me?"
She leaned back, eyes shut.

"Your brother Michael—he owns a car? A Rambler,
painted purple." She nodded.

"Fact. I've been driving it—mine's in the garage. Feel sort
of—selfconscious—that color. See it a block away. Easy to
find in a public lot, I'll say that."

"I'm sorry we can't explain, but a car that color has showed
up in something we're investigating, and we'd like to contact
your brother to ask him his whereabouts between eleven A.M.
and one P.M. last Wednesday."

She gave a little spurt of laughter. "Same like *Dragnet*.
They're still running that, you know? It's good. Whereabouts. You mean, him and the car?"

"That's right, Miss Boyd. Where—"

She propped her eyelids open with two fingers and said,
"Gah. *Nine* o'clock. You don't look old enough to be a cop."

Landers suppressed rage. "Where can we find him, Miss
Boyd? Where does he work?"

"At the Santa Monica Airport. He's a mechanic. I couldn't
take a job I had to get to before noon. At least. I'm a waitress
at the Bel-Air Inn. But you don't need to see Mike. I can tell
you. They wouldn't let you in anyway. Visiting hours two to
four, seven to eight." She yawned.

"What— Well, we'd rather see him personally." Landers
stood up.

"Have it your way. Come to think, a cop stopped me the
other night and asked who owned the car. Funny. You really
don't need to bother Mike. Lessee what time you—Wednesday? Wednesday morning? The Rambler was in the garage
out back, I was in bed of course, and Mike was right where
he's been ten days, poor guy, in the Santa Monica Hospital
with one leg in traction and some broken ribs and a fractured
skull. I told him he was a fool to ride with that Randy Pierce.
But he'll be O.K."

70

Landers was exasperated. "And just why didn't you tell that to the officer who stopped you on Thursday night, Miss Boyd?"

She yawned. Her blue eyes widened on him. "But he didn't ask me that," she said.

Higgins, Palliser and Grace were still working the Defor-rest-Parker thing. Before parceling out names from the address books, Higgins called Ballistics. "Whatever you've got on the Laveta Terrace thing," he said to Fisher. "I suppose Bainbridge sent up the slug out of Parker?"

"Oh, yes. It was in good condition. It's out of a Ruger Single Six .22 revolver. I'd guess a fairly new gun—not used much anyway. That's about all we've got for you so far."

"Oh, thanks so much," said Higgins. It was enough. He broke that news to Palliser and Grace. "So, that makes it look a little different."

"Does it?" said Palliser. "Does it really? We said, the Lesbian angle, another butch after Parker. Maybe the Ruger belongs to that one. There was a fight in that place—anything can happen in a fight, with guns in maybe inexperienced hands."

Higgins shrugged at him. "I can't say that's not so."

"I think I'd like to take another look at that apartment," said Palliser. "Before I go call on any more friends of theirs." They had left the apartment sealed. He drove down to Laveta Terrace. They had already talked to the other tenant, an elderly widow who had the second upstairs apartment. She hadn't heard any disturbance that night, but she admitted that she habitually took sleeping pills. The landlady, it turned out, was deaf in one ear.

Palliser broke the seal on Anne Parker's apartment door and went in. The ground-floor rear apartment; and the next block over was all single houses, so between the back door here and the nearest sleeping citizen was an alley, a deep back yard. He looked at this living room. It was a shambles. The lab had finished what the fight started. Furniture overturned, blood on the carpet, china ornaments smashed where they'd fallen, the coffee table lying on its side, one leg broken, with a vase of dead flowers, a porcelain ashtray, magazines spilled from it. And then the lab men had come along and dusted fingerprint powder over every likely surface, outlined the bodies in chalk, chalk-marked where physical evidence had been . . . The gun, he remembered, had been about there, a couple of feet from Deforrest's hand. As if she'd dropped it when she fell. One shot fired from it.

The Deforrest woman about five-nine. Palliser was six feet even. He stood over the chalk marks where Deforrest had lain, drew his Police Positive .38 and lifted it. Allowing for the three or four inches difference in height, the muzzle pointed in a line just over an upholstered chair halfway across the room. It had fallen on its back.

"Well," said Palliser thoughtfully. He holstered the gun, went across to the chair and set it on its feet. And there, hardly noticeable unless you were looking, was the faint scorch mark on the brown nylon cover of the seat-cushion. He probed with a cautious finger and there, by God, it was: the bullet. A bullet, anyway. The bullet from Deforrest's gun? In all likelihood. He took out his knife, slashed the cover, pulled out a little kapok stuffing, and there it was. Not much damaged.

He looked at it and wondered if it said anything; but at any rate, it was always so nice to steal a march on the lab—the holier-than-thou lab.

About eleven o'clock that morning Higgins came to one Mr. Stacy Barron, attorney-at-law, who was listed in Wanda DeForrest's address book. His office was on Hill Street, high up in a Security Bank Building. He didn't keep Higgins waiting, but came out to the anteroom himself to usher him into his office—a quietly masculine and old-fashioned office, paneled walls, no Impressionist reproductions, an old square mahogany desk, man-sized ashtrays and a general air of unpretentious prosperity.

"It's about Wanda," said Barron without preamble. "Sit down, Sergeant. You did say Sergeant?" He offered Higgins a cigarette. He was a man about fifty, probably, but you wouldn't guess that at first glance; he'd kept his dark hair, his white teeth were all his own, and his gray eyes keen; a good-looking man. Right now he looked rather haggard. He lit his own cigarette after Higgins', and sat down at the desk. "It doesn't seem possible she's gone. Not possible. I'm—her executor, I had notice of the inquest on Monday. My God—an inquest on Wanda." He was silent, looked up. "Any way I can help the police, Sergeant, but I don't know how I could. I hadn't seen her since the night before it happened."

"Oh?" said Higgins. "You knew Mrs. Deforrest fairly well, sir?"

"For a number of years," said Barron. "I was her husband's attorney—and executor, which was how we met. I looked after the few investments he left her, advised her." Barron looked away, out the window.

"I see." Higgins debated with himself. This might be just the man to tell him a few things. An intelligent man: very likely a cynical man: he had known the woman in a business way, had known the husband: he might be quick at getting the nuances.

"What could I tell you about it?" said Barron; he spread his hands—well-shaped manicured hands. "It was a shock—a great shock. To hear about it on the radio, in the car, on my way home—God. I—went there, of course, but you'd all gone then and all the landlady could tell me—I gather, a burglar breaking into the apartment downstairs. And of course Wanda would have gone running to protect the Parker girl like a—like a she-bear with her cub in danger."

"Did you know Miss Parker, sir?"

Barron gave him an automatic quick smile, humorless. An attractive man. "Knew of her from Wanda, that's all. She sounded like a nice girl. She was an orphan, no people at all. Came to the big town from Ventura, happened to take that apartment, and Wanda—took her under her wing."

"Mr. Barron," said Higgins," I'm going to be frank with you because I think you're in a position to help us. You knew Mrs. Deforrest in a business sense, call it, over quite a long period of time. You're a—man of the world, to use the cliché—" Barron shot him a rather ironic glance—"and, well, to be quite frank, sir, we've got more than a smell of some Lesbian angle on this thing, and I'd like to ask you, in the time you knew Mrs. Deforrest, whether—" He stopped.

Barron began to repeat, "*Lesb——*" and stopped too. For a moment he just looked completely astonished. Then he barked a short laugh, and put a hand to his temple and said, "My God. Oh, my God. The most unkindest cut of all. And how furious she would have been." He didn't look at Higgins; he said, "I would suppose, Sergeant, that in your job you know something about the realities of life too. Yes. If I can speak in—er—confidence? She wasn't domestic, you see. The little home-maker. Which was quite all right with me—I've been a widower for ten years and I'm quite comfortable in my apartment. We were both adults without any families, and in any case—" He put out his cigarette. He was still looking out the window. "In confidence, Sergeant, I can assure you that Wanda was quite definitely a very normal female." He looked sad, amused, and angry all at once.

"Oh," said Higgins. "Oh, I see."

So what did they think about now?

"I'm sorry," said Roman Coppola, looking anxiously at Mendoza and Hackett standing over him. "I know I shouldn't ought to've done it. But honest, I got so fed up with that

74

damn sergeant. My dad said, Army'd be good for me, but it wasn't. I didn't like it no ways. I got drafted after they threw me outta college, see, and I got sent out here—and—I never got no leave, there was always something against me—and I—" He stopped, and sniffed, and said, "I was real careful with the Rolls-Royce, I didn't hurt it none."

They looked at him. With the formalities, and the long drive back to town, it was getting on for ten-thirty now. The Rolls would be towed up and eventually shipped back east to the family. When they'd got the lab evidence on Coppola, they'd automatically applied for the warrant, which was on Mendoza's desk now.

Coppola was twenty-one, but he didn't look more than seventeen: not very big, dark, the irresponsible face, thought Mendoza, knowing Hackett was thinking that too. The shadow of a dark beard showing, but the voice the immature one of adolescence. And just how the hell he'd ever got into college in the first place—but they were taking anybody these days, the lowered standards or the nonexistent standards.

"So, go on," said Hackett. "You're sorry, are you?"

"Sure. I—I—I wanted to see Disneyland!" burst out Coppola. "And I never got no leave—" He was AWOL from Vandenberg Air Force Base. "That close, and I never—so I just went. All the orders all the time, yessir, yessir, I couldn't stand it. And when I got here on the bus, I—well, I didn't have much money, for a room or anything, and I went in that big hotel—high-class hotel, I hung around, I thought maybe I could get into some room and get some money. I noticed that guy, he looked real rich, and once I saw him go out the front door and get in that Rolls—garage man brought it round for him—so I knew it was his. I just thought—I just thought—I wasn't going to keep it!"

"And the travelers' checks?" prodded Mendoza. They weren't having any trouble with him; he was anxious to explain, excuse himself.

"Oh—those things. I thought he'd have real money—cash. But I'd watched him, and a couple others, they'd sign those things at the desk and get real money for them." Quite incredibly, they were to discover later, he had signed four of the travelers' checks with his own name, and a downtown bank had cashed them. And probably Coppola wouldn't have known a bank might cash them, but as it turned out he had overheard the desk-clerk apologizing for not being able to cash a large check and suggesting the bank. The sea of paper floating around—

"How'd you get him to open his door?" asked Hackett.

"I said I had a telegram for him." And Spaulding, probably waked suddenly, not stopping to think that the desk would have phoned. "Didn't he tell you?" asked Coppola. "About that? I guess I oughta apologize—I shouldn't have done that to the guy. An older guy too. I shouldn't ought to've. I just couldn't think any other way—I—I'd got this piece of pipe out of an alley, when he opened the door I just hit him a couple of times, put him out, you know, and then—and then, well, it was a couple days since I took off, so I took a bath and shaved and put on some of his clean clothes. So as to look better. There wasn't no trouble about getting the Rolls, and honest, I took real good care of it. And now that guy gets her back all right, and all, and maybe if I apologize to him—" He looked at them anxiously, and then suddenly he gave them a beaming bright smile. "I been at Disneyland ever since, I seen everything and went on all the rides and it was great, just great!"

They looked at each other. There really wasn't anything to say.

Now, about an hour and a half to work on the new one, before lunch.

As Mendoza and Hackett came up to the big round table in the corner at Federico's, Higgins and Palliser were just sitting down. Adam, the tall Jamaican waiter, hurried up; everybody but Mendoza ordered drinks; and as they were served Landers and Piggott came in and automatically joined them.

"All I say is, it'd do no harm to lean on Pope a little."

"I don't suppose. All I say is, I don't believe in miracles. I hear we've got a new one," said Landers, sitting down next to Palliser.

"For our sins," said Mendoza. "Looks like another rape. Baby-sitter, fifteen."

"My God, another?" said Higgins.

"Back door forced, girl beaten up—Bainbridge will say, rape or not."

"And nobody knows nothing," said Hackett lazily, lighting a cigarette. "Naturally." He picked up his Scotch and soda as Adam set it before him, and Palliser reminded him of the calories in it. "You go to hell. Been meaning to ask you, George, how's Steve's leg?"

"Fine," said Higgins, smiling. "Brace came off last month, he still limps a little but the doctors say he'll be fine." They had never caught up to that hit-run driver, nearly killing Stevie Dwyer.

They all glanced at him with absent, hidden affection: Higgins the loner all of a sudden falling so helplessly for Bert Dwyer's widow and acquiring the secondhand family; now, a family of his own. And Mendoza wondered academically just how often they'd all sat around this table, kicking the current cases around, optimistic, discouraged, swearing at the tough ones, complaining about the tedious routine that went on forever. Sometimes only a couple of them, sometimes most of them happening to knock off for a Code Seven at the same time: and men from other offices in the big, busy Police Facilities Building that was Central Headquarters, L.A.P.D. Big, sandy Hackett, big, wide-shouldered Higgins with his craggy unhandsome features, dark, plodding Piggott seeing the devil's busy hands at work on all sides, boyish, fresh-faced Tom Landers, tall, dark Palliser looking rather gloomy these days over the house-payments, solid, middle-sized Henry Glasser, and their latest addition brown, soft-talking Jason Grace. How often? And probably Alison was right—he complained about the thankless job, but he wouldn't know what to do with himself without it.

"That Warthol thing," said Hackett. "What still gets me is the Hollywood Bowl. Why?"

"You can't ascribe any logical motives to one like that, Art," said Mendoza. "It may just have been the first place that came to his mind."

"But damn it, if he was so all-fired hot for a female why'd he take her anywhere at all?"

"Don't ask me—I didn't do it. The steak sandwich, Adam."

"Ditto for me," said Hackett.

"And me. Extra well," said Landers. "That Boyd female. They didn't ask her. Brother. Well, he's out of it anyway. Depending on Traffic to spot purple cars for us, my God." He felt his shoulder. It was still raining in a half-hearted way. He started to tell Mendoza about that. Piggott sat looking morose.

They kicked the new one around a little, and Warthol. There'd be the inquests coming up Monday and Tuesday. Just as Adam brought up a big tray, deftly set it on the folding rest and started to serve them, Jason Grace drifted up to the table. They made room for him. "And where've you been?" asked Palliser.

"I went backtracking," said Grace, sitting down. "Skip the drink, Adam, and bring me the small steak—I'm starving."

"Yes, sir. Medium."

"Backtracking?" asked Mendoza.

"Thought it'd do no harm—" he lit a cigarette—"to see what kind of reputation the Parker girl had in her own home town. Ventura. I went up there and asked around. Everybody told me she was a very nice girl. Orphan—raised in an Episcopal children's home there. I—"

"Oh, by God," said Higgins, "but I never passed *that* on—the boss monopolizing the conversation. You're flogging a dead horse, Jase. What I found in my travels was the Deforrest's boy-friend." His grin died; he said, "I shouldn't laugh. He's a nice guy—widower, about fifty, but still very much all male. And he's feeling it. They'd known each other some time. I gather, neither of 'em particularly interested in the domestic scene, but at the same time still human. Their business. He assured me, in confidence, that Wanda was definitely all normal female."

Hackett laughed. "You don't say! Well, so that's that. What angle do we look at now?" Piggott said something about the ways of strange women and they all looked at him indulgently.

"Well, sometimes," said Mendoza, "we do tend to read complexities where they're not—"

"And see who's talking," said Hackett.

"*Irreverente, amigo.* A couple of people told us they were like mother and daughter. That might be the simple truth. Deforrest never had a family—she was the right age to feel motherly toward Parker, the orphan. And considering the state of those two apartments, and the fact that the door to Parker's apartment wasn't forced—" Mendoza stopped and stared into space.

"Yes?" said Higgins.

"And the Deforrest woman apparently left her place upstairs in a hurry, left the door open—I think," said Mendoza, "that we go asking around about Parker's boy-friends. Possibly a recently acquired one. Whom she had let in, and then maybe he got a little too—mmh—assiduous, and she yelled for help and Deforrest heard her and came running. Only Deforrest hearing her."

"Which reminds me," said Palliser, "I've caught the lab in a boo-boo. I—"

"Don't mention the lab," said Higgins. "They haven't sent a report up on Warthol yet. Better jigger them up some, Luis."

"And then there is Jane Doe," said Mendoza in a dissatisfied tone. "Damn it, I cannot understand why she hasn't been missed by somebody—"

And all the routine still to do on the new one. . . .

A deathly hush prevailed in the living room of the house on Rayo Grande Avenue. Humanwise it was occupied only by Mendoza. Cedric the Old English sheepdog was curled up dutifully at his master's feet: and enjoying the warmth of his big body, Sheba and Bast were curled up on either side of him, with Nefertite between his immense paws. El Señor the miniature lion, aloof from everybody, was probably at his self-appointed post of watch-cat in the nursery. Mrs. Mac-Taggart had washed and groomed Cedric to proud elegance this afternoon: the steel-blue parts of him shone and his white shirt and paws gleamed snowily.

Mendoza was somewhat somnolently rereading *Rewards and Fairies*. Since his strange enthrallment had seized him, he had discovered that Kipling can be reread indefinitely: age could not wither nor time spoil the genius of a master.

Alison appeared in the doorway with a small stack of sealed envelopes in her hand and regarded him amusedly. "Woof," said Cedric in amiable greeting, and Mendoza looked up.

"I will never understand it," said Alison.

"Very few females appreciate Kipling sufficiently," said Mendoza. "What have you been up to?"

"Invitations," said Alison. "Angel and I are giving a baby shower for Mary Higgins."

"Oh."

"And if it happens to be a girl," said Alison, "I don't envy

Mary. The most spoiled brat in seven states, unless she really puts her foot down. Your George Higgins I've only met a few times, but men I know. His acquiring a family at his age—"

"You and Art insulting me," complained Mendoza. "He's only thirty-eight. I was—"

"Rules don't apply to you, Casanova," said Alison. Mendoza got up and advanced on her with a glint in his eye and she hurriedly deposited the stack of invitations on the credenza. The phone rang down the hall.

"Hell," said Mendoza.

"Just like a doctor," said Alison with mock resignation.

"Mendoza here."

The phone sneezed violently at him. "As if we weren't busy enough!" it raged. "The daily routine piling up, my good God Almighty, and why the hell can't they hang *onto* them when they *get* them?" Another sneeze. "Where the hell did I put the Kleen—— And you are just as busy as I am, damn it, you don't need to tell me—"

"What's up, Saul?"

Lieutenant Goldberg of Robbery and Theft sneezed again, said, "Damn allergies. Doctors saying, avoid tension. My God. You'd better come see this. I'm at the Riley and Bell Pharmacy on Sixth. Galeano's here."

One of the two pharmacists who'd been on duty was D.O.A., shot through the body. It was a chain pharmacy, not a regular drugstore, specializing in the prescriptions. Sergeant Betts of Goldberg's office was there, taking notes as he listened to the other pharmacist.

The manager was a little fat fellow, bald, unexpectedly under control and cool-headed. A Robert Coleman. "They didn't get much, Lieutenant. There wasn't much here to get— we are in the process of moving to a new location on Wilshire, practically all of the stock had been transferred by yesterday—that is, of the type they'd likely be interested in, the barbiturates and so on. It was just before closing time, as I told you—anything we can do to help you, sir, I don't mind going over it again—but, my God, young Forsythe dead—and for nothing really—"

"All I want you to tell Lieutenant Mendoza," said Goldberg with enormous restraint, "is what you told me. You identify this photograph as one of the men who held you up tonight?" He shook it under Coleman's nose.

"I can. I do. There were two of them, and that was one of them," said Coleman. "I couldn't say about the other, it all happened so fast—I tried to keep my head—but that was one of them all right."

Goldberg sneezed, snarled and handed the glossy photograph to Mendoza. "And haven't we expected them, Luis?"

"*¡Por mi vida!*" said Mendoza, looking at it. "We have indeed, Saul." It was a mug-shot of Roger Starr.

So they were here. Trasker, Starr and Killeen. For pretty sure, all three of them.

6

THAT, of course, was the hottest news on Sunday morning—that trio of cons being definitely here. It had been a relatively quiet weekend so far in Central's territory: a few brawls, a knifing, muggings, but nothing for Homicide. Which was just as well, considering the load they were working. And now the escaped trio had come to town.

"Nothing to do about it, *naturalmente*," said Mendoza. Until and unless they showed up somewhere else on another job. And that was all too likely; they hadn't picked up much loot last night, and the fact that they'd pulled a job at all meant that they needed the loot. Not a straightforward heist last night: they'd been after the eminently saleable drugs; and two of them had dealt in those before, they'd have contacts. It was likely they'd be heard from again, soon.

Meanwhile, Homicide had its own work to do. Everybody was in today; theoretically Mendoza was supposed to have Sundays off, and sometimes he actually did. They couldn't descend on the citizens before nine o'clock at least, but by then they were starting off on the routine.

Traffic had turned up three more purple cars, in Torrance, Glendale, and Pacoima. And this was the top force anywhere, but the job wasn't made any easier by the fact that this was also the biggest city in the world in square mileage, if not population: and the county area was ten times as big again.

Landers and Piggott started off to look at those cars. Higgins and Palliser went out looking for more friends of Anne Parker's, concentrating on her now. Grace took the first call of the day, a body over on Main; Glasser stayed in to take anything else coming along. Mendoza and Hackett went out on the new one, the baby-sitter Linda Ulner.

"Messing up my living room, cops," said Mrs. Ruthena Kling. "I suppose it's got to be, such a thing, but a nuisance." There were still evidences, in this rather shabby living room, of the lab-team's routine: fingerprint powder, chalk marks. Mendoza's eyes strayed to the outline of the body there in the middle of the archway between living and dining rooms. An eloquent outline: legs wide spread, arms up, head twisted. The classic, all-too-usual, case.

"I told the cops all I know already. The other cops," said Mrs. Kling. "Friday night. Is it all right to clean all this up now?"

"Quite all right," said Hackett. "Had you hired Linda as a baby-sitter often, Mrs. Kling?" They had already had a painful interview with Mr. and Mrs. Ulner next door. Linda an only child; by her school photograph, a pretty girl, blonde and dimpled, with an impish grin. Why did it have to be Linda, they were asked. That question Homicide never could answer.

"Sure," she said. "It was handy, her right next door. The kids liked her all right." Rather a waste of time, talking to the kids: Jeanette, ten; Ricky, eight; Patricia, four. They'd been asleep; they hadn't heard anything. "Linda was fine with them. See, Rick—my husband—he's on the swing shift, we can't go out at night together, movies or that, it was only once in awhile I had to have a sitter." She looked at them, the two men from Homicide, slightly incongruous in the cluttered shabby room, their dark suits and ties, formal white shirts a contrast to her slightly dirty pink housecoat and old mules, and she said a little nervously, "It was awful—I've been terrible sorry about it, I guess I didn't sound—but it was an awful shock, find her like that. I knew Linda since she was a little thing. But—"

Her husband wasn't there; he'd gone to church, she said.

"I'm sure it was, Mrs. Kling," said Mendoza. "You don't mind if we look around?"

"Oh, no, I know you got to investigate. Try to find out who it was. These fiends, attacking innocent young girls like Linda." She was about forty, a sharp-featured woman once very pretty, with a good figure, probably tinted reddish-brown hair, a little too much make-up.

Mendoza wandered through the dining room back to the kitchen and said to Hackett, "You said the back door was forced."

"Schenke said so." They looked. It was an ordinary back door, solid, with a screen door beyond. That was an old one, the wood rotten and the screen full of holes: ordinary strength would suffice to have forced the staple holding the hook to give, which it had. A simple lock on the door, and in-adequate screws on the hinged side; a screwdriver or a strong knife would have easily forced it open far enough to break the lock, and by the marks on the door and jamb, that was what had happened. If Linda had had the radio or T.V. on, likely she wouldn't have heard a thing. And the radio or T.V. covering whatever noises she made after he got hold of her. The classic case. See if the lab came up with any latents, any other physical evidence.

Mendoza's long nose twitched; he looked round the kitchen. A neat clean kitchen, if oldfashioned: no dirty dishes in the sink. A bottle of hand-lotion sitting beside the sink; one of those fancy ceramic ring-trees there, to hold a lady's rings while she washed dishes. The curtains at the one window were pink and ruffled. There was a magazine lying open on the kitchen table: *True Romances.*

"The classic thing," said Hackett, still looking at the marks on the door.

"¡Qué más?" murmured Mendoza. "What else?" Hackett turned to look at him.

It wasn't exactly raining today, but it was gray and cool with a mist in the air. Landers' shoulder was still giving an occasional twinge. They were using Piggott's Chevy today.

Down in Torrance, they found Bob Spencer at home, and gave him a severe fright. He was a high-school senior; he owned a 1957 Ford painted purple; and he happened to be a Negro. When he saw the badge in Lander's hand he began stuttering in panic. They went in as he backed before them; he managed to introduce his parents, who looked merely bewildered at the badge: a pair of plumpish placid people, in a neat single house well-maintained by its white paint and green stretch of lawn in front. Landers attempted to soothe the boy, and Spencer Senior said, "Now, Bob, don't you be foolish. You got nothing to hide, you tell the officers whatever they want to know."

Spencer Junior, who was a nice-looking boy very neat and clean for Sunday, regained some self-possession. "For gosh sakes," he said, "I'm not scared o' cops—why should I be?—but for gosh sakes, any o' those guys at school and around, those SDS guys and them, they find out I had cops come see me, I'm dead for sure! I tell you—"

Landers pointed out that they were in plain clothes, which reassured him somewhat. "I just don't want them guys thinking—I just stay away from that kind!"

He had been, last Wednesday morning, at school— "Anybody tell you, only for gosh sakes, you go asking about me and them guys—" The car had been at a local gas station for an oil-change. The Spencers looked like upright citizens; Landers and Piggott thanked them and started out for Pacoima.

It wasn't, of course, very likely that anybody who lived in

Pacoima would be coming all the way into L.A. after a rape victim. But you never did know.

In Pacoima they found a stolid middle-aged construction worker by the name of Henry Schultz, who had a 1960 Ford sedan painted purple. He told them he'd just bought it last month, a good transportation car. "Belonged to this kid down th' street, high-school kid—leastways, his dad bought it for him when he was old enough to get a license. Now his dad takes it away, and a good thing, kid gettin' tickets all over the place and fallin' behind in school. It was a bargain. I been meanin' to get it painted a decent color, feel like a damn fool drivin' around in a circus wagon like that." Last Wednesday he had been on a construction job in town with some thirty other men, all day, the car parked on the site. "And everybody ribbin' me about the color."

"You know, Matt," said Landers, "this is sometimes a drag, this job."

"When we have to do it the hard way," agreed Piggott.

They started off for Glendale.

"Well, she wasn't—if you know what I mean—very outgoing," said Rose Baird. She looked at Higgins rather doubtfully across the little dinette table in this neat, small apartment. She looked as if she wasn't sure that tough-looking, rugged-featured George Higgins knew what a nuance was, least of all would be able to understand one. Rose Baird worked at the same brokerage that Anne Parker had, and turned out to have been one of her closest friends. "I—I just couldn't believe it at first," she had said. "Anne, getting murdered. Not—a thing that happens to people you know." But she wanted to help, and had asked him in, even offered him a cup of coffee. She was an attractive, dark-haired girl about twenty-five, with a pleasantly crooked smile.

Now she was saying, "Boy-friends? She didn't date too much—I think, just little things she said, she'd had a sort of bad experience with some fellow awhile back, he walked out on her or— She wasn't very outgoing. What? I think that was up in Ventura, before she came to L.A. I don't know his name. Anne—she didn't talk much about herself, ask for sympathy. It just doesn't seem fair she should—"

"But she did go out with men sometimes? Would you know who?"

"Sometimes, yes." She stirred her coffee, sipped. "Not steady with anybody. I guess the latest one she'd been dating was this Sam MacDonald. I'd never met him, but the way Anne talked—when she did say anything, she was a quiet one, you know—she liked him quite a lot. She met him at the painting class—"

"Painting class?"

"Yes, she'd always been interested in painting, and she finally enrolled in an adult course when the semester started in February. At Hollywood High School. She liked it. That's where—"

"Sam MacDonald. You know where he works, what his job is—where he lives?"

She shook her head. "He's in an architects' office somewhere, but I don't know which one. There'd been some talk of us going out on a double date—I'm engaged—but it hadn't come off yet."

"Know any other fellows she'd dated?"

"Only a couple she'd mentioned." Higgins took unobtrusive notes. He thought this Sam MacDonald was one to follow up. You worked it as you could; what showed you went and looked at, and sometimes you hit the jackpot. Just sometimes.

It was nearly eleven o'clock. No locating MacDonald on a Sunday; they'd have his address at the high school, of course. Higgins had a look, just for fun, in all the telephone books, and found eleven Samuel MacDonalds and nineteen S. Mac-

Donalds. He did find a MacDonald and Sons Architects in Pasadena, but that was no use either on a Sunday.

He went on to find the next name listed in Anne Parker's address book, one Margaret Kay. Not many names in the address book; a quiet girl living quietly, an orphan without any family. Margaret Kay lived in Hollywood.

Mendoza sat at his desk, swiveled around to stare out at the panoramic view. Not so much panorama as obscurity, today: gray fog, gray mist, no hint of the Hollywood foothills on the horizon. Same like all these damned amorphous cases, he thought.

The lab had finally sent up a report on Brenda Warthol. Dr. Bainbridge had sent up an autopsy report. Neither said anything. Brenda Warthol had been raped and strangled. Period. Not even any indication whether the kill had been intended or not; sometimes, in fact often in such cases, it wasn't. The lab said there was material under her nails where she'd scratched and fought him. It had been analyzed. Short dark hairs from a Caucasian, human skin tissue ditto. That was a big help, thought Mendoza. There had been plenty of fingerprints in the Warthol kitchen and service porch, on the rear door, but they all belonged to Brenda or the other Warthols.

And that baby-sitter—his nose twitched again. Like any experienced detective, he knew that what it looked like was usually just what it was. Except for the times it wasn't. Nothing he could put a finger on exactly, but— Wait for the autopsy, for the lab report. And if they couldn't do any better than they had on Brenda Warthol—

There was Jane Doe in the morgue, lovely, anonymous, and—familiar? Looking like not just anybody. Why hadn't somebody missed her? And what had happened to her—naked as a jaybird in an alley along Figueroa, suffocated and raped?

"Me doy por vencido," he said to himself, "I give up." He

got up, took down his hat and went out to lunch. In contrast to yesterday, there wasn't one other man from Homicide at Federico's. Lieutenant Pat Callaghan of Narco, incredibly bigger than Hackett or Higgins and redder-haired than Alison, was deep in discussion with Sergeant Steve Benedettino. Mendoza went over to join them.

In Glendale, Landers and Piggott found Steve Rosney at an apartment on Stocker Street. Rosney had a 1962 Plymouth painted purple. He had not been expecting a Sunday call from cops, and the apartment—which, they found later, contained nearly no furniture but several mattresses and an expensive stereo outfit—was occupied by seven people of assorted sexes all high on something. Landers and Piggott, greeted by an amiably grinning youth who opened the door to let out a heavy waft of marijuana smoke, didn't attempt to ask him any questions. They said they'd rung the wrong bell, found the nearest phone and called up the local forces of law, chasing down to Glendale Headquarters to join the party.

There was a little donnybrook before they got all seven of the joy-riders fetched in and booked; they left the Glendale lab men still examining the apartment, and foregathered with Sergeant Walsh at the detective bureau at Glendale's very handsome new Police Headquarters.

"Well, we're much obliged to you," said Walsh genially. "Funny thing. You boys following up a routine lead on a homicide, and turning up the users for us. And I suspect, from what we came across there, very possibly a seller too. We'll sort it out with the lab. One thing about this job, we swear about all the damn routine, but you never do know just what you're going to run across next. The surprises." He shook his bald head.

"We've been having kind of a spate of those lately, downtown," said Landers. "But this Rosney—he did just show on the thing. I don't think it's really likely that he was downtown abducting this woman last Wednesday morning, but we'd better look at him. Question him."

"You won't get any sense out of him way he is now," said Walsh cheerfully. "What put you onto him, anyway? From Central?"

Landers exchanged a glance with Piggott. Evidently Walsh hadn't heard about the SOS to Traffic detail all over the county. Landers was almost ashamed to tell him. The L.A.P.D. did pride itself on being the most progressive, scientific, precisely regulated force in existence. To confess to their sloppy piece of investigation, just at random the patrol-cars roaming the streets taking notice of the purple-painted cars— the one faint lead they had— He cleared his throat as preliminary to confession.

Walsh offered him a cigarette. "You know," he said, "you don't look old enough to be a cop, let alone a ranking detective."

Landers uttered a strangled sound and Piggott laughed. "I guess I could say it for you, Tom. You too, Brutus? I'm always telling you the devil's pretty busy these days. Going up and down."

"I wouldn't say no," said Walsh, looking slightly taken aback. "But—"

"Never mind, sir," said Landers austerely. "We'll have to see this Rosney when he's rational. If that kind ever is, entirely."

"Too true," said Walsh. "He'll be in the Memorial Hospital, at your service. Tomorrow, maybe."

Mendoza came back from lunch to find Jason Grace sitting at his desk in the sergeants' office, with his eyes fixed on space. A completed triplicate report, carbons not yet separated, lay beside his typewriter. He had pulled his tie loose, and sat smoking a cigarette, the smoke curling slowly upward.

"Inspiration struck you?" asked Mendoza.

Grace jumped convulsively. "Sneak up on a fellow like that! I don't know. I don't really know. There's just a little something came to my mind, and likely it doesn't mean anything at all. It's so—mmh—nebulous that I'll keep it to myself for the time being."

"What was the new call?"

"Nothing," said Grace. "Routine. Old lady found dead in bed in a cheap rooming house just this side of the Row. Pensioner. She'd been an out-patient at the General—various chronic diseases. Without much doubt the natural death, but the paperwork goes on forever, doesn't it?"

"Like the routine," said Mendoza. He wondered if anybody was getting anything useful, wandering around town on a gray Sunday on the legwork. Talking to people. Asking questions.

He went into his office and sat down at his desk. He thought about Brenda Warthol and the Hollywood Bowl. About Deforrest and Parker. About the baby-sitter Linda Ulner. And he thought about Jane Doe. Found Wednesday morning: dead since Tuesday night. And this was Sunday, and nobody had missed her yet. Why not?

He heard Lake say, "Central Homicide, Sergeant Lake . . ." He opened the top drawer and took out the cards.

Grace looked in. "Something new—I'll take it."

"*Bueno,*" said Mendoza, and began to shuffle the deck.

At ten minutes past two that Sunday afternoon, two excited and alarmed men burst into Police Headquarters in Beverly Hills. The desk-sergeant tried to unravel their story, finally sent them up to Sergeant Macy's office. Macy got them calmed down; they were both normally intelligent and rational men, but they were frightened. They told him the story in a more coherent way, and he took down the description and asked questions.

As he looked at the written description of the woman it

rang a small bell in his mind; Beverly Hills was no part of L.A., but citizens of L.A. County being very mobile, the various police forces were in constant contact with each other, exchanging information of one sort and another. The small bell connected this incident to Wilcox Street in Hollywood, and he excused himself and went away and called that precinct. He got a Sergeant Barth.

"No," said Barth, "we found that one. Jean Everett. Hit-run—not very serious—she hadn't any I.D. on her, that was all. But that description— Central had an M.P. report out on one like that, almost the same—unidentified body I think. Maybe you'd better check with them."

"O.K.," said Macy. It wasn't likely—that beat down there hardly where you'd expect to find one like this—but they had to go by the rules. He called Central Homicide. He got Mendoza.

At three-thirty Mendoza faced them in his office. After some difficulties. Fortunately, Higgins and Hackett had both turned up, stymied on the routine by the fact that it was Sunday. They had escorted the two down to the morgue. Griffith Clevenger Junior had passed out and then been sick, and been taken to First Aid; Griffith Clevenger Senior had groped for his digitalis ampoules and they'd called an ambulance, but he'd recovered and insisted on staying, on talking.

Now they sat numbly side by side on chairs in Mendoza's office and looked at the three Homicide men with grieved and angry expressions.

Griffith Clevenger Junior was perhaps thirty. He was a good-looking man, tall, dark, normally an assured and confident man: regular features, thick eyebrows over a masterful nose, a wide mouth, a cleft chin. He looked like his father: the older man's thick crown of hair was pure silver and he had the same heavy brows, prow of a nose, cleft chin. And everything about them said Money: their quietly excellent tailoring, their discreet jewelry, their manner even in shock and grief.

"But why—how?" burst out the younger man. "I don't understand—Lily! How did it happen? Why was she down here? Why—"

"Now let's just take it easy, Mr. Clevenger," said Mendoza; but a kind of warm satisfaction was in him, at that: his instinct had not been wrong, Jane Doe had been somebody. "One thing at a time. You've identified a body as that of your wife. Lily Clevenger. Can—"

"My God, my God, yes—but, Lily! I don't—I can't—" He put his hands to his face. His father laid a hand on his shoulder, spoke to him quietly. They both turned ravaged faces to Mendoza. "It doesn't seem possible," said young Clevenger a little more steadily. "You can't imagine what I—what we felt when we came home—just this afternoon—and she wasn't there. Hadn't been there. When did you say— There aren't any servants living in, just Olga and James coming—a couple of times a week, or if Lily was giving a party—and Mrs. Vickers next door saying she hadn't noticed the car for—but I don't understand how—"

Mendoza went on soothing them into more coherence. The Clevengers constituted something called Estate Management Incorporated: they arranged absentee management of a number of extensive properties, ranches and other large estates; and they had been away from home for nearly a week inspecting a piece of property in Arizona which had just come into their hands. They had been, they said, in the field, part of the time roughing it in camp, and as Lily had known that, there hadn't been any attempt to contact each other.

"She was busy, she had appointments," said young Clevenger. "This try-out in Pasadena, and her agent— But where's her car? You said— She'd have been driving, she— Oh, God, her agent must have tried to reach her, didn't Olga say he'd called, Dad? I—"

"Easy, Mr. Clevenger. Her car? What was she driving?"

"A Porsche, navy blue—1969," said Clevenger automatically. He was shaking. "I don't see how—you said—said she was raped and—? Oh, my God, Lily."

Hackett bent over him. "We don't know much about it yet, sir, you must see that. We know you're upset and shocked, but if you could just pull yourself together to help us, please. A try-out? Her agent?"

Clevenger made an effort to steady himself. "I'm sorry. I realize that. We've got—to help you—however we can. To find who—" He swallowed and accepted the cigarette Hackett offered him. "I'm sorry. It wasn't that she—needed the money, or—but she had a—a very good voice. A trained voice. She had done—some professional entertaining—before we were married. Night clubs, and so on. That was—we were married two years ago." He got out a handkerchief, pressed it to his mouth. "It wasn't necessary—but just lately —she thought she might—go back to it, just to keep occupied."

The older man looked up at Hackett. "She couldn't have a child," he said steadily. "She was very disappointed and unhappy over that. She—we all thought—perhaps if she had something to occupy her time—"

"I see," said Hackett.

"She had—did you say it happened Tuesday night? When she was—? She had a try-out engagement set up," said the husband. "At a place in Pasadena. Her agent arranged it. At a place called the Aquamarine Club. One of those—what they call—intimate supper-clubs." He added the agent's name dully: Bernard Sohl, an address in Hollywood. "I didn't—didn't like it. I didn't say anything— Dad said maybe in time she'd be reconciled— But you mustn't think," he said suddenly, "that Lily was—was like the people in that business. Show business. No. She—it was only an accident she got into that line of it at all. She wanted opera—but her voice wasn't that—that big. She went to the Juilliard School, you know. Her family—oh, God, we'll have to call them, tell them, my God—her family —very prominent people—New York, the Stoddards. But I don't understand how it could have happened!" He looked at the Homicide men wildly.

"Do you know the plate-number on the Porsche, Mr. Clevenger?" asked Hackett. "The license plate-number?"

"I—it'll be listed somewhere—on the insurance papers. I can look— But how could that have happened to Lily? Here? Downtown? She wouldn't have been anywhere *here*—Tuesday night—she'd have been in Pasadena—and then—just coming home. To Beverly Hills. How could—"

The Homicide men looked at each other. How indeed? How had their Jane Doe, no longer Jane Doe, ended up naked in an alley along Figueroa? On the way home from Pasadena, the most convenient route would have taken her down the Pasadena freeway to the interchange downtown, and then the Santa Monica freeway. And what had happened to the Porsche?

"Mr. Clevenger," said Hackett gently, "we're sorry to badger you at a time like this, but you understand we've got to ask the questions—"

"Any way we can help you. Anything. To find out who— did that—to Lily. But I don't understand how it *could* have happened. Lily—"

And it was gratifying to have his instincts about Jane Doe justified, but identified, she seemed to pose more questions than she had as Jane Doe. Lily Stoddard Clevenger, of one of New York's first families. Not quite talented enough for opera, but enjoying success as a sometime night-club entertainer. (He had probably seen a publicity photograph of her sometime.) How the hell had she ended up minus her newish Porsche in an alley off Figueroa? Raped and suffocated? Her body immersed in grease of some kind—an attempt made to wash it. . . .

Mendoza had been pacing the living room for some time. The cats, Alison and Cedric had retired discreetly elsewhere as his mood became evident. On a sudden stray thought he stopped in his tracks and said aloud, "*¿A son de qué? Me gusta un poco*. That could be. But at that time of night—" See the agent, ask at the intimate supper-club. What time would it have been? He lit a new cigarette and went on pacing; and the phone rang down the hall.

"Mendoza here."

"Oh—Lieutenant. It's Mary Higgins. Lieutenant, I'm sorry to—but it's George. Something's happened to George. I—" Her voice shook just a little.

"*¿Cómo?*" Mendoza was startled. "Mrs. Higgins, what—"

"I don't know!" she said. She was trying to hold her voice steady; as a sensible intelligent woman, she was keeping her head, and she'd been a cop's wife for a long time—first Bert Dwyer and now George Higgins. "I don't *know*. He went out a good hour ago—up to the pharmacy to get my prescription filled—and he needed cigarettes. He took Brucie with him for the walk—I'm sorry, you don't know—our dog, Brucie."

"Yes," said Mendoza.

"I wondered why he wasn't back, but— But Brucie's come home, just now, alone—his leash still on—and I can't leave the children, you see," she said tautly. "I—please, Lieutenant—"

"I'm on the way. We'll be out. Where was he heading for?"

"That pharmacy up on Glendale Avenue—Graham and Dwight—"

"I'm coming," said Mendoza.

7

He called Palliser and Landers, as being nearest; told Landers to call Hackett. He threw four explanatory words at Alison in the bedroom doorway, snatched up his jacket, ran down the hall, nearly fell headlong over Cedric slurping from his water bowl in the service porch, and fifteen seconds later the Ferrari's motor roared to life. *Por Dios,* he'd been swearing for a year he'd have a siren installed in this thing—

Down the twisting canyon road too fast, to Hollywood Boulevard, and Sunday night, thank God, not as bad as Saturday night, but enough traffic. He made what time he could, beating the lights, thinking toward the turns ahead. He knew this city like the palm of his hand. He caught the light at La Brea and sat swearing steadily in two tongues until it changed. Down to where Hollywood Boulevard became Sunset Boulevard at its beginning; left on Fountain to Hyperion, and around the great reservoir of Silver Lake to Rowena, sharp right to twisting Glendale Boulevard. He thought he marked that pharmacy—one like the other one last night, a big dispensing pharmacy, not a drugstore—a faint first pang of fear hit him. Just past where Fletcher Drive angled off to the left—

The Ferrari screeched too fast around the last curve and he set a violent foot on the brake. Too many cars gathered down there to be normal for Sunday night; and then his headlights showed him the familiar high-domed black-and-white shape of an L.A.P.D. mobile lab unit. He swerved the Ferrari sharp into the curb under a *No Parking At Any Time* sign, got out and ran, pulling out his billfold with the badge pinned to it.

As he ran, automatically his mind was telling him that whatever had happened here had happened awhile ago. There wasn't another black-and-white anywhere around: the Traffic men, first to answer a call, had gone back on patrol. Civilian cars, men in civilian clothes, a dozen of them inside the place—he ran through the propped-open door, a man reached to stop him, challenged angrily, and up there by the prescription counter he spotted a familiar face.

"Barth!" he gasped. "What goes on here? When?"

"Mendoza—what are you doing here? Heist job," said Sergeant Barth. "The pharmacist was shot. No, not fatal, he'll be at the receiving hospital by now—"

"One of my men—maybe something to do with it—one of my men missing," Mendoza told him. "Sergeant Higgins—he started up here over an hour ago, his wife said—they live over on Silver Lake—have you found—"

"What?" said Barth. "One of your— Well, there wasn't anybody here but the pharmacist when the Traffic men got here. He managed to call in after the heister ran. Robertson —when was this one clocked?"

"Seven-fifty, sir. There was a black-and-white here in five minutes."

Mendoza looked at his watch. It was a quarter past nine. Over an hour ago, Mary had said. Give George what, fifteen minutes to walk the four blocks here, with the dog—he could have walked right in on it. He said that to Barth; he said, "And if he did, he wouldn't have stood by without taking a hand. My God, if he walked in on it, he'd be more or less committed—he wouldn't see anything wrong until he got inside, and if I know George, when he did spot the heister he hauled out his gun and tried to take him—"

"Then where is he?" asked Barth.

"*¡Estúpido!*" said Mendoza. "It could have gone any way—we don't know—but what his wife said, he could have got here just about when the action was going on. The dog came home alone. George didn't. Heist-men don't think twice about shooting. Listen to me—" he shook Barth's arm—"I want the helicopters out with the search-lights, I want an inch-by-inch search of six blocks around— I want the dogs—he could have chased them, he could be lying bleeding to death under a hedge in the next block—"

"All right, all right," said Barth. He ran for the lab truck and the radio. Palliser dodged him, coming in, and Landers was just hurrying past the big plate-glass window. Mendoza explained rapidly, filling them in.

"I don't know what Wilcox Street has got yet, the search is the important thing right now. By the times, he could have walked right into the middle of it— I'm thinking now, maybe he only saw one man, maybe there were a couple, and he got jumped or shot from behind."

"Not shot dead," said Palliser instantly.

"*Pues no,* he'd have still been here. No, it's possible he chased after, tried to get a look at their plate-number—we don't know, damn it, but if he's lying wounded around here somewhere—"

Which could well be; beyond the boulevard and its tall arc-lights, this was a section of little dark residential streets, narrow, with tall trees at intervals and few street lights. Barth came back. "The helicopters are on the way, and six cars."

"We can't wait for them," said Mendoza. "A flashlight—hell, there's one in the car." He ran to get it, and Landers and Palliser to collect theirs. When Mendoza came back he had a Hollywood street map flapping wildly in his hands. "Now look, Barth—*Dios,* it's your beat but my man—we'll cover from here in south to the lake—between where Armstrong cuts in and Silver Lake joins Glendale. O.K.? You deploy the rest of the men the other side of Glendale—"

Five minutes later, as they began their search down the little dark pockets of streets, three of the big L.A.P.D. helicopters attached to Traffic came hovering over them. They sent their brilliant great searchlights groundward, lighting up the area and that surrounding it as bright as day. Barth had a man sitting in the lab truck, in touch with them by radio, directing them; they were a godsend.

And in the end, they were the biggest help in proving to the frantic searchers that George Higgins, dead or wounded, wasn't anywhere within twelve square blocks around.

At a quarter past twelve they called off the search. They foregathered back at the pharmacy, still brightly lighted up: Mendoza, Palliser, Landers, Hackett, eight uniformed men, Barth.

"But where the hell *is* he?" raged Hackett. "So he walked in on the heist, for God's sake, Luis, how could that—"

"It's got to be something to do with this caper," said Mendoza tersely, coldly. "I don't believe in that big a coincidence, that he vanished for some other reason just when this was getting pulled. Barth! You said the pharmacist was shot—unconscious when you got here. Bad?"

"I don't think so. Body shot."

"All right. Art, you know what I want. A man with him every minute." Hackett turned and ran for the truck. "He could place George here—maybe tell us a lot. So what do you know, Barth, what showed before this came up?"

"Not much." Barth was worried and hurried too: at times like this, cops drew together. "It looks like the heist after the dope. A place like this. By the looks, that was what loot they took—out of the stockroom back there. We got here about a quarter past eight, the lab boys a few minutes later. One thing I can say—the only blood anywhere was around the pharmacist." He nodded toward the counter. "Back there, on the floor."

Mendoza let out a long sigh. "All right. Does that say

George wasn't wounded? But—" He stopped and stared into space for ten seconds, and then he said, "*¡Santa María y José y Jesús!* Last night—last night—"

Hackett came back. "It's set up, Luis, I got—"

"Trasker, Starr and Killeen!" said Mendoza. "*Dios, Dios—* they missed the loot last night—did George walk in on them here tonight?"

"My God!" said Hackett. "But even so, Luis—"

"Why in hell would they—you're saying maybe they took him? Hostage?" said Landers. "Why? We don't, for the love of God, even know what they're driving. We're not on them, not even close. Which they must know. Why—"

"Trasker, Starr and Killeen," said Mendoza in a whisper. "Read it, boys—just read it. They knocked over a place twin to this last night, and by a fluke got nothing. I know it's not for sure it was them here tonight, but the odds say it could be. All too likely. And George walked in on it. In the middle? As they ran? You know George. He wouldn't have stood and watched. He'd get out the gun, wouldn't he? Try for them anyway. And—he'd—have—the badge on him."

"Christ," whispered Hackett. "What are you saying?"

"I don't pretend to know how the ones like Trasker, Starr and Killeen got that way," said Mendoza, "but the way they are I know. Just read it, Art. He walked in on them. What happened then? Please God the pharmacist will tell us something when he comes to. But one guess I'll have, *amigo.* George was alive. If he was dead they'd have left him. Why didn't they? There's no sign of his gun anywhere. I think they found out he's a cop, Art—and just on the spur of the moment, maybe, took him along—for fun."

"What the hell?" said Barth. "Crazy—they must be holed up somewhere, Mendoza—why would they kidnap a hostage?"

"I don't know—but you're a detective too. What's left after everything else is ruled out must say something. I don't believe in coincidence. Those three have been getting around, Barth, by the trail they've left. It could be they're planning on the quick deal for this loot and goodbye to L.A." Mendoza dropped his cigarette and put a deliberate heel on it. "They've all got long pedigrees, they're tough and mean and experienced, and they don't like cops one damn bit. They picked up some loot tonight, and all of a sudden—God damn how it happened—they find they've got a cop too. A real man-sized cop. They didn't kill him. They took him with them—maybe —to have some fun with—later on?"

"No," said Hackett. "No, Luis. That kind aren't—that subtle. They wouldn't—"

"I wouldn't take any bets," said Palliser, "what those three might take into their heads, Art."

"It couldn't be—" Landers looked frightened.

"So where is he?" asked Mendoza. There was a long, terrible, oppressive silence. Hackett let out his breath; he'd forgotten to light the cigarette he held. "We had better go talk to his wife," said Mendoza.

She was in control; she was being good. And it wasn't kind to tell her foolish reassuring lies; Mendoza told her what conclusions they had come to bluntly. "You know we're on it— we're doing all we can."

"I know that, Lieutenant," she said steadily. The children were in bed. She wasn't likely to sleep. Mendoza went to the phone and called Alison, told her to send Máiri down here at once, told her what they thought.

"Oh, Luis," she said. "Luis. It—just couldn't—happen to her again? Losing Sergeant Dwyer—and now Higgins? The baby due in October. Luis, it couldn't happen. Yes, I'll send Máiri. But— I can't feel—anything so *wicked* could happen, *amante*."

Mendoza bent his head to the cool impersonality of the phone. And wholly without volition (in the naked moments of life, involuntarily, the things instilled in childhood return to power) he found he was repeating over in his mind, *Padre nuestro, que estás en el cielo, santificado sea tu nombre*—Thy will be done, but—

"Luis?"

"I don't know, *cara*," he said. "I don't know." *Dios te salve, María, llena eras de gracia, el Señor es contigo*— Pray for us sinners now and at the hour—

He went back to the living room. He remembered suddenly that after Bert had been killed, Mrs. MacTaggart had come to stay with Mary, look after the children. It couldn't happen again, could it? He asked her, "Do you want us to call your sister?" She had a sister somewhere in Oregon.

She looked up at him: a pretty woman, Mary Higgins, with her black hair and gray eyes and matte-white complexion. She shook her head. "I guess not, Lieutenant. She—disapproved of my marrying George. She said—I was a damn fool—to marry another cop."

And there was nothing to say to that. Nothing at all.

He waited until Máiri came. She was a brisk and efficient as always; she'd be a tower of strength here, until they knew —one way or the other.

She said to him, "I willna believe the Lord is that cruel to take away her second man in violence too. It willna be. We'll all do some hard praying on it, man, and I'll be making a Novena on it too. God wouldna do such a thing. The man is safe somewhere."

"We can hope that, Máiri." It was a commodity that cost nothing.

"Now we know all things are possible with God. I'll make a Novena on it. I don't flatter myself that I'm that deserving, but a remarkable few times God has answered my prayers before," she told him earnestly.

He looked at her sturdy, silver-curled, round-faced placidity and a strange warm comfort touched his heart. Quite irrational, of course.

"You just do that, Máiri," he said and went out.

And he never knew that Mrs. MacTaggart, looking after him, said to herself contentedly, I'll be getting the heathen man safe back into the church yet, one of these days.

Monday morning, and things to do. Clevenger, Junior had called in asking what they found out about Lily, and been apologized to by Lake. Piggott and Glasser were supposed to be off, but the night men had called them with the news, and they both showed up at eight o'clock. They still had these cases to work, whether they felt like it or not; and there'd be new things showing up too, probably.

Mendoza told them the conclusions they had reached, on Higgins; there were things to do about that, he'd been down here until three o'clock this morning doing them. Meanwhile the daily routine went on, and the best way they could help was to carry on with that.

There was the Deforrest-Parker thing; Linda Ulner; Brenda Warthol, and the purple cars— Traffic had called in four new names overnight. They all nodded at him quietly and went out to carry on the routine; Hackett stayed, lighting a new cigarette.

"That kind," he said. "Trasker, Starr and Killeen. I can just see it, Luis. Only just. What might be in their minds?"

"Contrary to popular opinion, I don't carry a crystal ball in my back pocket."

"No. You don't need one for this, do you? They must know we're not within miles of them—they don't need a hostage to hold us off. Just a cop to—push around." Mendoza hunched a shoulder at him. "He could be tied up, gagged, in any dirty hole in east L.A., with the cigarette burns, the knife— All right, I'm going. The routine." He went out quietly.

Mendoza swiveled around and stared out the window. Foggy again today: no hint of the hills on the horizon.

Things to do. He had done them. Teletypes to all law-enforcement agencies in ten western states. Probable that Trasker, Starr and Killeen were now holding an L.A.P.D. officer as hostage. Description: George Allen Higgins, six-three, one-ninety, brown and blue, Caucasian, thirty-eight, no marks. There was a man sitting at the hospital bedside of Ronald Chidsey, the wounded pharmacist. The hospital said he was doing fine: shot once in the body, a second shot creasing his skull, but eventually he'd wake up and answer questions. One thing—by the Saturday night caper, and those pulled up north, that unholy trio weren't making any attempt at the disguise. Experienced men, they relied on swiftness of execution, surprise, to confuse the victims; they knew that eyewitness identification can be very shaky in a courtroom.

He had arranged for all the mug-shots to appear in every newspaper in the county. Too late to get them into the morning *Times*, but they'd be in all the afternoon and evening papers. Appeal to the public. Something might turn up from that.

Had it been that threesome, last night? Or were they jumping too fast to conclusions? Please God the pharmacist could tell them.

He hadn't slept much; he passed a hand across his eyes. He'd known George Higgins a long time.

Sergeant Lake came in and handed him a lab report. He was looking subdued. "Damn it," he said, "it couldn't happen to that poor damned woman twice, could it?"

"*No se*, Jimmy. I don't know." He opened the report inattentively, and it was with a little vague surprise that the gist of it penetrated his mind, as he read it. Ardlow. That one. The bleeder. Eventually, reported the lab, by using oblique-light technique, they had been able to raise several usable latent prints from Ardlow's worn leather billfold. They had turned up in L.A.'s Records, and they belonged to one Jesse Lee Nash, who had a long pedigree of various minor felonies in several states as well as here: petty theft, mugging, threat of bodily assault, robbery from the person, breaking and entering. His last term in had been in the pen in Arizona, for B. and E. He'd been out, and off parole since 1968. Known associates listed: he liked poker, women and liquor.

Mendoza regarded the report in somnolent surprise; he'd never thought they'd get anybody on that one. At least they knew who it was, on Ardlow, whether they ever picked him up or not. He ought to put the word out on Nash: put out an A.P.B., alert the pigeons.

He thought back to that time when Art had almost got himself murdered. Well, that had come out all right. Maybe—

But he knew the ones like Trasker, Starr and Killeen all too well. There was no mercy or compassion in them, only the random violence; and they didn't like cops.

Hackett was a good cop and a good detective. He'd known George Higgins a long time too, and at the back of his mind the worry and fear for Higgins sat like a black devil nagging him; but the work had to be done. They were doing all they could do about Higgins; mere worrying never accomplished anything.

Worrying, he went out on the routine, with the photostat of Anne Parker's address book. He came to Rose Baird, at the brokerage on Spring where Anne Parker had worked, and she was surprised, let him buy her a cup of coffee on her morning break. "But I told the other man all this," she said. "Yesterday—a Sergeant Higgins."

And of course he couldn't explain about that. He was vague; she told him, patiently, what she'd told Higgins yesterday. Like Higgins, he thought he'd like to talk to Sam Mac-Donald, and went up to Hollywood High School to get his address. He got handed around some, finally wormed the address out of them: an address on Norma Place in west L.A. There, he found a Mrs. MacDonald who told him her son was at work, told him where: an architectural firm on Sunset. He found Sam MacDonald, finally, at twelve-thirty, seated on a bar stool at the London Grill over a martini.

Sam MacDonald was an amiable-looking young fellow, not handsome, but attractive in an All-American-boy sort of way, with good shoulders and a direct gaze. He sobered at Hackett's self-introduction of himself. "About Anne," he said. "That was a shock. Did you say Sergeant? Can I buy you a drink?"

"Against regulations, sir, but I can buy one." Hackett ordered himself a drink, and damn the calories.

"I know you have to ask questions. Anne—such a quiet girl. A nice girl," said MacDonald. He stared at his drink. "I guess —if you want to know, Sergeant—I was halfway to deciding to propose to her." He took a quick swallow. "One of these louts breaking in and—"

"Well, it doesn't seem it was," said Hackett. "Door wasn't forced. Whoever it was, she'd let in."

MacDonald stared at him. "Somebody she knew?" he said, taking that implication at once. "But that's—"

"Let's say, somebody she thought she knew," said Hackett.

"Oh. Yes, I see. Well," said MacDonald thoughtfully. "I'll be damned. But you know, she wasn't—just so very shrewd, Sergeant. At sizing people up. Even if she'd lived in the city awhile."

"Is that so?"

"That's so. I am not a fool," said MacDonald tiredly. "You have to look everywhere, I know. I'd been dating her. It happened Thursday night. I don't know what time—you will. Well, I was at home all that evening—my mother was there, and some of the time a neighbor, Mrs. Knudsen. I went to bed about eleven, and Mother stayed up to watch the late movie so she could say I didn't leave the house."

"Thanks very much," said Hackett. "You do realize—"

"Oh, yes," said MacDonald. "You have to look. I just hope you find him, Sergeant—not that it can do Anne any good. It doesn't seem fair—she never had much out of life at all. No family, and then—" He lifted his glass and finished his drink quickly.

Landers and Piggott were out pursuing purple cars.

"It couldn't happen to that poor woman twice, could it?" said Piggott. "I can't believe God would let that happen, Tom."

"I don't know," said Landers. "The Lieutenant'll be doing all that can be done. Which isn't much. But if he walked in on those three—and they didn't kill him outright, Matt—and he's vanished—well, you know as well as me what that kind are like."

Piggott had been a cop awhile too. "It does say," he observed, after a little silence, "that Satan shall be given power for a little time. Kind of hard to figure out dates and times from what it does say, Tom. But there are times I think it's right now Daniel was talking about. What with the spiritual wickedness in high places, and all the kids on dope, and the pornography floating around, not to mention all the wolves in sheeps' clothing in the N.C.C.—" He was silent again, and said, "I guess it wouldn't do any harm to put in some good hard praying for Sergeant Higgins."

And Landers, who hadn't been inside a church since he got too old for Sunday School at the Central Christian Church, said soberly, "I guess you might be right, Matt."

Most of the purple cars, of course, were owned by teenagers and slightly older young people. On this cast they found, first, a Sidney Kerr in Burbank, with a 1963 Ford sedan. He was twenty-two, Negro, very surprised but not apprehensive at being singled out by cops, and he worked at Lockheed as a skilled mechanic. He had no record, he looked like an honest citizen, and last Wednesday he'd been at work as usual all day, as his supervisor could—and did—say.

They wandered on. They found, in Culver City, a high-school boy named William Cowan who owned a 1960 Plymouth two-door sedan painted purple. He was young for his age, awed at being approached by cops; he could only have a car, he said, by earning the money for it himself, his dad had said, and he had; he had an after-school job at a service-station, he was too busy to go gadding around any; and last Wednesday he'd been at school, of course.

"This is the silliest damned way to *investigate*," said Landers. "We never followed up that dope in Glendale. I don't say he's *likely*—"

And both of them went on worrying about Higgins.

The Clevengers had given Homicide the plate-number of Lily Clevenger's Porsche. It had gone on the hot list this morning. That was another one they ought to be doing some work on; and the vague notion that had struck Mendoza about it should be followed up. Lily, on her way home from Pasadena to Beverly Hills—

There was a peculiar feeling permeating that whole tall building at 150 Los Angeles Street, today. A feeling of solidarity; of family concern and worry. Of all the five thousand odd members of the L.A.P.D., not many knew George Higgins personally, only the men he had worked with over seventeen years on that force; but every member of that force knew he was a cop in trouble, and there, and at all the precinct houses, and at other police headquarters around the county, there was the silent concern: the silent anxiety, and maybe more than one prayer put up for the cop in trouble.

Palliser and Grace were groping around on Linda Ulner. Very probably any useful lead they would get on that would come from the lab; but they had to work it as they could.

They had asked around the neighborhood, any recent prowlers or disturbances of any sort? They turned up one little thing: about six months ago a high-school boy who lived down the block had been picked up as a Peeping Tom, put on probation. A Lionel Liggett, seventeen.

He was just a possible; they found him at school and brought him in to talk to. And they went on worrying about Higgins.

"Why the holy hell," said Palliser, "would they, even if it was those three, Jase? Take him as a hostage? Off a job? But what other answer is there?"

"That kind don't add up to sense," said Grace.

What none of them knew about, and thus didn't take into consideration, was Killeen's sense of humor. That, they would hear about in due course.

At four-forty on Monday afternoon Ronald Chidsey opened his eyes. The man on duty at his bedside was a rookie, Pete McDowell, and this was the first time he'd been delegated such unusual and interesting duty, helping out the detectives. It had been damn boring, at that, just sitting here, watching the nurses tend Chidsey, if different from riding the black-and-white with his experienced partner. He had specific instructions what to do when and if Chidsey came to. And he'd only been in the L.A.P.D. six months, only four months on the job after attending the Police Academy, but he'd never have joined at all if he hadn't respect for the uniform. Like every other L.A.P.D. man, he knew there was a cop in trouble, and that Chidsey might be able to give them valuable information.

When he saw Chidsey was awake, he was excited; he bent over him. "Mr. Chidsey?" he said. "You hear me?" Chidsey turned his head weakly and his eyes focused on McDowell. "Police, Mr. Chidsey. You remember what happened? Can you tell me—" Chidsey nodded.

"Want to—help you—whatever," he gasped.

"I've got some photographs to show you, sir." McDowell got them out. "Now take your time. We want to be sure."

Chidsey shook his head at the mug-shot of Starr, nodded affirmatively at those of Trasker and Killeen.

"That—was them."

"Good, sir. Was there another man?"

Chidsey made an effort and raised himself on one elbow. "I remember," he said painfully. "Want to help—another man came in the store—just as they were leaving— I knew him— Higgins—there were three men, and that one—that one in the photograph—hit him from behind, he didn't know—didn't see—the little dog ran out—"

McDowell ran for the telephone.

8

THAT WAS definite; and Mendoza and Lake got on it right away, with the follow-up teletypes everywhere. Oregon had been asked last night to look up all known associates of those three up there; probably they were still looking for whoever had aided and abetted the breakout. But whatever Oregon might turn up, it would be past history. Right here was where the action was.

Trasker and Starr were in L.A. Records, of course; both had been picked up here as first offenders. That was awhile back: 1955 for Trasker, he'd been seventeen; 1954 for Starr, ditto. It was anybody's guess when and where they'd hooked up with Killeen; they had, it was thought, pulled several jobs as a trio before Killeen drifted up to Oregon—or maybe they'd all gone up there together—and eventually got married and later killed his wife. Killeen had been in the pen seven long years for that: Trasker and Starr only four. Both had served terms in San Quentin before that, on two convictions. The damn fool parole board, let them out after a minimum term—but the damage was done now.

Since this morning Records had been gathering what information L.A. had on Trasker and Starr. The last L.A. had heard of Trasker and Starr was in 1963, when they had both been paroled from Quentin on a sentence for armed robbery. That was a good while back, considering the way pros drifted around; maybe they were out of touch with pals here, but also maybe not. You came back to a place you'd once called home, you went looking up old friends—when you had time.

And they'd need contacts to dispose of the loot. Records, looking back through its microfilmed files, had come up with three known old pals of Trasker's by ten A.M., but two were dead and the third was in Folsom. They went on looking, and came up with more; by two o'clock Mendoza had Grace and Glasser out hunting, and as men reported in, called them back to go out on that, neglecting the current homicides. He hadn't left the office himself—they'd been pretty sure Chidsey would talk this afternoon sometime—until McDowell had called in; then he went over to the hospital to see Chidsey before starting the legwork himself.

By then Chidsey was feeling stronger and more coherent; he was sitting up. He greeted Mendoza eagerly. "I want to help—all I can," he said. "I was so *surprised*—we've never been held up before— I suppose that was just luck. With all the drugs—normally in stock. . . . Three men, yes. I could only swear—to the two. But Mr., I should say Sergeant Higgins—my goodness, I knew him, of course—Mrs. Dwyer's, I mean Mrs. Higgins' Cytomel, and now the prescriptive B-complex, of course I knew—"

"Just what happened, what you saw, Mr. Chidsey. I don't want to tire you."

"Oh, yes—but I'll be fine. I hope— I do hope the sergeant wasn't hurt." His brown eyes were anxious. "They were just leaving— I had very foolishly tried to trip the alarm, and the taller one shot at me—I'd been lying there sort of playing dead, sir—I didn't *think* I was badly hurt—and just as they came out of the stock room, I saw Sergeant Higgins come in. And he—the one man, the tall one, just lashed out with his gun—"

"Had the sergeant spotted them, do you think? Was—"

"Oh, no, sir, he'd only just come in the store—the man just

struck him with the butt of his gun as they ran out, just to—to knock him out of the way like—but he didn't fall down. He got out his gun quick and turned and ran after them. Out the door. And then I must have—have fainted. The loss of blood. When I came to myself again I managed to get to the phone—call the police."

"You didn't hear any shots fired outside? See which way they went? The sergeant—"

"I'm sorry, sir, that's all I could tell you. I don't know." Chidsey was apologetic. "I do hope the sergeant—"

"Yes. Thanks very much," said Mendoza.

At least there hadn't been any blood anywhere in the street. But that was definite. George had gone after them. And how often had Mendoza said that the man who automatically jumped toward trouble instead of away from it was the born cop. And then?

But, then, they knew. Things to do on it here and now. He sat in the Ferrari and looked at the list of previous known associates of Trasker and Starr, dating back to when they'd lived here, awhile ago. He started back for his own beat, where they all were to be found—if they were still here. He was at Sunset and Western, stopped for the light, when the phone rang on the dashboard. He picked it up. "Mendoza."

"We just had word from Oregon," said Lake. "They found a couple of guys who admitted they organized the breakout. They don't say whether they offered 'em lollipops or twisted their arms, but they parted with the info that Trasker and Company were in a nearly new gray Pontiac. No plate-number."

"Well, you know they won't be in it now. They're not fools," said Mendoza.

"Landers and Piggott are still out, and Hackett."

"All right. When they show up, give them the rest of the names."

"Will do. I just thought you'd like to be up to date."

Hackett, after lunch, had gone to do some work on the Clevenger thing. Not one blessed thing had been done on that, the mysterious and exotic Lily Clevenger who had so intrigued them as Jane Doe. He drove over to Pasadena, worrying about Higgins, and found the Aquamarine Club tucked away on a side street in the middle of town. It wasn't officially open, but he hoped by this time of day there'd be somebody there and banged on the door until an irritated-looking middle-aged man opened it and told him to go away, they didn't open until six. Hackett showed him the badge and irritation gave way to alarm and questions. A liquor license cost something in this state; possessors of such were very co-operative with the law.

"Lily Stoddard?" He blinked at Hackett across the little desk in his cubbyhole of an office beyond the dance-floor, the ranks of tables, the door to the kitchens. "Why, sure. Last Tuesday night." He had introduced himself as the owner-manager, Morton Greenberg; he was a natty smallish man with sharp tailoring, two rings, a Brooklyn accent and an unexpectedly charming smile. "A try-out? Well, it wasn't exactly that—you said Sergeant? I liked her. She hadn't worked professionally since she got married, and not long out here before that— I think more back East. But I'd heard her, three-four years ago when she was at the Acapulco in Hollywood. I was glad to hear she was taking engagements again. I like that girl. Maybe I'm a square." He laughed. "Me, I'm no pro musician, but an ear I got. It's a regular pain in the —well, a pain to me, these strictly no-talent kids slipping and sliding around, half-notes, quarter-notes, my God, they can't hold a note straight—the moaning and groaning, the rock—" he shut his eyes. "Lily Stoddard, she's class. I'm a square—and I'm forty-eight years old." He twinkled at Hackett. "She does the oldies, you know—specializes. The goodies with the tunes to them, the solid time. *Honeysuckle Moon,* and *Dinah,* and like that. Sure, she's coming here for a thirteen-week stay, beginning—"

"Well, I'm afraid she's not," said Hackett, and told him why. Greenberg was astonished, shaken, incredulous, grieved. "Dead? She's dead? *Murdered?* How did you s——raped and— Oh, my God! What a thing! What a goddamned awful— It doesn't seem right," he said suddenly. "A lovely girl like that—and with her voice. To kill something beautiful and good like that—"

Hackett asked him questions about Tuesday night. He spread his hands. "What can I tell you? Nothing. She was singing in two spots, eight-thirty and ten-thirty. She got here about eight. She looked wonderful. You know, she was even prettier close to than under a spotlight? But her agent told me—Bernie Sohl—he said, she's mad in love with her husband, she's a lady, no funny stuff with Lily. Not that I would have," he said absently. "She was class, and I'm just a Jew kid from Brooklyn that made a little money with luck. She was great. She gave them *Meet Me Tonight in Dreamland,* and *Harvest Moon,* the first spot. They loved her. Even the younger people who don't remember back to then, or were just kids, they like the goodies. They like a tune you can sing. I went and took her to a table, says won't she have something on the house, but she says she never eats much when she's singing. She had about half a martini and a couple of spoonfuls of our Eggs Benedict. She was— he looked at Hackett— "like champagne. Sparkling, sort of. Right on top, Sergeant. She was—fine. She gave them *Good Night, Sweetheart* and *Lovey Mine* and *Me and My Shadow* the second spot, and they ate her up. She had them in her hands—me too. My God, to think of that beautiful thing dead. Dead. All that sparkle and life—"

"When did she leave here? She was alone?"

"She was. I asked her. I told her to be careful—a woman driving alone these times, at night—she says she always keeps the doors locked. She left right after the second spot, maybe ten-fifty, eleven o'clock. I told her she'd never needed any try-out with me, I was sold on her already. She thanked me and said Bernie'd see me about the contract— I was surprised I hadn't heard from him, but I knew it was O.K. and—God. It was that night?"

Hackett said yes. But how and why? She'd have headed straight for home, on the freeway. As a cynical cop, he did think of the extracurricular boy-friend—the husband away from home—but even just what they'd heard about Lily so far, he didn't think much of that. Griffith Clevenger looked like an eminently satisfactory husband, and Lily had evidently been a respectable wife. How had she ended up down on Figueroa Street?

It was three-thirty. He called in. Lake told him to come back and do some important work for a change, and he started downtown in a hurry.

Landers and Piggott had found another teenager with a purple car, spotted by Traffic in Montebello last night. He turned out to have a minor pedigree as a j.d. and they questioned him at length, but his employer—a Shell station manager—alibied him and they let him go.

They had two more new ones to look at, in Maywood and Inglewood. Landers was driving today. They didn't talk much; they were worrying about Higgins.

The purple car in Maywood was owned by an offbeat character, one Bella-Mae Durward. She was fat, forty and friendly, and she ruled her life by astrology mostly, but had a few other ideas too. Purple, she told them, was her lucky color; she never wore any other color. Even her front door was painted purple. In her fussy-frilly living room were bowls of artificial violets and pansies, and her fingernails were painted purple and her lipstick was purple.

They got away from her just after four-thirty and called in

just in time to hear the news that it was definite; Chidsey had told them.

"Come in," said Lake. "We've got about a dozen names from Records—old pals or sometime pals of Trasker and Starr or both. We'll all be doing the overtime."

Alison had called Angel Hackett at two o'clock. "It just couldn't happen," she said.

"You'd think not," said Angel. "We'll hope not. Have you seen her?"

"I just got home. Máiri's there, of course. Of course she's taking it all right—she's under control—but, Angel, the children aren't. It's awful. They're terribly fond of George— I— I think he came around just as they were missing their own father so, and they're—upset. Bewildered. It makes it worse for Mary. It's the waiting, not knowing. God knows how long. They're all doing the overtime downtown, but—"

"Alison, you know we'll have to phone around—all the invitations out for the shower—we *can't*. Not knowing."

"Yes, I know. But surely we'll know—one way or another —by next *week*?"

"One way or another," said Angel sombrely. "Well, it's no good talking, is it? They're doing what they can on it." And what neither of them said, of course, was that they were cops' wives too, and these days, anything could happen to any cop, any time.

Up to six-thirty, the hunt for the known old pals had turned up exactly one: a Jerry Parcher, at one time a pretty good friend of Trasker's; and he was no use to them at all. Since those days, Parcher had turned into a wino; what mind he'd ever had was preserved in alcohol, and obviously no half-way intelligent escaped con would trust him with any secrets.

Mendoza and Hackett knocked off for dinner then, and went uptown, out of the greasy-spoon area, to Chasen's. Over a drink (and damn the calories, he needed a drink) Hackett passed on what he'd got from Greenberg. " 'Class,' he said. She seems to have been. I can't see any illicit romance there, anything like that. She'd have started home on the freeway. What got her off it? Nobody could force her off the freeway, in a car. And what's happened to the car?"

Mendoza took a swallow of rye, sat back and lit a cigarette. His eyes looked rather savage, but he knew that raging up and down and swearing was an unproductive exercise; they were doing what they could. These other cases on hand too. To be worked somehow, sometime.

"¿Qué significa eso? I had one small thought about that, Arturo. I know you're going to swear and say you're an idiot not to have thought of it. We've had this and that thrown at us in a hurry, and now—George. But—" he looked at his cigarette—"tooling around town with a twelve-cylinder engine, I'm lucky to get twelve miles to the gallon or so. Of course the Ferrari's got a thirty-two-gallon tank. A Porsche's only got room to carry about thirteen."

"My God!" said Hackett. He set his drink down with a bang. "My God! She was out of gas—"

"It just could be." Mendoza shut his eyes and emitted a long stream of smoke. "Driving around in that thing, that'd get nearly thirty miles to the gallon—only four cylinders, of course—" Mendoza didn't really recognize anything under six cylinders as a legitimate automobile—"you'd be more apt to get low on gas before noticing it. It was just a thought. The Clevengers' place is on the west outskirts of Beverly Hills. Thirty-five, thirty-eight miles over to Pasadena, and back again. Say she hadn't thought about the gas tank. All of a sudden, maybe just as she's on the last lap of the Pasadena freeway toward the butterfly interchange downtown, she notices the tank is low. Maybe nearly empty. What would she do?"

"My God, but what fools we were not to see it! It's about

the only answer, isn't it? She'd get off the freeway and look for a station. But that time of night—"

"What time would it have been? She left the club at ten-fifty, eleven—and there'd be nothing on the Pasadena freeway then. A week night. Put it between eleven-twenty and eleven-thirty she'd be off the freeway looking for a station open. Some of them stay open to midnight."

Hackett looked at him aghast. "On top of everything else we've got, we just go looking at random for every gas station downtown that stays open to midnight? And no leads other than that at all— And come to think, Luis, if that was the reason she got off the freeway, nothing says where. It could have been in Eagle Rock or—"

"But she ended up downtown," said Mendoza. "It's the likeliest thing, Art. That she got off it at the interchange. And there, she had a choice of main drags where the stations are, but not much. Figueroa, Washington, Venice, and that's about it."

"Yes," said Hackett, "that's a fact. But there'll still be quite a few, Luis. And so we look, and the attendants say, 'No, she wasn't here,' what then?"

"*Paciencia*," said Mendoza and picked up his knife and fork.

Two of those they were looking for were Johnny Knight and Harry Becker, who had been pals of Trasker's when he was here. Both of them had pedigrees along the same lines as Trasker's and Starr's, if not as long or as sinister. But that went back to 1959, 1960, and in that length of time the men like that drifted around. The latest address they had for Knight was from 1964, the latest on Becker, 1962. They started out with those and found they had both moved away, but if they were still here at all, they would tend to stay more or less in the section of town they knew, where they felt comfortable.

By eight-thirty that night they were reduced to wandering

in and out of the bars, asking if anybody had seen Knight or Becker lately. As the neat, clean plainclothesmen they ordinarily were they'd have stood out like sore thumbs, and they had all taken their ties off and tried to look shabby and blend with the scenery. Hackett, coming out of a bar on Third Street, ran into Mendoza and told him he looked like a paid hand for the Mafia, with his normally smooth thick hair on end, minus a hat, tie or jacket, with his moustache looking somehow sinister. "No luck?"

"*Nada*. Maybe some of the other boys—let's call in to see."

Palliser and Landers came across Harry Becker unexpectedly, over a beer at a bar on Main Street. The bartender pointed him out casually, and they took him back to headquarters in a hurry. Unfortunately neither Palliser nor Landers looked especially tough or threatening, however much. they might feel that way; but as luck had it Mendoza called in just as they got there and brought Hackett back with him. Hackett, six-three and a half, two hundred and twenty, was enough to intimidate almost anybody, and he was just in the mood to do it too.

So it was four of them stood around the bewildered Becker, unsure why he'd been pounced on, there in the interrogation room. "Come on!" said Hackett roughly. "You were a pal of Rod Trasker's, don't tell us he didn't look you up when he hit town! You read the papers, Becker? You know he's here—and he's holding a cop, did you know that, Becker?"

Becker stared at him, his mouth open slackly; he wasn't very big, a sandy bowlegged man about five-five, and he said nervously, "Listen—listen, you got no call pick on me—Rod T-Trasker?—Jesus, I knew him way back but I ain't seen him in years—I didn't know he was back—honest, I'm clean, I don't know nothing—"

"You'll come apart, Becker, if you stay here all night," Hackett told him grimly. He bent over him menacingly.

"You don't suppose we care what we do to anybody hurts a cop? You don't suppose the doctor wouldn't say you had an accident, fell downstairs?" Play-acting, he thought tiredly.

Becker looked at them wildly. "But I don't know nothing! Honest, I ain't laid eyes on Rod Trasker—" he gulped. "All right, all right, I seen in the paper—about him maybe bein' back here. He wouldn't—wouldn't want nothing to do with me now! He's big-time, Rod—since I knew him—*I don't know nothing!* Don't you hit me—"

They kept on at him, but that was all they got. And as he hadn't taken much breaking, he was probably telling the truth.

At eleven o'clock they shut down the hunt for the night. They had run into a couple of men who told them they used to know Johnny Knight, but hadn't seen him in a long time.

And on Tuesday morning they had, of course, a new body. The body in a car parked along Flower Street, routinely tagged by Traffic as illegally parked, and the patrolman had naturally noticed the body and reported it just as the night crew was leaving Homicide.

Palliser and Grace were supposed to be off, but they had both come in. There was the Warthol inquest at ten, the Ardlow inquest tomorrow. Everybody else but Glasser had gone straight back to the hunt for Trasker's former friends. Palliser went, perforce to look at the new body. As the body was lying quietly in the rear seat, Traffic had mounted a quiet guard over it until a Homicide detective was available.

The car was a 1965 Impala, white. The body was that of a youngish man, nondescript from what Palliser could see through the windows. He thought they'd better get the lab straight on this; he didn't dare open a door. There wasn't anything around the car, on the street or sidewalk, that looked significant, so he called for a tow truck and had the car towed into the garage. There, after Duke had dusted the car and lifted some latents, they finally opened a rear door and had a good look at the body.

It had pretty obviously been a body from the start: a couple of bullet-holes right through the face. The interns said, some time last night, maybe about midnight.

Palliser went through the corpse's pockets. A billfold, empty of bills, plenty of I.D. One Lester Rhys, an address on Norton Avenue in Hollywood: valid driver's license, membership card in an Elks lodge, BankAmericard, a leather case filled with business cards: *Mr. Lester Rhys, Attorney-at-Law*, an address on Fairfax Avenue. Change loose in his trouser-pocket, a memo-pad in breast pocket, ballpoint pen. No rings, no tie-clasp, no watch.

Palliser riffled the memo-pad, saw writing and spread the pad open carefully. In a precise copperplate hand on the first page of the pad appeared a message: "If I should be found dead at any time or place, even though it may appear to be a natural death, I beg that the authorities will make a full investigation. My life has been threatened *and attempted* on several occasions by my wife Myra Rogers Rhys and I fear she will yet succeed in murdering me. I have left a deposition to this effect with my partner Jacob Lockyear, 1909 Normandie Avenue, Hollywood." It was signed *Lester Rhys.*

"What the hell?" said Palliser. He was annoyed and intrigued. As if they hadn't enough on their hands—

The autopsy report on Linda Ulner was on Mendoza's desk when he came in on Tuesday morning. He had just finished reading it when Hackett came in.

"So, the continued hunt?" asked Hackett.

"*Dios.* All these other things— But that's funny," said Mendoza. "What did I think about that at the time? I don't know —nothing I could put a finger on, but—"

"On what?"

"Linda Ulner. The baby-sitter. She wasn't raped, Art. Just

beaten to death with the blunt instrument. Bainbridge says something like a wrench."

"What? Well, that is funny. It looked like such a classic case —the Peeping Tom spotting her alone, and—God," and Hackett passed a hand across his face. "I can't think straight, Luis. George. Those unholy three bastards—whyever they took him, what they might have done by now—God. And all this coming along at the same time—"

"*Vaya despacio*," said Mendoza softly. "*Sé.* We go on doing what we can. And holding the positive thoughts, Arturo." He looked a little washed-out this morning, taut and pale, but dapper as ever, and groomed. "There's a new body —a rather peculiar body. John's on that. Things a little hot and heavy. The Clevengers have just informed us that Lily would have been wearing her engagement ring—a one-carat solitaire diamond set in platinum. Yes, swear. Description out to the pawn-shops. And there's Deforrest-Parker. Ballistics just now tells us that that bullet John found where they'd missed it is from Deforrest's gun. The Hi-Standard .22. I don't know if that gives us anything."

"It doesn't," said Hackett.

"*Donde menos se piensa salta la liebre*," said Mendoza. "One never knows. You and John go work the other ones, today. O.K.? We may get a break—but odds or evens, the jobs have to get done, damn it. Somehow."

"I know that. I know that, Luis, but— Oh, all right. Where do I go first?"

"George was going through Anne Parker's address book. He turned in a report Saturday night. There's only two or three names left. Go look at them. On Warthol—damn it, we've got five more purple cars spotted by Traffic, from Tarzana to Artesia, and —*¡diez demonios desde el infierno!*—when there's even a chance that one of these old pals of Trasker's or Starr's might tell us something— But the whole job—"

125

"In fact, time is of the essence," said Hackett tiredly. "All right, I'll get on that."

Lily Clevenger would just have to wait. And Brenda Warthol. The new one—well, obvious things to do there. Another funny one.

At eleven o'clock that morning, with Palliser on the new case, Hackett on Deforrest-Parker and Mendoza still doing a little academic wondering about Linda Ulner—which had looked so much like the usual thing indeed and now didn't—at eleven o'clock that morning they found Johnny Knight.

He had moved around since he'd built a little j.d. record at about the same time as Rod Trasker; he had served one short term for burglary and got out in 1958. That was the last L.A. Records had heard of him. And actually, the Homicide men hunting around Central's beat didn't find him; he found himself.

Sergeant Lake, trying the phone in the Ferrari every two minutes, finally got Mendoza and told him—Knight had come in. Of his own volition.

Mendoza, Landers, Piggott and Grace shot back to headquarters in a hurry.

"Now look," said Knight. He was a big tough-looking man, broken nose, acne scars, scant dark hair and shoulders as massive as Higgins'. "Look. Sure, I made the mistakes. I done the time. But I make the brag, I ain't no fool, see? It don't get you anywhere—" he eyed them with a glint of humor—"you guys are always smarter. I come out, I intend stay out. Play it straight. And I have. I was always good at hand work any kind, I went and took a course in mechanics, I got a good job, next in line to manager, big garage— Stoner's—up on Vine. You know you got no count on me after that first one. I got married to a nice girl, we got two good kids."

"So, Mr. Knight?"

"So, Rod Trasker don't know that," said Knight. He

looked at them straightly. "You don't want to think I dragged my heels on it. No. I never seen the paper—the *Herald*—till this morning. I don't read a paper regular. Then I see it, an hour ago maybe—all that about Rod and the other guys. I come as soon as I saw it. *I* didn't know about Rod—that he'd moved into the big time on the bent, see. I been straight. Rod, he shows up at the garage where I work—says he'd asked around for me, I don't know who told him where. He says he needs a place to stay, he and some pals of his. Look, what do I say? He was a friend of mine— I ain't seen him in years but he used to be a pal." He looked up at them standing there listening to him; he said, "I don't feel about cops—way I did once. Stupid. There's got to be cops. The fellows like Rod. And that Killeen— God. Rod says it was just maybe overnight. I says they could use our garage—out back of the house, I mean. We got no room take them in. That was Sunday night, they came. I didn't feel right about it all yesterday. I suspected they were on a job—or goin' to do a job. But then last night—last night—"he wet his lips—"they'd left the car in the garage, Rod put a padlock on the door which I didn't like so good—and when they all come back from somewhere, get the car, I went out to see them. I was gonna tell Rod I'd changed my mind, see. I go in the garage, and there's Rod with the hell of a roll in his hand. Money, sure. And then I see there's a guy all tied up in the back of the car, out cold he looked—and I want no part of this no more. I told Rod, I said, you're on a caper some kind, no dice, I said, and what's with the guy all tied up? I said—"

"Could you tell—the man in the car—dead or alive?" asked Mendoza tautly.

"I don't know. I didn't want no part of it. When I saw that roll I knew Rod had pulled something. I told 'em to get out."

Contacts Trasker would have had, to fence the loot taken Sunday night.

"They took off then?" said Mendoza. "What was the car?"

"I can't give you the whole plate-number. There was mud and dust all over it. It started out AGC, I think—California plates, sure. The car's a Caddy, 1967, white over blue."

9

MENDOZA called off the hunt; they knew as much as they would probably get of that threesome's movements up to last night. Knight didn't know whether they were leaving the area or just his vicinity. But Mendoza sat at his desk smoking rapidly and exercised his one rule for detecting: "Haven't I said it before, make like the idiot boy looking for the lost horse! What we do know about them, Art, they've been on the go up to now, ¿cómo no? Loose since a week ago Sunday, and they've pulled the capers in Sacramento, Bakersfield, now here—and they must know they're hot. Especially since they must guess we know they've got George—"

"That's why I think they'll dump him," said Hackett shortly. "They'll kill him and dump him, Luis."

"No se. Who knows? We hope not. Meanwhile Landers and Piggott have gone to get what description we've got of the car on the air. If that car is anywhere in three counties around, it'll be spotted. But, Art—but—" he put out his cigarette and looked at Hackett pensively. "They got about seven C's from the Sacramento job. How'd they get rid of it so fast that three days later they're pulling a job in Bakersfield for under a century? And the day after that they're here in a hell of a hurry to go after more loot. Why?"

Hackett opened his mouth and shut it. "That hadn't struck me."

"What do the pros do when they've made a hit and have it to throw around?"

"They throw it around," said Hackett. "All ways."

"Women, liquor, gambling," said Mendoza. "So? How far is Sacramento from the Nevada border?"

"Nevada—" said Hackett. "You think that could be? With George in the back seat, Luis?"

Mendoza's mouth tightened. "No," he said. "They've been busy fencing the loot. Maybe they haven't had time to have fun with the cop yet. That's why I want that car found fast. They took off, what, fourteen hours ago from Knight's place. *Dios*, they could have killed him, dropped him somewhere and be across the border by now." He got up. "But get that on the air—just a possibility they're headed for the border."

He went up to see Pat Callaghan in Narco. "It's flogging a dead horse, but you might put the word around, try to find out about the deal. What might they get for that kind of haul, Pat? Wholesale value, about ten G's in the barbiturates, bennies, and so on?"

Callaghan rubbed his red-stubbled jaw with one enormous hand. "Quite a roll, Luis. The stuff—any of it—is in short supply since the crackdown on the Mexican border. We've been getting—as Goldberg could tell you—the pharmacies and doctors' offices knocked over, ten times as many as a couple of months ago. They might have got as much as twenty G's."

"*¡Por vida!*"

"And I don't think much of Higgins' chances," said Callaghan soberly. "That kind, they're unpredictable. Tough, mean, hair-trigger. And impulsive. It was a crazy thing to do, kidnap a cop. Now they're stuck with him. Just like you say, they'll be in a rush to blue the loot. Maybe one blessing, Luis."

"So tell me."

"They maybe took him to, like you said, have fun with a

cop. The cigarette burns, the knife, the— But now, in a hurry to enjoy the loot, maybe a quick bullet in the head and they dump him."

And the same thought had come into Mendoza's mind. He said savagely, "Don't even think it—no, I won't think it."

"You don't really suppose they're still driving that Caddy, do you?"

"*¡Que Dios te envíe a otra parte!*" said Mendoza violently. "Just a little ray of sunshine, aren't you? I don't know anything, Pat. We have to work it as we see it." He went back to his own office.

There was now nothing at all they could do for Higgins than they had done. Hope the trio had kept the Caddy; hope it would be spotted somewhere. It was very unlikely, even if Callaghan should find out about the Narco deal, that anybody at all knew what their immediate future plans were but Trasker, Starr and Killeen. This one they were playing by ear.

And all these other current cases ought to have some attention paid to them, some of the routine work done. Nothing the Homicide men could do for Higgins but wait and hope. And set about the routine on everything else.

Clevenger, Junior had called in again this morning, demanding results on his Lily; but there were just so many men and so much time. They'd get to Lily eventually.

Mendoza sat at his desk and lit a cigarette and remembered back to that time when Art lay in the hospital between life and death. Time had slowed down, it seemed weeks had passed and then it turned out to be only a day, two days. He remembered suddenly that Angel had been pregnant then too— And Mrs. MacTaggart the tower of strength with her. . . .

All these other things. Linda Ulner: another funny thing. Not raped. Lily Clevenger; should follow that up. Brenda Warthol, the damned queer lead of the purple car, and that

kind of random investigation could go on for months. Deforrest-Parker: that, really, could be anything. The new
body: Palliser was on that. And, damn it, inquests coming up
—he'd got the Ulner inquest postponed until tomorrow, but
there were others to come, Rhys, Ardlow—

"*¡Demonios!*" he said to himself. That lab report: they
knew who they wanted, on Ardlow. He went out and told
Lake to put out an A.P.B. on that Jesse Nash.

He thought he ought to do a little work himself. It was
after twelve but he wasn't hungry. Lily Clevenger. . . .

Hackett had seen Higgins' latest report, as of Sunday. The
last name in Anne Parker's address book he had been looking
for was a Margaret Kay, address in Hollywood, Tamarind
Avenue. Hackett didn't want much lunch, left a sandwich
half-eaten at a drugstore counter, drove up there. It was a
newish apartment building; he got no answer at the apartment
door and tried the manageress downstairs. She told him, after
staring curiously at the badge, that Miss Kay worked at Capi-
tol Records.

He drove there, to the eye-catching big round building on
Vine, and found Margaret Kay at the receptionist's desk in
the lobby. She was a nice-looking blonde, about twenty-five,
and she looked surprised, then comprehending, then grieved
when he introduced himself.

"About Anne," she said. "I was terribly shocked. It didn't
seem possible. I knew her all her life. But I don't know anything to tell the police." But she let him go to lunch with her,
talk to her. He sat across the little table in a booth and drank
black coffee absently and asked her this and that.

"We were in the Episcopal Orphanage together, up in
Ventura—that's where I knew her. All our lives we knew
each other. Well, I've only been here a couple of years, she
came here before I did, but of course we'd kept in touch. We
didn't really see each other often—both working and all—but

we'd phone each other and—I—there was a notice in the paper about the funeral—" her eyes filled with quick tears. Yes, Barron being efficient, thought Hackett.

"When did you talk to her last?"

"It was the night before—it happened. She sounded just so —like herself, and ordinary and— Of course she didn't know anything was going to happen to her."

"Remember what you talked about? Anything she said? About a recent date, or anybody at all?"

"Well, we were just talking. No, I— Oh, I do remember one thing, not that it could mean anything—to do with—that. She said, guess who she'd come across yesterday, and I said who, and she said Jerry Trenton. She said she'd met him at lunch that day, and was so surprised to see him down here."

"And who's Trenton?"

"Goodness, I hadn't thought. of him in years," she said. "Oh, he was raised in the orphanage too. I never knew him, to say *knew* him—well, they were pretty strict, the boys and girls were in separate buildings, but in class— I don't think Anne knew him well either, just to know who he was, you know. But anybody from your home town—"

"Thanks so much," said Hackett. "Did—"

"But it can't *mean* anything," she said. "Some awful criminal breaking in and murdering—and that nice Mrs. Deforrest too. She'd been so good to Anne—Anne thought so much of her."

But they never, of course, knew what might mean something. "Did she say any more about Trenton? Is he working here?"

"Oh, he told her he'd been trying for a job at one of the brokerages down there—answering an ad. The one where she worked. That's all I can think of. We were just talking. She'd just got a new dress she liked, and she was going to have a permanent and new styling—"

"Well, thanks, Miss Kay."

"So she did," said Jacob Lockyear mournfully. He looked at Palliser sadly; he was a mournful-looking man, long and thin and gangling, and he had melancholy brown eyes and a long jaw and a long nose. "I thought she'd get him sooner or later."

Rather taken aback at this casualness, Palliser began telling him just how and where Lester Rhys had been found. He had found Lockyear in the Fairfax Avenue office listed on Rhys's business card: a rather shabby set of offices but equipped with a horse-faced middle-aged secretary and many file-cases. Evidently the law partners doing a thriving business. "There was a—message—written in a memo-pad in his pocket. He mentioned a legal deposition in your charge, sir. You were his partner, I understand."

"Yes." Lockyear folded his long bony hands together and laid his chin on them. "Poor Lester," he said. "Poor devil. That goddamned woman. Yes, she'd tried for him before— we both were convinced of that. Had that soup analyzed, and there was arsenic in it all right, but of course she could have claimed it was accidental, and God knows she's such a messy housekeeper, it could have have been. Oh, he'd left her, of course, but that made no difference—she was still after him. He got some sample chocolates sent him through the mail about ten days ago—of course he was an idiot to eat even one, but he did. Sicker than a dog."

"But—wasn't all this reported to the police, sir?"

"What good would that do?" asked Lockyear simply. "You're thinking of fingerprints on the parcel and so on? Wouldn't think so. Very smart woman. I'd take a bet she murdered the first husband too. Said he died of food poisoning. Hah! It was the insurance, of course."

"Insurance?" said Palliser. "But if Mr. Rhys suspected that she was trying—if he'd left her—"

"Oh, he'd canceled the policy, certainly. Wouldn't put it past her," said Lockyear, "to kill him just because she was

134

mad that he had suspected her. Damn fool to've married her on the spur of the moment—he was on vacation, of course, on some damn cruise or other—but then she's a very attractive woman. Charming. For all we know she's murdered half a dozen husbands. So she finally got Lester. Poor bastard. I was afraid she would."

Palliser regarded him dumbly. For the first time in his life he didn't know what to say. He said finally, "Do you know where Mrs. Rhys is living, sir?"

"Certainly. We had a private eye on her up to a couple of weeks ago. Apartment on Cahuenga. She's working as a hostess at a restaurant on La Cienega. But she was still mad at Lester for getting away from her." He looked up at Palliser then with belated comprehension in his eyes and said, "Did you tell me he was *shot?*"

"That's right, sir. In his car, parked on Flower Street downtown."

"Now that does surprise me," said Lockyear. "I wouldn't have expected her to be so violent. Not after the arsenic in the soup, and the chocolates. I wonder where she got hold of a gun."

"Excuse me," said Palliser, feeling that he had somehow strayed onto the pages of Lewis Carroll, "but we have to have a formal identification of the body. If Mr. Rhys hadn't any relatives locally, we'll ask you to—"

"Oh. Oh, certainly," said Lockyear. "Poor Lester. I was afraid she'd get him—hell of a temper, that woman—but I am surprised, I must say, that she'd shoot him. Really very peculiar. Oh, you want me to come now? Certainly, certainly."

Mendoza was out in Beverly Hills, at the Clevenger place. Estate would be a better word for it, he thought; it occupied nearly half an acre of land, and the house, while not a mansion, whispered slyly that Money lived here. An unpretentious house, French Provincial, but no expense spared—big rooms ankle-deep in carpet, every convenience and comfort. But neither the Clevengers nor Lily, apparently, ostentatious or very social: there were just the two servants coming in twice a week, or on special occasions for a party. Olga and James Anderson.

The Clevengers, father and son, were out: they had a business to keep up, whatever personal grief they suffered.

The servants were there: Tuesdays and Fridays, said Olga Anderson in her placid voice. James did the gardening, whatever needed to be done in the way of handy work; she cleaned the house. But interestingly enough, Lily had been loved by her servants too; the woman's round face was drawn with grief and she had been voluble on telling Mendoza what a sweet lady Mrs. Clevenger had been, so quiet and easy and good to everybody—a real lady. How sorry everybody felt, and how terrible it was that such things should happen, and poor Mr. Clevenger—young Mr. Clevenger that was, though his father had thought the world of Miss Lily too—

Not much formal gardening to do here, thought Mendoza. The natural wild growth had been left untouched, a small grove of California oaks, a hillside planted with trailing wild shrub and vine. Only a small plot of lawn at one side of the house, and much expensive cement-work round an oversize swimming pool gleaming blue: tables, umbrellas, chairs. And now he was talking to James Anderson, middle-aged, weather-beaten, amiable, who was telling Mendoza how much everybody had thought of Miss Lily and what a terrible shock it had been.

"Did you take care of her car—the Porsche?"

"Why, yes, sir. Washed it and so on, same as the other two cars, the Cadillac and the Continental. I used to—"

"Could you tell me," said Mendoza, "the day she—a week ago today, did the Porsche need its tank filled?"

Anderson stared at him. "Why, how'd you know that, sir? Almost the last thing I said to Miss Lily—before we left that day—I said to her, don't you forget to get that tank filled, Miss Lily. She was going out that evening, and when I was vacuuming the Porsche I noticed there wasn't but a bit over two gallons in the tank. How did you—"

So. A little over two gallons. The little four-cylinder job, that would have been enough to take her to Pasadena and a good part of the way home. And then she'd suddenly noticed the tank nearly empty. Forgot to get it filled because she was excited at the prospect of the new job? Possible.

All those gas-stations. . . . He thanked Anderson absently and walked back to the Ferrari in the circular drive.

It was funny about Linda Ulner.

And Brenda Warthol and the Hollywood Bowl. Purple cars, *por Dios.*

And what had happened at Anne Parker's apartment? The quiet girl living quietly?

And the new one.

And what was happening to George Higgins, while they all necessarily went at this damned routine on the bodies forever turning up to be looked at? What? He could deny it, he could refuse to look at it, but Pat was right, of course. A trio like that—and unpredictable, yes, yet all too predictable in some ways. . . . a guy all tied up in the back of the car. . . . and now all the nice profit to blow, the cop they'd picked up a nuisance. Get rid of him the easiest way.

And he could not face Mary Higgins; there was nothing to say to her. We've done what we can. You know how we feel. It was nothing. Nothing.

He had smoked a cigarette nearly through before he suddenly realized what he really felt: a curious sort of shame. Shame that he was even thinking about any other current case than Higgins. That he was giving any time at all to anything but Higgins.

But they were helpless; they had done what they could, and that was it. Period. Now they waited.

He tossed his cigarette out the window, and the phone rang on the dashboard. He snatched it up. "Mendoza."

"We've got the Caddy," said Lake in a muted tone. "Empty. Left just this side of Barstow on a secondary road. The C.H.P. just turned it up."

"*Es el colmo*," whispered Mendoza, but the next moment his mind denied it, not George, it couldn't happen that way, and—Barstow. He said sharply, "Barstow! Northeast toward the Nevada border—Jimmy, get that on the air again, they may be headed for the border—I want every law officer between there and the border out—the National Guard if necessary—the tracking dogs! If they're heading for Nevada they may have dumped George before they left the car. Listen, you get Barstow—I want a make on every hot car they've listed in the last twenty-four hours!"

"If they've dumped him, you know they shot him first," said Lake.

"I do not know any such damned thing," said Mendoza savagely. "I'm coming in. Get on it!" The Ferrari roared to life like an angry lion.

Then, they sat on the radio and the teletype down in Communications: Mendoza, Hackett, Palliser. Mendoza had just grunted when Palliser passed on the Alice-in-Wonderland reactions of Jacob Lockyear to the murder of his partner.

Other law-enforcement agencies were concerned for the cop in trouble too. The California Highway Patrol diverted two dozen cars up to that area, patrolling the back roads around Barstow, looking; every officer between Barstow and the border had the list of hot cars from that area fresh in his mind, looking; and the border guards were alerted. Every car passing into California was stopped and examined, the ridiculous fruit-fly bit; but they usually didn't bother about cars going the other way. And there was the hell of a lot of border to California, plenty of back roads where a car could slip over unnoticed into Nevada.

The day wore on, and nothing came through. Periodic reports. Nothing. "No news is good news," muttered Hackett once, and Mendoza and Palliser looked at him with cold eyes.

Barstow police pounced on one of the stolen cars about six o'clock. It had been hopped by a teenager just for kicks. Mark one off.

At seven o'clock they all went home. They'd be called if anything turned up.

"Darling," said Alison, "I know how you're feeling, but you ought to eat something." Absently he ate what she put in front of him. He sat in the living room with Bast and Sheba coiled complicatedly on his lap, their shaggy dog Cedric dutifully at his feet, and Alison went to get the twins to bed, and time kept expanding and moving slower and slower. Had he remembered to put out an A.P.B. on that Nash? Ulner—very peculiar about Ulner. And that new one. The peculiar things sometimes happened. The surprises.

"Darling," said Angel, "I know how you feel but it's no good worrying, Art. Accomplishes nothing."

"I know, I know," said Hackett. "It's not a—a voluntary thing, is it? You know something," he added suddenly, "I just realized. It's a silly damned thing, but—all the time I was talking to that Kay woman, I was feeling so damn guilty—because I was giving any time to anything else. Than—"

Palliser went home, to answer Roberta in monosyllables and pace. Grace went home to his Virginia, who looked at him with anxious eyes. They all went home, and presently Schenke and Galeano took over the night shift, and they all went on worrying about Higgins, helpless to do any more to help him—if he wasn't already beyond help.

Mendoza got up at five o'clock, having slept heavily from

midnight to two and then waked for good. He shaved and dressed quickly, for once scarcely noticing what he put on, and backed the Ferrari out and started downtown. The night crew was gone when he arrived; the office was empty. He got a cup of coffee at the machine down the hall and contacted Communications. Nothing.

Overnight reports from Schenke and Galeano: a corpse on Main Street, looked like a hit-run: a knifing on the Row, X in custody, witnesses available. The paper-work, going on forever.

He went down to Communications. Nothing had come through. The C.H.P. was restarting their search around Barstow and points northeast. The Forest Rangers at the Angeles National Forest station had promised a couple of helicopters.

And eight o'clock came, and the Homicide men came in: it was Landers' day off but he showed up.

And however they felt about it, they were the Homicide crew and there were still the other cases to be worked: people to talk to, statements to get, reports to type.

Deforrest-Parker. Hackett passed on what Margaret Kay had told him about Jerry Trenton from the old home-town. "You'd better get onto Ventura and check on him," said Mendoza. "Query Records too." Hackett said he'd thought of that himself.

Ulner. Where to go on that? See if the lab turned up anything.

Warthol. The purple cars. Traffic all over three counties still spotting those and faithfully reporting. A very sloppy piece of investigative work. Now, four more purple cars, the owners still to be looked at.

Landers said, "I hate like hell to leave the office, Matt. It's a silly feeling, but—"

"Oh, I know what you mean," said Piggott. "You know, Tom, I keep thinking of the sermon last Sunday."

"What was it about?"

"Well, it was *about* sin—but I keep thinking about that piece of Scripture the minister quoted. It comes in Ecclesiastes —I'd have to look it up. 'Lo, this only have I found, that God hath made man upright, but they have sought out many inventions.' You come to think of it, Tom, that just about sums it up, why there have to be cops."

"I guess it does," said Landers soberly.

Palliser, feeling guilty at being out of the office, busy on anything but helping Higgins, went looking for Lester Rhys's wife. He didn't find her.

Jason Grace went out to get the witnesses' statements on last night's knifing and spent the morning cleaning up the tedious paper-work, worrying about Higgins.

Hackett waited for some answers to his query of Ventura about Jerry Trenton. Trenton didn't show in their own records. He fidgeted around the office smoking too much and calling down to Communications every five minutes. "Nothing," he said mechanically to Mendoza after every call.

"And if you tell me no news is good news, Arturo—" Mendoza had the cards in his hands, practising crooked deals.

Glasser went out on the newest call, which looked like a suicide, said the patrolmen.

Landers and Piggott had cleared up the latest batch of purple cars by twelve-thirty; these four had all turned out to be high-school kids—Hawthorne, Huntington Park, Downey and South Gate: three white, one Negro. They all looked ordinary, none of them had records, and they had all been in school a week ago today.

"It feels like it should be later," said Piggott. "I mean, it seems like time's got stuck or something."

Landers said he knew what he meant, and they weren't far

off home base, go up to Federico's for lunch? Call in first and see if anything had turned up.

Nothing had. The C.H.P. had picked up another hot car off Barstow's list, but it was N.G. Another juvenile.

They came into Federico's, glanced at the big table in the corner and saw Grace and Palliser there: went to join them. As they came up, Palliser said, "Nothing yet."

"I know," said Landers. "We checked." There wasn't anything more to say on that. The waiter came up and he said, "Straight Scotch, Adam, and the small steak." Piggott ordered, and the waiter brought Grace and Palliser's already-ordered drinks.

And they'd said all there was to say about Higgins, about Trasker, Starr and Killeen; but of course they said it all over again, over the quick lunch.

"It's a little crazy," said Palliser, lighting a cigarette and finishing his coffee, "but I feel a little guilty—spending the time at anything *else*. Nothing more we can do."

Grace said in his soft voice, "Oh, yes, John. I know," and asked Landers how they were coming with the random lead on Warthol.

"Random you can say," said Landers half angrily. "Of all the ways to do the routine—we could be at it for a year and get nothing. And at that, the only possible lead on Warthol at all. That Hollywood Bowl thing still gets me—"

Grace lit a cigarette. He said, "Things coming along kind of fast at us, and I sort of got deflected off that since we first got it, but I had one little idea about Brenda Warthol. The Lieutenant got me to question the boy, you know—Douglas. Nice little boy. And the boy said one thing that just set me wondering a little."

"What?" asked Landers. "All he could say was about the color of the car. And of all idiotic ways to have to—"

"Well," said Grace dreamily, "the boy said the big man came in and hit Mommy and she fought with him and hit him and he let her go but then he got hold of her again and took her out to his car and drove away."

"Well?" said Landers.

"I just had the thought," said Grace, "she wasn't—Brenda Warthol—a very big strong female. Not at all. So how did it happen that she hit him hard enough to make him let her go? Even once? So the boy said he was a big strong man—that's nothing, a five-year-old isn't to be relied on judging adult sizes—but he had to be a fairly big strong man at that, didn't he? The boy says he picked her up, carried her to the car."

"You have a point in mind?" asked Piggott.

"I have. She hit him and he let her go—" Grace looked at his cigarette. "And if you recall, the squad-car men got there to find the hot iron burning through the board. She'd been ironing her husband's shirts."

Landers said, "So? I don't see—"

And Palliser said, "My God, Jase! You mean—"

"Well, it just occurred to me," said Grace. "Woman attacked unexpectedly, in her own kitchen, not a very big woman, but it's instinctive to fight back, isn't it? And she had the—"

"Hot iron in her hand," said Palliser. "And she—"

And Landers and Piggott looked at each other, and it hit them both at once like a bombshell.

"That band——" they started to say together. And then they both got up and ran for the nearest exit.

10

THEY DIDN'T do much talking on the way; Landers got onto the Golden State freeway and it was a slack time of day, not much traffic. Piggott said this and that about miracles in a reverent tone, and Landers said repressively, "We don't *know,* damn it."

They came into town, and again they were lucky. The blindingly iridescent purple car was sitting in the drive, and he was just coming down to it from the garage. Landers and Piggott marched up to him and he paused, a hand on the driver's door, and stared at them.

"What you want, here again? I told you—"

"You, I think," said Landers.

"What? I don't—" his eyes moved nervously.

"Is your cut better?" asked Piggott. "Where you fell off the ladder?"

"My—oh, yeah, yeah, it's—"

"We'd like to see it," said Landers. "You mind letting us see it?"

"Yes, I do mind! You can get to hell off my property!"

"As soon as we see it," said Landers. "Come on, just unbutton your shirt." He put out a hand, and the other man aimed a fist at him; he ducked. "Now, Mr.—" The next blow connected with his shoulder; he staggered.

"If he wants it that way—" said Piggott and yanked the

man off Landers roughly. Landers straightened; the big man was struggling with Piggott, who had got both his arms clamped behind his back.

Landers reached out and in one motion ripped the blue cotton work-shirt open. "No—you got no right—you let me alone—"

"Jackpot," said Landers.

There, smack in the center of Edward Goeltz's naked chest, marking him like the brand of Cain, was the healing burn: the perfect imprint of the hot iron.

They brought him in with no trouble. When he knew they'd seen it, he quieted down and turned silent and slack. They brought him in, after necessarily reciting the piece about all his rights; he just nodded dispiritedly. And Piggott kept talking about miracles. "One of the first Traffic turned up, just looking at random—"

And Landers said, "It's one for the books, and I think the boss had better sit in on it," and went to look for Mendoza.

He was, of course, down in Communications. Where nothing was coming through. He listened to Landers and said, "¡Caray! That is a tale. The mark of Cain."

"I've been hearing nothing else from Matt. We thought you'd like to sit in."

"I would."

In the interrogation room, with surprisingly little persuasion, Edward Goeltz talked. He seemed, even, glad of the opportunity to do a little boasting.

"I don't know how many," he said. "Hundreds maybe. For years. Women, they're funny, you know. They don't like to say they've been—you know, raped. They keep quiet. I lived down here all my life till six years ago. You know something? I went to school down here with that Brenda Davis. I forget what her married name was. I lived right down that block, in the same street, up to six years back. It wasn't till my uncle died, left me the place in Van Nuys, I moved out there —and my folks was dead then anyways, in that accident. I don't know how many women—I couldn't count. Since I was sixteen. It's the only way I get a kick out of it, see. I don't know why."

"What about Brenda, Goeltz?" asked Mendoza.

"About Brenda," he repeated dully. "Could I have a cigarette? Thanks. Yeah, well, it was funny, that. I wasn't even thinkin' about a woman that day, up to then. I told you guys the truth," he nodded at Landers and Piggott, "I was at old lady Gunn's house in Hollywood that day, fixing things. But I had to come down to L.A., downtown, for some plumbing parts, warehouse down here—and kind of passin' through my old stampin' ground, I don't know, just all of a sudden I was thinkin' about Brenda Davis. I knew where she lived, acourse, right up from where I useta. I just—I don't know—after I got the parts I went there. Snotty old Brenda—she always kind of turned up her nose at me, and she wouldn't go to that football game with me, that time—I just— Well, I went in the kitchen and there she was. But that was a little bit different than all the other times—they was mostly all after dark, down here— other places. All over. She tried to scream, she hit me with the damn iron, and that made me mad. It sure did—it hurt like hell, I tell you! I smacked her good, but I'd thought before— before I went in there, take her away somewheres, on account maybe somebody'd see me, reckanize me. I lived that neighborhood quite a—I just thought—"

"So you took her away. Why the Hollywood Bowl, Goeltz?"

He looked blank. "It just happened, sort of. I belted her good, keep her quiet, and I took her out to the car, and drove. I got on a freeway, and what was kind of in my mind was that park up in Hollywood—Griffith Park—but at the interchange I got shunted off, I was in the wrong lane, and first I knew I was in Hollywood but way the other side, and then I thought about the Bowl. Not open, empty place. That's all. She come to and fought me, time I got her outta the car. I didn't mean to *kill* her. I never meant—it's just, it's the only way I get a kick out of it. It's just how I am."

"Did you kill any others, Goeltz?" asked Mendoza.

He licked his lips. "I never meant to," he said in a low voice. "I never meant that. I found out—after the first ones—down here—most of 'em don't never tell. Police or anybody. They're kind of ashamed. So it was safe, safe as hell. Just wait —on a dark street somewheres. I don't know how many there was. After I moved to the valley, well, it was just the same. But I useta come back down here too—I knew the streets, the best places, down here. Hundreds, maybe, there been—since I was just a kid. I—there was another one," he said suddenly. "I saw about it in the paper, after. I didn't mean to *kill* anybody. A dame in a parking lot. Wolf or Elk or something."

The Homicide men looked at each other. Isabel Fox.

"I shouldn't've thought about Brenda that day," said Edward Goeltz. "All her fault. Just because she had that damn iron in her hand when I come in—" he squinted down at his chest with the merciless telltale brand on it, and up at the men standing over him—"what call she got to hit me like that?"

"A miracle," said Piggott. "I can't get over it. Out of the first batch Traffic turned up."

"Well, one off our hands anyway," said Mendoza and went back to Communications."

Landers took Goeltz down to the jail on Alameda and booked him in, while Piggott started the machinery going on the warrant. At least they had this one cleared up, and the Fox thing at the same time: gratifying. Mendoza was fond of saying when one thing came unstuck, another was sure to follow; he was to be proved right today.

But at that particular moment, they had just been handed a new one, and Jason Grace had gone out to look at it. Landers started to type a last report on Brenda Warthol, and Piggott started to tell Glasser about the miracle.

Down in Communications, something finally came through. Barstow was not, of course, a very big town, and the list of stolen cars, missed in that area during the twenty-four-hour period when, probably, Trasker, Starr and Killeen had picked up new transportation, had numbered only six. Four of those had now been recovered by the C.H.P. or Barstow police. Trasker, Starr and Killeen, for about eighty-five percent sure, were driving either a 1965 Pontiac, white, or a 1967 Chevy station-wagon, green. The plate-numbers were out on the air, urgently, all over again.

Helicopters were out, but by the reports coming in weather conditions over there were not too good. Fog and rain getting worse eastward. A direct phone call from the Chief of Police in Barstow came through about three o'clock. He said, "You know, there's still snow lying on the high ranges. It's icing up some now above five thousand."

The reports came in and added to nothing. A great big nothing.

"There's a lot of empty land out there, Luis," Hackett reminded him.

"But, damn it, that trio—they'd head for the bright lights! They've got to be spotted somewhere—"

"And they're smart boys," said Hackett tiredly. "We think we're so brilliant, deducing. What says they didn't pick up new transportation right here, or San Berdu or some place, and just abandoned the Cad up there to lead us off the—"

"*¡No seas tan exigente!*" said Mendoza. He lit a new cigarette from the stub of the old one.

Jason Grace contemplated the living room of a small, shabby house on Constance Street. It was an old frame house on a narrow lot, the ambulance was waiting in the drive, and a distressed young woman was talking compulsively at Grace, the interns, the squad-car men, anyone who would listen.

"We *told* her she ought not to live alone! Sure, the rise in crime but we didn't think of that so much as—I mean it wasn't just that—she was nearly seventy, she could fall, break her hip or something—it wasn't as if she was forgetful or anything, way some people that age are, but anything could happen, her alone in the house—but she was so independent, she wouldn't hear about moving. Giving up the house. She could've moved in with Ray and me or Vina or Bob or any of us—glad to have her, Mother Reiner a good help and no trouble—"

"If you don't mind, Mrs.—? She was your mother?" asked Grace gently.

"Not *my*—my husband's mother—I'm Wilma Reiner. Ray was her youngest, she was forty-five when he was born. I couldn't get her on the phone all yesterday or today and we were worried, so I came—" Suddenly she burst into tears and one of the interns led her away to a chair.

A very modest little place, but everything looked as if it had been neat and clean—until the burglars started hunting for loot. Drawers pulled out, dumped on the floor, in here; in the first little bedroom off this room, too; and on the bed there, Mrs. Ellie Reiner, tied up with clothesline, gagged with a pair of cotton stockings, and apparently strangled manually.

Grace reflected sadly that he would take a bet on this one. So often the rumor got around, any old person living alone, that there was cash in the house, hidden away. Probably the poor old lady on the state pension.

He moved into the kitchen and halted. A little surprise. The canisters had all been dumped out on the counter, the cupboards ransacked. But on the kitchen table was scattered a pack of cards, in two little piles opposite each other, chairs pulled out as if the players had risen hastily from their game;

149

between the piles of cards a milk-glass dish had been used as an ashtray, overflowing with cigarette butts.

"Well, do tell," said Grace to himself. "Talk about surprises."

At a quarter to three Landers came into Communications, to summon Mendoza back to his own office. "I can't make head nor tail of why Juvenile should be after you, but they are. Most urgent."

"What the hell does Juvenile— All right, all right." In his office, he took up the phone and said, "Mendoza. What do you want with Homicide? . . . . Oh. Oh? . . . . Oh, really! The teacher. . . . the hell you say. . . ." His eyebrows climbed and he put out his cigarette in the tray on his desk. "Where? All right, I'll be there. *Pronto*." He put the phone down. "They do say, never two without three. Now maybe— And maybe not, too."

"What was that all about?" asked Landers.

Mendoza brushed his moustache back and forth. "Maybe," he said, "a vindictive liar. And maybe not."

Palliser came in looking morose and said, "Anything yet?"

"*Nada*. We just—"

"Well, I can't get hold of this Myra Rhys. The restaurant people where she works say she's off on vacation. She's not home, anyway. I—"

Mendoza got up. "So you can come with me and listen to another surprise. Just maybe."

The public elementary school was on Temple Street, an old red brick school with a generous playground, the usual chain-link fence around it. An old building, and permeated with the usual sealed-in odor of chalk, books, young perspiration, ink. At the principal's office Mendoza and Palliser were met by four harassed-looking, shocked-looking people, who introduced themselves all at once. Mr. Wilkins, the principal:

Mrs. Shapiro, teacher of fifth grade; Sergeant Lilywhite of Juvenile Division, L.A.P.D.; and the school psychologist, Mr. Nevers.

"I could see something was on her mind, all week," said Mrs. Shapiro, dividing her gaze among Mendoza, Lilywhite and Nevers. "But I never *dreamed*—and if I didn't know Jeanette for a truthful little girl—I couldn't *believe*—but she was so upset—"

"Children of this age so often fantasize," murmured Nevers. She threw him a hostile look.

"And *I* could scarcely believe," said the principal faintly, "that there was anything to—but the child was so earnest—and I finally—"

"Brought me into it," said Lilywhite, who was an abrupt beetle-browed young man in untidy clothes. Mendoza had never had much to do with Juvenile Division, which came under the Patrol Bureau rather than the Detective Bureau. "And being a cop of sorts, Lieutenant, in my simple way I thought I'd better check with Homicide to see if there'd been such a killing. And sure enough there was, so a Sergeant Lake told me—and so we fetched you in. You'd better listen to this kid."

"Who?"

"This Jeanette Kling." Lilywhite cocked his head. "I thought I'd seen and heard everything, but I can still be surprised. My good God almighty. Come on. She's down the hall with the school nurse."

She was ten. She was small for her age, a thin, pale, freckled child with china-blue eyes, a shabby stained cotton dress, ankle socks, runover moccasins. Her sandy hair was stringy and untidy, and she had been crying and her eyes were reddened. Mrs. Shapiro, a young and rather pretty dark woman, sat down beside her protectively there in the nurse's little office.

"I'm not afraid," said Jeanette in a thin little voice. "When

I—when I—*had* to tell somebody, I was scared, but I'm not scared now. Now I've told. I'll tell *anybody*. Because it's *so*. And—I—liked—Linda. I did. She was always so nice to us— she talked to me like I was—was real, not just—a kid. She—"

"You just calm down, dear," said the teacher. "Just take it easy."

"I want to tell, now. I was scared of Mama—I was scared even tell Daddy—I *couldn't* because Mama's always there when he is, there wasn't no chance—and I don't know if Daddy'd b'lieve me anyways, he's always saying Bible says it's wrong talk bad about anybody, and he prob'ly wouldn't—but ever since. I felt just so bad—I was scared Mama'd do what she said, kill *me*—"

Mendoza squatted in front of her, to put their heads level. "Linda?" he said. "Linda Ulner, Jeanette?"

She nodded, and the stringy hair bounced on her neck. "She lived right next door. And her mother 'n' father cried and cried, they felt so bad. So did I—in bed, where nobody'd see —I loved Linda. But Mama said she'd kill me. If I told. She— she's hit me before, that time, hit me a lotta times with the broom, and Daddy's belt sometimes—I was littler then and didn't have no sense, and I ast her about the man come after dark when Daddy was to work. I never, ever, since—and there've been lots, since. But—she didn't know, I *saw*—about Linda. Till after. And then she said she'd kill me too. But—"

"Kill you too?" said Mendoza softly.

"Yes, sir. You'll—you'll do something to her for it, won't you? So she can't hurt nobody again? I was scared—but all week I had this awful pain right—right—" she put one scrawny hand on her chest. "I—just—had—to—tell—some-body!" She started to cry. The teacher hugged her.

"Just—just tell the officers what you told me, dear."

"Y-yes, ma'am." She blew her nose and sniffed. "I—I saw her, see. That night. Daddy didn't know, but she goes out a lot at night when he's to work. Sometimes there's men come after dark, but then she always locks the bedroom door, where us kids sleep, I mean. But mostly she goes out, and Linda—stayed—with us. Sometimes. Even if Mama didn't pay her. And—that night—when Mama come home, I'd been asleep but I heard her yelling and I got up to see what was the matter—and she was hitting Linda and hitting her and hitting her, and she kept calling Linda awful names, she was nosy and she talked too much and— And she hit her and Linda fell down and Mama just went on hitting her—she had something in her hand—and then she saw me and come at me and—and said she'd kill me if I told—and next day—next day I found out Linda was *dead*—"

"*¡Carape!*" said Mendoza. He stood up. He said to Lily-white, "I thought I'd seen everything too, *compadre*."

They found Mrs. Ruthena Kling at home and brought her in for questioning. They got nothing from her but sullen silence, and then when she heard how they'd dropped on her, a string of obscenities impartially directed at damn tattletale brats and smart-alecky teenagers sniffing around where they hadn't any obscenity business.

Maybe the lab could turn up something on a potential blunt instrument around the Kling house.

And, another one cleaned up: at least they knew who on Linda Ulner, if they never got any concrete evidence on it. In any case, a judge would probably listen to Jeanette. And if it hadn't been the utterly brutal kill of a fifteen-year-old, they might have been grimly amused at husband and father Richard Kling: the thing burst on him with complete surprise; it had never crossed his mind that Ruthena was anything but devoted wife and mother.

He couldn't take care of the kids alone; they were taken down to Juvenile Hall. At least temporarily.

And nothing more had come in from Barstow, or anywhere, about the two hot cars or anything else. Barstow said the fog was coming down thicker. The helicopters, useless, had gone back to base.

"Daddy read!" demanded Teresa imperiously. "Read *el cuento*—all 'bout *el Camello* an' his *joroba!*"

"Now, Terry, you mustn't bother your father tonight, darling—please—"

"*No Camello!*" said Johnny. "*El Gato* all by himself! *El Gato*—like Bast 'n' Sheba 'n'—"

"Johnny, no, your father can't—I'll read you *all* the stories, *enamorado*, but you mustn't—" Alison looked up at Mendoza as he shrugged into his jacket, got out the keys. "Luis, I—you'll give her my love. If there's anything, anything at all we can do—"

"Yes, *cara*."

"You're just torturing yourself, you know."

"I have got to see her," said Mendoza. "You know that."

As he went out toward the kitchen door, Alison was saying firmly, "We'll read all about *El Rinoceronte* and how he— All right, all right, then *El Gato*, Johnny, but quiet down!"

And of course Mary was bearing up. Like the good soldier she was. Mrs. MacTaggart was cheerful and sensible; she'd be seeing that they got meals on time, the housework done. He could say what he had to say to Mary; he told her what they had done, what they were doing, what they thought. Every law-man between here and the border, a lot of law-men in Nevada, on it, anxious to help the cop in trouble. But there weren't any guarantees on one like this.

"I know that, Lieutenant," she said with the ghost of a smile. "It was—almost easier—with Bert. We all knew, right away."

"I know it's no help to you at all," said Mendoza, "to say that everybody's doing everything possible. But I've got to say it."

"Yes. Thank you."

But he didn't know at all what to say to Steve Dwyer. He didn't know Steve very well, of course. It came to him, when the boy came into the living room, that Steve Dwyer had had several bad things happen to him in his nearly twelve years, and he just hoped to God another bad thing wasn't going to happen to him now. Losing his own father when he was only ten: Bert had been so proud of his kids. Bert, dead in a pond of blood on the marble floor of the bank. Then the hit-run, and the long siege of therapy and the brace, but that had been after George's humble pursuit of Bert's widow, his incredulity when she agreed to marry him. At least it seemed Mary appreciated George—solid, lonesome, intrepidly upright George. But Mendoza didn't know what to say to Steve at all.

He came into the room still limping a little. He was going to look like Bert: sandy-haired, solidly built, getting his growth early, as tall as his mother now. "Laura's crying again," he said. "She couldn't do any homework." His blue eyes went to Mendoza. "You're Lieutenant Mendoza. From headquarters. Have you—have you found George yet?"

"No, Steve. I'm sorry."

"I'd better go to—" Mary started to get up, but Mrs. MacTaggart forestalled her.

"You bide quiet, Miss Mary. I'll see to the lamb. And never you fear, God wouldna do such a thing to a good woman, I'll not believe."

Mary gave a long sigh. "She is so good," she said. "But—"

"Sir." The boy came up to him. "George isn't—isn't dead, is he? That couldn't happen? Like—Dad?"

Mendoza shook his head blindly. "I don't know," he said. "I just don't know."

"I just—don't think I could stand it—if George was dead too," said the boy. Mary's face twisted; she put an arm around his shoulders. "I mean, we were all so—so excited, sort of, about the baby—and—and George said he'd teach me about boxing when my leg was all right—I mean, it was all like it was before Dad—"

"We don't know, Steve," said Mendoza.

"It's because he's a cop," said Steve. "I heard—some of what you all said, before. Those guys picking him because he's a cop and they—hate—cops. Sir. Lieutenant."

"Yes, Steve."

"I—I—if they killed George—those guys—or—or if they didn't, *I'm* going to be a cop too. Like my dad. Like George. I don't care what Mother says. She said, 'God forbid,' when I said that before. But I will be. I will."

Mendoza looked at Mary. She colored; she said straightly, "Well, I did say it. Wouldn't I?" But her arm tightened around Steve. "I'm ashamed I said it. Now. You'll do that, Steve. You'll be a cop, and a good one—as good as your father and George. And I'll be proud of you, Steve."

There wasn't anything to say to either of them. Mendoza went home, not to sleep.

He got up at six, leaving Alison sleeping heavily, and dressed and drove down to the office. He wasn't hungry; he got coffee at the machine down the hall.

Reports on his desk from Schenke and Galeano. Nick Galeano, probably, putting up the foolish prayers at the altar, same like Máiri MacTaggart. Another unidentified corpse along the Row. A quiet night for Homicide.

Lily Clevenger. Should do some routine on that.

That Ulner thing. Talk about offbeat. Turn the lab loose on that house. He went out to the switchboard; he'd sat at one of those awhile, on this thankless job, and manipulated it automatically, got the lab, left a message for Duke.

Lester Rhys. *Cherchez la femme*, he thought. Palliser on that.

The new ones coming along. Grace had told him about the Reiner woman. The cards on the kitchen table. Peculiar.

That Goeltz. No telling how many rapes he'd pulled. Maybe he hadn't killed before Isabel Fox, Brenda Warthol. The rapists didn't kill frequently. But in some fifteen years, he'd probably been responsible for a lot of the rapes thrown into Pending. And a lot, as he said, never reported. Probably, now, the head doctors would get him sent up to Atascadero.

He went down to Communications at eight o'clock, just after the men began to come in. Hackett went with him. It was supposed to be Hackett's day off. In the elevator, he told Hackett about Steve Dwyer. Hackett hunched his shoulders. "What is there to say, Luis? Can you think there's still a chance?"

"There's always got to be a chance, Art. Until we know for sure."

Nothing had come in. The C.H.P. was out in force again, searching. The Rangers' helicopters were out. The only encouraging thing was that the fog had lifted, visibility was better.

Hackett brought him another cup of coffee. "Palliser's out on that Rhys dame. Grace on Reiner. We ought to be doing some work on Lily Clevenger, you know, Luis. We ought to—"

Mendoza took a swallow of scalding coffee, gasped and swore. "Damn it—Sé, sé, I know! Damn it, all these men out hunting—why they haven't spotted that car—"

"Lot of wild country out that way," said Hackett.

There was. Inaccessible terrain.

At ten-thirty there came through a direct long-distance call from the Chief Ranger in command at the Walker River Indian Reservation station in Churchill County, Nevada.

A carful of tourists from back East, exploring the reservation, had stopped at the ranger station to report an accident off a mountain road up Walker's Canyon. They had gone up to look, called the sheriff's men to help. The car had gone over the side of the road down a steep cliff; it was a total loss.

It was a 1967 Chevy wagon, California plates. Three bodies had been recovered, and had been identified by the sheriff's men from the mug-shots L.A. had supplied: Rodney Trasker, Roger Starr and Donald Killeen.

II

"WHAT ABOUT our man?" asked Mendoza sharply. "Sergeant Higgins?"

"No sign that anybody else was in the car, sir," said the ranger. "It's not a heavily wooded area, quite open, if there'd been anyone else in the car we'd have found him right away." Mendoza had automatically switched on the amplifier and recorder, and Hackett swore, hearing that. "No, sir, nothing caught fire—they just missed an easy curve and went over a hundred-foot drop. It's possible that all three had been drinking, there was beer and Scotch in the car—"

"All too likely," said Mendoza grimly. Good riddance to Trasker, Starr and Killeen. But—

"They were all going armed," said the ranger. "A Smith and Wesson nine-millimeter automatic, a Ruger Black Hawk three-fifty-seven magnum, a Colt Super thirty-eight." Mendoza said yes impatiently. No use wondering where they'd picked up the guns. All the ridiculous clamor about gun-registration: all that did was disarm the honest citizen, and he seemed to recall that the whole idea was contrary to the Constitution. The pro-hoods could always get hold of the guns, and usually did. "Was—"

"There was another gun in the car. A Police Positive thirty-eight in a shoulder-holster."

"Have you got it there? Give me the serial number." Mendoza nodded at Hackett, who snatched out a ballpoint pen and took it down as the ranger read it. "Will you hold on while we check that, please?" Hackett fled. There would be a record of the serial number of Higgins' gun in their files. The ranger went on telling him about the accident: the sheriff's men were still at the scene. "They think it probably happened yesterday sometime. We've had quite good weather, no fog— the snow's just going off the higher slopes. But of course if they had been drinking—"

Hackett came back panting. "It's George's gun all right."

"*¡Pues bien!*" said Mendoza. "Listen—that thirty-eight belongs to our man, to Higgins. They had him—which we knew. Just in case, I want a massive search made in that area. You hear me? I want everything you've got on it—helicopters, dogs, all the men you can turn out. Just in case."

"I've got that," said the ranger unemotionally. "You think they may have left his body somewhere in—"

"I don't *know!*" snarled Mendoza. "Let's look, that's all. All right, thanks. Thanks very much." He put the phone down. "And wouldn't you know," he said to Hackett. "That trio of—of maniacal idiots, the typical pros, doing what comes naturally, getting themselves killed in a silly damn accident. Tanked up, missing a curve. And what the hell were they doing in the middle of an Indian reservation, for God's sake? They'd have headed for the bright lights—women, liquor, gambling—an *Indian* reservation? *¡Por Dios!* But, you know, Art—" He stopped, and very deliberately lit a cigarette. "You know what all that says."

"*Ya lo creo,*" said Hackett soberly, "like you'd say."

"We may never know," said Mendoza. "When or how or where, about George. There is the hell of a lot of wild empty land out there, Art. Even between here and Barstow."

"That is a fact," said Hackett.

"But," said Mendoza, automatically still functioning as the professional detective, "the idiot boy and the lost horse—yes

—Sunday night. Sunday night. And Knight told us, on Monday night, a guy all tied up in the back of the car. The Caddy. They must have been a little busy on Monday, making the deal for the loot they got on Sunday night." He put out his cigarette, lit a new one. "Read it. The ranger said they probably went off that cliff sometime yesterday, which was Wednesday."

"Indubitably. You heading somewhere?"

"*Finalmente.* Where's an atlas?" Mendoza looked around. The Communications office was bare of reading matter. "Hell, there's one in the office—" He got up and took Hackett's arm. In his own office, he riffled open the atlas and laid a ruler to the California map, muttering. "Fifty-nine statute miles to the inch, yes, all right, call it ninety miles up to Barstow, another hundred and twenty to the border. Walker River Reservation, the ranger said—that's another hundred and twenty from the California border, and actually they had time to go farther than that. Even with stopping to eat and sleep. They took off from here Monday night. They wouldn't have bothered with any motels, where the plate-number'd be asked for. Heading for Nevada—the gambling tables. How the hell did they end up— But they left the Caddy outside Barstow, afraid it was getting a little too hot. And nothing says—" His voice trailed away. He took up the phone. "Jimmy, get me the C.H.P." With the local headquarters on the line, he passed on the information from Nevada rapidly. "Now listen. I'm thinking it's possible they— got rid of Higgins before Barstow. Where they switched cars. I want the search concentrated on that area—all the way up from civilized parts as it were."

"Call it Pasadena or so?" said a quietly sarcastic voice. "I get you, Lieutenant."

"That'd be about right." And there was a lot of empty country there too. That area, from civilization on northeast, took in that vast mountainous area of the Angeles National

Forest, mountains and valleys and canyons left entirely wild, a great game sanctuary where the wild life abounded. It took in the left-to-nature resorts, Lake Arrowhead and Big Bear Lake, and on over the mountain range to Victorville, and down to the desert—the tail end, at this end of the continent, of the great American desert, empty and desolate, where shifting winds changed the sandy contours of the land daily. There weren't many towns along the way—little desert communities. And past Barstow, nothing—nothing at all for forty miles up to a town called Baker, and then only a few more up to the border. Mendoza shut the atlas.

"You can see it's possible," he said to the phone. "We've got to look."

"So I'll put the word out, Lieutenant. I see what you mean. At least those three are no loss. But—well, I see what you mean."

Mendoza put the phone down. "And if anybody can tell me why I stayed on this damn thankless job—"

Palliser, worrying about Higgins, had gone out doggedly again on Rhys. The jobs were there to be done, damn it; they were all worried as hell about Higgins, but they couldn't just drop everything else. The routine had to be done. And Lester Rhys—that was really a very damned peculiar thing, wasn't it? By what Lockyear said. Arsenic in the soup—poisoned chocolates. And Rhys apparently so afraid of the woman he carried that note on his person.

She lived at an apartment on Cahuenga, but he hadn't got any answer there so far and the manageress didn't know anything. "I don't take any notice, they pay the rent or they don't, that's all I know." She worked at the Cock's Walk restaurant on La Cienega, and they told him there she was off on vacation.

The autopsy report, and the report from Ballistics on Rhys, ought to show up sometime today.

Just casting around, he tried the apartment again at ten o'clock Thursday morning. To his surprise the door opened to him. "Mrs. Rhys?"

"At the moment, yes," she said. She wasn't exactly pretty, but there was a direct sensual lure about her any man would feel like an electric shock. She had rather untidy short black hair, an olive complexion, long-lashed brown eyes, a full mouth, a good figure carelessly displayed, but that hadn't a thing to do with it. The electric charm, the instant lure, was something in the woman herself. Palliser regarded her warily. He got out the badge.

"So, a cop," she said. "What do you want with me?"

"It's about your husband. May I come in, Mrs. Rhys?"

She shrugged. "Be my guest." The apartment was sterile. The only word for it. A rented place, furnished, and she hadn't added anything to it because she wasn't here often, wasn't interested in her surroundings particularly. She sat down on the couch, lit a cigarette. She had on a pink chiffon negligee, pink silk slippers, and he suspected nothing else. "Lester?"

"You've been away, Mrs. Rhys?"

"I've been away," she agreed mockingly. "Just got back last night. You asking where?"

"I'm asking."

"Vegas. Why?"

"How long were you there, Mrs. Rhys? When did you leave here?"

"Aren't we full of questions," she said lazily. She smoothed her hair; her nails were painted iridescent pink. "If it's any of your business I went over there Sunday night. Is it your business?"

"I see," said Palliser. And that might be a very clever alibi indeed. Check in at a hotel or motel, and you were officially in Las Vegas; but most people went there for the one reason, and if you said, I was playing roulette at the Sands, or

~ *163*

blackjack somewhere else, how could a team of detectives prove you weren't? The croupiers and dealers were too busy to notice who, of the roaming public, was present when. He said again, "I see. I'm sorry to have to tell you, Mrs. Rhys, that your husband is dead."

He watched her, but he wasn't prepared for the reaction he got. "*Dead?*" she exclaimed. She sat bolt upright and dropped her cigarette. "*Lester? Dead?* Well, I will be goddamned!" And if she wasn't another Sarah Bernhardt, that came straight from the heart. "What happened to him? How did—"

"He was shot," said Palliser.

"Shot? *Lester?* Now you've got to be kidding," she said. "Come on! Lester? That guy would die of heart failure if anybody showed him a gun. I tell you. If he ever volunteered to give blood, they'd take one look and offer him some. Honestly. Lester—"

"He was found on Tuesday morning," said Palliser, still watching her. "He'd been shot twice in the head."

The astonishment was still naked in her eyes. "Well, I'll be damned. Shot, my God, how'd it happen? *Lester.* Mister, that guy really had me fooled. He looked good—just on the surface, tall, dark, good-looking—brother! It didn't take me three hours after I married him, find out about him. The original Milquetoast, and I'd take a bet he'd never laid a female before in his life. Well, anyway now I don't have to pay for a divorce."

"Both he and his partner Mr. Lockyear have made," said Palliser, "certain allegations. That you had attempted to murder him. Have you anything to—"

"Anything to *say?*" she picked him up. "Sure as hell I've got anything to say! You just automatically believe anything you hear, cop? That damn idiot listening to Lockyear—why the hell should I want to murder Lester? Divorce is easier. That Lockyear—Lester under his thumb all the way—they had one of those mutual benefit, whatever they call it, insurance policies, before. And Lester canceled his part and wrote it over to me. Ask me, Lockyear was telling the poor bastard all those wild tales about me, get him back in on that deal. And if he had, mister—and Lester got himself murdered, Lockyear's the hell of a better suspect than I am!"

"What?" said Palliser. "You mean one of those partnership deals—life insurance recrues to the partner?"

"Like that, sure. To sum *up*," she said crossly, running fingers through her hair, "Lockyear didn't like me because I'd got Lester away from him and upset that deal, and Lester got to be afraid of me—me!—because Lockyear fed him a lot of bull—and I didn't like either of 'em, Lockyear on general principles and Lester because he turned out to be such a damn rabbit. A nothing. When he looked so good on the outside. If you want to know, I lived with him twenty-four days and that was enough, thank you. I could pick a better man just reaching out blind in a crowd at the state fair."

Palliser laughed involuntarily. "That might change the picture some," he said cautiously. "But can you tell me where you were last Monday night, Mrs. Rhys?"

She looked at him lazily, the rather crude sensual lure of her nearly tangible in the room. "You got a name?"

"Sergeant Palliser."

"Well, yes, Sergeant Palliser, I can tell you where I was Monday night. I was with a gentleman by the name of Nick Graziano, over in Vegas. We had dinner together about eight o'clock and we saw the first floor-show at the Sands and we did a little dancing and then we went back to my hotel room at the Dunes and went to bed, Sergeant Palliser. And lest you are thinking, Sergeant Palliser, that Nicky will back me up on that just to be obliging, I'll add that he seems to be a V.I.P. in Vegas, everybody knows him, and the manager at both places came to speak to him and his chauffeur waited at the Dunes to take him home, Sergeant Palliser—he has a house in Vegas. And that was about four A.M., and I should think—"

"So, thanks very much," said Palliser dryly. The Syndicate saw to it that Vegas stayed a very clean town. They had too many fingers in too many pies there to risk any open trouble. And this might be a constructed alibi indeed but he didn't really think so, now. Myra Rhys was something less and more than the subtle murderess he'd heard about from Lockyear. He was thinking more seriously about Lockyear, now.

If he had persuaded Rhys to reinstate that mutual-benefit partnership policy—

After that, it was quite an anticlimax to find, when he got back to the office, that the lab had cleaned it all up for him. Nobody was in the office but Lake, sitting at the switchboard; he just shook his head at Palliser and said, "Nothing. I just checked with Communications. The boss is still down there, with Hackett." He went on to tell Palliser about Trasker, Starr and Killeen.

Palliser told himself there just couldn't be a chance that Higgins was still alive, after this while. Since Sunday night. He told himself not to be a pessimistic idiot, there had to be a chance. Just had to. He sat down at his desk and pulled the typewriter toward him, and the inside phone rang on Hackett's desk; he made a long arm and reached it. "Homicide, Palliser."

"Duke. Say, this Rhys—the guy in the car?"

"Yes? You turned up something on the car?"

"And elsewhere. Maybe all you need. It was plastered with latents—good, bad and indifferent. A lot of his, sure. But among others, quite a few that showed in our records. One Luke Abell, quite a pedigree. Picked up first at thirteen, burglary. It goes on, burglary, robbery from the person, five counts of that—B. and E., narco possession, more burglary, mugging, etcetera. His prints were plastered all over the steering wheel, gear-shift. I think he was the last one to drive the car. I presume you'd like his description?"

"You presume quite right." What the hell, thought Palliser.

"You don't ask why he's loose," said Duke, "with such a pedigree."

"I'm not a fool," said Palliser. "That part I don't have to ask about. The slaps on the wrist, the abused civil rights, the probation, and maybe last time he was let off because it was Be Kind to Criminals Week."

"Oh, yes," sighed Duke. "He's on parole now, matter of fact. The pedigree says he's not a permanent user—Mary Jane, H, speed, whatever—just sometimes the pot, or bennies. What he prefers is gin, and it turns him mean. You got a pen? All right. He's six-two, a hundred and ninety, Negro, black and brown, thirty-seven, and his latest known address was Lebanon Street downtown."

Palliser wrote that down and stared at it. "Thanks," he said. Duke wished him good luck and hung up.

But how very funny indeed. Rhys the rabbit, coerced by Lockyear into thinking his wife had designs on his life? Rhys actually more in potential danger from Lockyear? If the life-insurance deal had now been reactivated? And Rhys, running into a dangerous punk like Abell just by coincidence?

Ours not to reason why, he reflected. Jason Grace came in and he told him there was nothing on Higgins yet, and then told him about Rhys and Abell. "It's funny, you know."

"We seem to be getting nothing but," said Grace. "The queer little things. The surprises." He sat down at his desk looking grave and lit a cigarette. "Sergeant Higgins. Are you taking any bets?"

Palliser shook his head. "After four days? Did you hear about those three? Went off a mountain road and—"

"I heard from Jimmy. So maybe we just never will know about Higgins," said Grace.

That had occurred to Palliser too. "They could have dumped him anywhere, damn it."

Landers came in with Piggott. "Have you heard about

those—" began Landers, and Palliser said they'd heard. "Damn it, he could be anywhere," said Landers, and sat down at his desk. He looked tired. "They're doing all they can do. I know that, but I feel guilty doing anything *else*. We've been trying to get something out of that Kling woman. No dice. But the lab's turned up a wrench from that house they say could be the weapon. God, what a thing. A fifteen-year-old —Kling getting the idea she was spying on her and her boy-friends—"

"Which maybe she was," said Grace. "Ever think? Just be-cause she was only fifteen doesn't say she was the angelic innocent."

"I suppose," said Landers. He looked at his watch. "It's ten past twelve. Anybody interested in lunch?" Nobody appeared to be, much.

Grace said, "I ought to get out a follow-up report on Reiner. I'm just a little curious about those cards. It turns out just the way I thought—rumor going around that the old lady had a lot of cash hidden away. She was on the state pen-sion, family helping her out. More of the punks."

Lake looked in. "If you're interested," he said, "a pigeon just called in—a shy pigeon who says Sergeant Palliser can pay him any time—he tells us this Jesse Nash is staying with a pal at the Maple Leaf Hotel on Grand."

"Nash?" said Palliser. "Nash? Oh! The one on Ardlow. That one."

"Just in case you're interested," said Lake, and went back to the switchboard.

"Damn, I suppose we'd better go look," said Palliser. He got up. Grace said he'd go with him, and straightened his tie and reached for his hat.

Landers and Piggott sat there in silence for a minute. "Can we think there's still any chance, Matt?" asked Landers. "After four days?"

"I don't know," said Piggott. "Like the man said, 'The affair is in the hands of God.'"

"I—" And Sergeant Lake called urgently and they both went out to the anteroom.

"New one," said Lake. "Four cars on it—Kohler Street. Corpse and-or corpses—it sounds kind of confused." He added the address.

Still thinking about Higgins, Landers and Piggott went out on that in a hurry.

When they got there, one ambulance was just leaving and another one waited. It was the expectable house, a little old stucco crackerbox of a place. They went in. A little crowd of neighbors around in groups outside, two uniformed men at the door. Inside the small square living room, two more patrolmen were standing guard over a big burly man handcuffed and leg-cuffed, who was sitting head down in sullen silence. He was about forty-five; he had a couple of days' growth of dark beard and exuded an odor of whiskey and sweat.

"At least he's stopped swearing," said one of the patrolmen to the Homicide men. "We had a little donnybrook here, sir."

"Landers, Piggott. What's been going on?" asked Landers. There was the body of a man lying on the other side of the room, just at the door to a small bedroom. Landers went to look at it. Somewhere a woman was crying loudly.

"Well, what we can make out, a Mrs. Golladay lives here, and she—"

"Mrs. Betty Golladay." They all looked around. A fat elderly woman in a sleazy pink cotton dress had spoken and was standing in the door to the hall.

"Mrs. Fitzsimmons, sir. She's a neighbor, she was here—"

"That's right. She's taking on something awful, I reckon she oughta see a doctor. Poor soul, I seen the whole thing. Often enough she told me about him. *Him.* Her husband."

She looked at the sullen man in righteous indignation. "Common criminal. In jail half the time, drunk the other half. Not supportin' her, and her with the little girl to bring up. A nice little girl, Rosalie. Mrs. Golladay's a nice respectable lady."

"The kid was hurt—interns said not too bad, but some," offered another patrolman. "Twelve years old, the kid. The body seems to be one Glenn Thayer—"

"A nice respectable man," said Mrs. Fitzsimmons. "I should oughta say, I'm next-door neighbors with Mrs. Golladay. I—" And the weeping woman came slowly out from the kitchen, a slight dark woman sobbing into a handkerchief.

"She's dead, isn't she? He killed her—and Glenn—all I had—they're both dead, aren't they?"

"I think maybe," said Landers, "we ought to have a policewoman here." One of the uniformed men went out to call in.

"Now, Rosalie's not dead, she's goin' to be all right, you gotta believe me, I heard the doctor say. I saw the whole thing," said Mrs. Fitzsimmons. "I can tell you. You'll be what they call plainclothes officers. Detectives."

"That's right, ma'am," said Piggott. "If you could just—"

"You don't look old enough to be in the cops," she informed Landers. "But I seen the whole thing, account of I'd dropped over to borrow a cup of flour. And poor Mr. Thayer there—never a wrong thought in his life, honest respectable man, and all the trouble poor Mrs. Golladay's been through, it don't seem fair, her just goin' to get a new start in life like they say, meeting Mr. Thayer—he has—he had—his own business, good hardworking man, variety store up on Olive and doing good. And then this—this *husband* of hers, they let him out on parole. Why in the name of time they do that? Once they get him, they oughta keep him! Why they let him out?" Landers couldn't tell her.

"Oh—oh—oh," sobbed the younger woman. "All my fault —Glenn dead, and Rosalie—I should have divorced him the first time, but I—oh—oh!"

"She'd seen a lawyer about getting a divorce, just last week. New start in life, and then this has to happen. Terrible. He came in just after I did—he wanted see his little girl, he said— she didn't—Mrs. Golladay didn't even know he was outta jail —on parole like I said—and he saw poor Mr. Thayer talkin' to Rosalie—a nice man, Mr. Thayer, he liked children and Rosalie liked him, he useta help her with her arithmetic— And *that* one," she nodded, "well, he was just like a madman—yellin' and shoutin' and swearin'—"

The sullen man raised his head. He said in a sudden resurgence of rage, "I ain't havin' no other guy have nothin' to do with my little girl—damn bastard puttin' his arm round Rosalie—pattin' her hand—damn him to hell, I won't have—they belong to *me*, my wife 'n' kid—" A stream of obscenities came out of him, and a patrolman went to shut him up.

Landers squatted over the body. What had been a nicelooking fellow about forty, gray suit, thinning brown hair, nondescript regular features. What you could still see. His skull had been smashed in and there was blood and brain-tissue all over the thin rug, the gray suit. Beside him lay an ordinary household hammer, stained.

Piggott went out and used the radio in a squad-car to call the lab down here. He passed on Golladay's name, told them to run a check on him. Ten minutes later headquarters reported back.

Leon William Golladay, in on a second count of armed robbery, a three-to-ten, had been let loose on parole just forty-eight hours ago.

"At least," said Piggott to Landers, as the policewoman efficiently soothed Mrs. Golladay, and the lab men started to take pictures, "at least we can say this one isn't exactly a surprise."

Hackett said, "Luis. You ought to have some lunch."
"*Sé.* I'm not hungry."

"Look, I know how you feel. So do I. Damn it, George and I were at the Academy together. But— Look, everybody's on it. Doing what they can. What can be done."

"*Sé*," said Mendoza again. "I know, Art." He stubbed out his cigarette and immediately lit another.

Nothing was turning up, from the wide search: nothing at all. The helicopters were out again, the C.H.P., the rangers. There was just too much wild country, empty country, to cover with anything like efficiency.

"Luis—" Hackett turned away. No good talking to him.

And the outside phone rang there on his desk where he sat mechanically shuffling the deck of cards; he dropped the cards and snatched it up. "Central Homicide, Mendoza."

"Protheroe," said a deep rich baritone. "Chief Ranger, Shoshone Range station, Nevada, Lieutenant. I called just as quick as I could reach a phone. To tell you you can stop worrying about your Sergeant Higgins. His guardian angel was riding with him all the way, and he's sitting right beside me drinking milk and cussing like hell because the doctor won't let him have a steak right away. He's fine. Comparatively fine."

"What—*¡Gracias a Dios!*" said Mendoza limply. "Where? What—"

"Couple of my rangers came across him about two hours ago, way up Apache Pass. He's got one frostbit toe and a bad cold, but he'll be O.K. Of course he's hungry as a bear, but the doctor says—"

"He's all right?" said Mendoza faintly. "He's—" he heard Hackett's loud questions but couldn't pay attention—"he's O.K.?"

And the baritone said, "All right, here he is," and Higgins' voice said, "Luis? Luis? By God, Bary bust be wild! You tell her—call her—I'b all right, I've just got a code—"

"Yes, George. What—"

"Add this dabbed toe," said Higgins. "That's all. Add I'b

starvig, add this dabbed doctor gives be bilk! Bilk! I've beed waddering aroud id the sdow—add it was addig idsult to idjury, Luis—those dabbed bastards, they forgot all about be!" He sneezed. "This dabbed code—you call Bary—"

12

MENDOZA handed the phone to Hackett and ran out to the anteroom where Sergeant Lake was listening in with a broad smile. "Get me Mary!" he said urgently. Lake plugged in and began to dial. In thirty seconds Mendoza was saying, "He's all right, he's fine—he's just got a cold— We don't know yet, but—"

Hackett appeared in the office doorway, phone-cord stretched out behind him. "The rangers are flying him down this afternoon—that is, Protheroe says if they can find any clothes to fit him—they'll—"

"Clothes?" said Mendoza, and to Mary, "Yes, yes—everything's fine—they're flying him home this afternoon— What? I don't know where— Art?"

Hackett asked questions. "Ione, Nevada. What?"

"Nevada," said Mendoza. "He—"

"—says they'll probably get into International about four o'clock," said Hackett, and to the phone, "We'll be there. What? Oh. Oh, I'll just bet. Thanks very—"

They beamed at each other, as Hackett put the phone down. "Protheroe said he figured we'd want to hear the story soon as possible, and quite a story it is."

"I'll just bet," said Mendoza. "The main thing is, he's fine." Sergeant Lake was busily calling every bureau in the building, passing on the bare news—the good news. "*¡Vaya, por Dios!*" said Mendoza suddenly. "I am starving, Arturo. Come on!"

They stopped at every floor on the way down to spread the good word and took the Ferrari up North Broadway to Federico's. Veering automatically toward the big table in the corner, they encountered the tall Jamaican waiter, and Mendoza said, "He's O.K., Adam, we just heard—they just found him over in Nevada, and he's O.K."

"Now praise the Lord," said Adam, following them to the table. "I been doin' some prayin' for Sergeant Higgins, Lieutenant."

"And I don't care what you bring me," said Mendoza, "just so it's quick. I am starving." Hackett said that went for him.

Adam flashed a smile. "Yes, sir. I fix you up all right." He brought drinks, and Mendoza said he really didn't need that at all and Hackett said he did.

"And damn the calories. My God, Luis, I feel ten years younger."

"And you know," said Mendoza, "that Máiri MacTaggart is going to claim it was her silly Novena, and all these earnest Christians putting up the supplications—"

"You going to say it maybe wasn't?" said Hackett.

"*¿Cómo dices?*" said Mendoza cynically. "The cards fall as they fall, Arturo." He swallowed rye, and set the glass down, and said, "*¡Caramba!* I never called Alison—" He ran for the public phone in the lobby.

Forty seconds later he was saying, "—quite O.K. We don't know the story, the rangers are flying him down this afternoon—he's got a cold but otherwise—"

"*Gracias a Dios,*" said Alison. "I can't believe it, but thank God." In the background he heard the twins conversing loudly and bilingually, and Cedric barking. "*¡Bastante!*" said Alison. "Quiet, you two, I can't— Oh, Luis, I know how you're all feeling— I'll call Angel. And Roberta."

"*Por favor.* I'm starving. I'll see you, *cara.*"

He and Hackett were just sharing the last French roll when Landers and Piggott came in, and immediately after them Grace and Palliser. Hackett stood up and beckoned violently, and regardless of the cultured hush lying over this genteel restaurant called out, "He's all right! They just found him, and he's O.K.!"

Heads turned; the other four men came up in a hurry. "What? Higgins? He's—"

"He's all right. Somewhere over in Nevada—the rangers are flying him back this afternoon." There was excited babble for a few minutes, the bare news exchanged, commented on.

"His guardian angel must have been with him all right," said Palliser. "I wouldn't have believed it. Thank God. And all of a sudden I am starving. Bring me the quickest thing, Adam."

"Me too," said Landers inelegantly. "My God, I never would have believed—"

"It just shows you," said Piggott seriously. "The valley of the shadow of death. But the sergeant's a good man, and I guess there were enough prayers put up for him."

"That might just be," said Jason Grace. "We don't know everything about everything yet."

Mendoza lit a cigarette. "And just what the hell," he said with sudden energy, "are we doing about all these cases we're supposed to be working? What's on hand and what's getting done? Lily Clevenger—the Deforrest-Parker thing—Ardlow —what's the damned rigmarole you were telling me about Rhys, John?"

Palliser grinned at him. "Rigmarole you could say. It's changed shape a little," and he told him about Myra Rhys and Lockyear and Luke Abell. "It just crossed my mind to wonder if Lockyear could have hired Abell—"

"Wild," said Mendoza. "But you'll fetch Abell in and lean on him some. The questioning in depth." Palliser said he intended to do just that.

Landers told Mendoza about Leon Golladay. "And no surprise, as I said," said Piggott, "but that poor woman. Of course she should have got rid of him as soon as she found out what he was."

"*Indudable.* But women so seldom do what they should, Matt."

"And there's Reiner," said Grace. "Poor old Mrs. Reiner. House ransacked, and the family says if there was fifty bucks there, certainly no more—and the cards left on the kitchen table. Where a couple of X's had played—I think—a game of black-jack."

"*¿Cómo?*" said Mendoza, interested. "You don't say!"

"I think," said Grace. "Not that I'm a compulsive card-player, but you do pick up this and that. At any rate, the fellow sitting west had a hand adding up to nineteen—ace, king, two deuces and four of spades. The other fellow held an ace, a deuce, four of diamonds, seven of hearts and seven of spades."

"Black-jack I don't know," said Landers. "What does that say?"

"Game's twenty-one," said Mendoza shortly. "Aces count one point or eleven. *¿No me digas,* Jase? That's interesting. And funny."

"Well, I thought it was interesting," said Grace.

Mendoza looked at Hackett. "What we said about Lily Clevenger. Gas stations down here. Have you done any looking?"

"No, I haven't."

"So get on that."

"There's Ardlow too," said Palliser, yawning. "That Jesse Nash—a pigeon called in—at the Maple Leaf Hotel on Grand. I checked, and he's registered, but he wasn't in. Shall we stake it out?"

"Is he our boy for sure?"

"By some good latents on Ardlow's billfold. And how surprised he is going to be," said Palliser thoughtfully. "Ardlow the bleeder. It'll probably end up as involuntary manslaughter at that."

"Well, we want him. Stake out the hotel," said Mendoza.

"The warrant came through on Goeltz," said Grace.

"*Bueno.*" Replete, Mendoza sat back smoking lazily. He looked his old dapper confident self again. They all felt as if they'd had a shot of adrenalin; they beamed at each other, and once again their minds were back on the job: the routine that went on forever. Mendoza said, "So, get with it, boys. Art, I'll meet you in the parking lot at three-fifteen—they might be early in, never can tell."

"Right," said Hackett.

And Hackett went back to the job feeling himself again too, not caring a damn that, damn it, the scales had showed two extra pounds this morning. The gas stations, he thought: Lily Clevenger, late at night a week ago last Tuesday, suddenly noticing that the Porsche's tank was nearly empty. (Where was the Porsche?) Their exotic Jane Doe, quite as exotic after identification, had intrigued them; Higgins had taken their minds off her; now Hackett was curious again. The Clevengers had been agitating at Homicide, what were they doing, what had they found out; and that was natural.

But before he got started on the gas stations, he was deflected over to the Deforrest-Parker thing by a teletype from the Chief of Police in Ventura.

"Your query Jerry Trenton," it said, "info required herewith. Raised Episcopal Orphanage Ventura released 1963 age eighteen graduate Ventura High School same year. Picked up auto-theft same year given probation. B. and E. 1965 six-month suspended sentence." Oh, really, thought Hackett. Evidently Ventura was plagued by some of these Be Kind to Criminal courts too. "Burglary charge 1966, one-to-three sheriff's farm, parole after ten-month stretch. Not known Ventura since. Official description six-one, one-seventy, Caucasian, brown and blue, no marks do you want copy official photo?"

"Well, well," said Hackett to that. He thought he'd rather like to talk to Jerry Trenton now. Margaret Kay had said Anne Parker had told her that Trenton had been applying for a job at that brokerage. Ask there; if he had, they'd have an address.

Meanwhile—until three-fifteen—gas stations. He sat down at his desk with the downtown telephone book and began to look them up: address of all those within, for a start, six blocks from the freeway interchange where all the freeways came together in a glorious muddle of under- and over-passes, and out-of-state visitors frequently panicked. Even residents of L.A. bore the traumatic scars of that butterfly exchange.

He started to list the phone numbers methodically. Make a start on the calls at least. Are you open evenings? How late? Were you open to midnight a week ago last Tuesday? There'd probably be quite a few which had been. Then, go look at the evening attendants.

Lily Clevenger, of course, quite something in the female line. And driving alone, late at night. . . . He remembered suddenly that Bainbridge had said something about the body having grease on it, an attempt made to wash it.

Grease? From a service station's stained cement paving? Hackett picked up the phone.

"I don't know what to think about Rhys," said Palliser to Grace. "It's just another damned funny thing. From what his wife said—Lord, what a woman!—he was a rabbit, under his partner's thumb and then he fell victim to Myra, and you'd expect her to be a better judge of a man but could be she saw him as a meal-ticket, who knows? But I really don't see Lockyear having the—the guts to hire a killer, and besides by his record this Abell isn't. Just a punk."

"A punk who likes gin," said Grace, smoothing his moustache. "Maybe we'll hear all about it when we talk to him. But it's funny, all right. Man so scared of his wife he carries that note on him, and then—maybe just by the coincidence—getting taken off by the punk."

"That woman," said Palliser. "*And* Lockyear. Well, the lab evidence is good, Abell's X, that we do know."

Lebanon Avenue. When they came to it Palliser said, "There you are. A short block off Flower, the same block where the car was found. With Rhys in it. And Duke said the prints indicated that Abell was the last one to drive the car."

It was an old two-storey house, the address they wanted with a sign in a front window, *Room for Rent*. They took off their hate; Palliser rang the bell. After a while a fat woman opened the door and he showed her the badge.

"We're looking for a Luke Abell. Is he here?"

"Cops," she said. She was chewing gum. "Goes to show I did right askin' him to get out. Yesterday I told him. And he got. He was behind on the rent. You unnerstand," she said to Grace, "I ain't anything against a person's color. But they's good and bad in all colors, and that one, gettin' drunk and behind on the rent—I wanted shut of. He was only here a month. That was enough."

"Well, I can't say I blame you, ma'am," said Grace, "but it's our bad luck. You don't know where he went?" She shook her head. "Or where he worked?" Another shake.

Palliser thanked her; they went back to the Rambler. "So, dead end," said Palliser.

"Put out an A.P.B.," said Grace. "Put out the word to the pigeons."

"Sure. We usually end up doing it the hard way," said Palliser.

Piggott was staked out at the Maple Leaf Hotel on Grand. It was scarcely the classiest hotel in town but it was, to all intents and purposes, an honest hotel; it didn't knowingly cater to the prostitutes, it was reasonably clean, and the desk-clerk hadn't shied away from the badge, but looked interested.

Jesse Lee Nash had, of all things, registered under his own name. Well, his pedigree wasn't a really bad one, of course, and he wasn't—so far as he knew—wanted for anything right now. Regarded in one sense, any pedigree was bad; but he was a small-timer, the petty thief and mugger living hand-to-mouth, holding the subsistence jobs when he had to, preferring it the easy way, getting along as he could.

"I just want you to give me the high sign when he shows up," said Piggott.

"Sure," said the clerk, who was a foxy-faced fellow with protruding teeth. "Sure, I'll do that. Cops after him, hah? I'll be glad to do that, sir."

Piggott retired to a corner of the lobby with its ancient furniture, to a chair where he had both the entrance and the desk in view, and sat back and thought warmly about Higgins. However he'd ended up over in Nevada, his guardian angel with him. Piggott believed in guardian angels. Some things couldn't be explained without bringing in the guardian angels. Anyway, thank God Higgins was all right.

He thought about Prudence Russell, that nice girl. He thought she liked him all right; she admired him because he was a cop, a detective at Homicide in Central Headquarters. And any woman was an idiot, thought Piggott, to marry a cop nowadays. Sit home wondering just when somebody would be calling to tell her he'd got shot, or bombed, or knifed, by one of these wild-eyed subversives or somebody on dope—

But at that, it would be kind of nice to have somebody to worry about him. There wasn't, as it stood, a single soul to care if Matt Piggott lived or died—except God and his guardian angel. And then he smiled at another thought; he thought about this last four days. That was a lie. Because

Matt Piggott *was* a cop, if anything should happen to him, there'd be thousands and thousands of people to care—all the cops who knew about it, and all the good citizens everywhere who knew that cops constituted the thin blue line between civilization and anarchy.

Feeling a little better, Piggot opened his newspaper, keeping an unobtrusive eye on the desk.

There was just time, after making a list of all the gas stations, to drop in at the brokerage. Hackett did so.

He was handed from secretary to secretary, finally introduced to a youngish man who admitted being in charge of personnel. "I'd just like to know," said Hackett, "whether a young fellow named Trenton applied for a job here recently."

Mr. Spencer said he could check their files. "Well, if you would, please," said Hackett. He waited impatiently, glancing at his watch. Spencer came back with a page in his hand.

"A Gerald Trenton made out an application form with us. Let's see, eight days back. He answered our ad in the *Times*. For a messenger-clerk. That's what we call it, actually it's a glorified office-boy's job. We didn't hire him."

"Why not?"

"Well, he'd had no experience in office work at all, and he did very poorly on the reading-comprehension test we ask applicants to take."

"Well, all I'm after really is the address he gave you." Spencer handed him the application form and Hackett looked at it interestedly. The usual blanks to be filled in: name, address, age, education, etcetera. It had been filled out very untidily, by somebody unused to holding a pen—a nearly illiterate hand. Hackett copied the address into his notebook: Bimini Place. He thanked Spencer.

It was three o'clock. He had left the scarlet Barracuda in a red zone at the curb; he drove hastily back to headquarters, went up to the office, and found Palliser and Grace there, idly talking.

"I thought we had work to do."

"Matt's staked out on Nash. We can't find Abell. Tom went out on a new call."

"Well, one of you might get on this," said Hackett, and passed over Trenton's address, the teletype from Ventura. "Parker told this Kay girl she'd run into Trenton. That was the day before she got killed. I don't suppose he's anything to do with it, a little pedigree, but somebody'd better talk to him. My God, I'm late—" and he ran.

Palliser went out to see Trenton; Grace started typing a report on Golladay.

Bimini Place was an old part of L.A., not the oldest but old. Academically Palliser wondered why Bimini: place-names were peculiar. He wasn't old enough to remember, as Mendoza could have told him, that awhile back, in that section just off Exposition Boulevard, there had been one of the city's first public swimming pools, bearing that name.

It was an old street. Courts, a couple of duplexes, at the end a larger house on the corner: that was the address. Palliser rang the doorbell, and a woman came to the door: a thin woman about fifty with her head tied up in a blue turban. Palliser opened his mouth and she said, "I don't take salesmen. Coming and going all the time, makes a body nervous. You look all right. No cooking in the room, acourse. It's my best one—twelve bucks a week."

"I'm sorry, I don't want a room," said Palliser, thinking of the payments on the forty-thousand-dollar house on Hillside Avenue. "I'm looking for a Gerald Trenton. Does he live here?"

"Oh," she said. "Him. He's paid all right so far. Yeah, he's in— I don't think he's got a job, and if he don't pay up this week out he goes. Left rear upstairs." She turned away and vanished down the hall.

Palliser climbed steep uncarpeted stairs, went down a dim narrow hall, knocked at the rear door on the left. There was a stir in the room; after a moment the door opened.

"Who're you?"

Palliser showed him the badge and he shied back. Well, the pedigree: innocent as day, he would shy back. "Sergeant Palliser. Mr. Trenton?"

"Yeah, I'm Jerry Trenton." He wasn't a bad-looking young fellow, regular features, wavy hair. "So what? I'm clean, I haven't done anything."

"Not saying you have," said Palliser. "Mind if I come in?"

"I can't stop you." Trenton went into the room, sat on the bed. It was a small square room, barely furnished. "So what you want with me? I told you—"

Palliser smiled at him. "Look, take the chip off. So you've got a little pedigree. I know you've just been trying for the honest job here. So you're trying to play it straight, and good luck to you. All we want from you is a few answers. That day you applied for the job at the brokerage, you ran across an old acquaintance. Anne Parker."

Trenton's eyes were wary. "Oh, her," he said. "Yeah, that's right. I—we never knew each other, it was just—we both got raised at that orphanage. A lot of kids there. She—we just said hello, that was all. Why?"

"Did you see her again?"

He shook his head. "They turned me down for that job. I guess she worked there. It was about noon, I s'pose she was on her way to lunch."

"You just said hello—that was all?"

"Well," he said unwillingly, "well, a little more, she asked what I was doing down here and I said, trying to get a job, we just talked a little and—and she wished me good luck. That was all." His eyes were on the floor.

"I see," said Palliser. That would have been natural, of course; they wouldn't have had much in common but the orphanage. "That was the only time you saw Miss Parker?"

"That's right," he muttered. "I—was surprised to see her, I knew she'd left town awhile back—Ventura I mean—but I didn't know for where."

Palliser offered him a cigarette and he said he didn't smoke. "Don't you see the newspapers, Trenton? Didn't you know that Miss Parker was murdered the next day? Shot?"

No immediate reaction; and then Trenton looked up at him slowly. "Shot?" he said. "No, I—I didn't know that. Was she? I don't read the papers much. I didn't know."

The big Cessna with the Forest Rangers' insignia on its side set down on one of the non-commercial runways at International Airport at four-twenty. Mendoza and Hackett, let through the private gate, were halfway out to it when the door opened and a uniformed ranger got out, followed by a familiar burly figure. They ran to pound his shoulders, convince themselves he was there, solid and sound. The ranger turned out to be Protheroe.

"I must say," he said, "it's been one of my more interesting experiences in the service. Come across a city cop wandering around the mountains in just his shorts—"

"What?" said Mendoza and Hackett together.

Higgins sneezed and groped for a handkerchief. He looked very un-Higgins-like, in a rather loud-patterned chalk-striped suit and a cheap blue shirt, no tie. "Oh, just wait till you hear," he said in a thick voice. "By owd dabbed fault, of course, these thidgs always are. Ab I glad to be back! Is Bary all right—the kids?"

"We've all been just waiting to celebrate getting rid of you, of course," said Mendoza. "My God, George, you can guess! My God, the whole C.H.P. out, the helicopters, the dogs— well, *naturalmente*, she's been out of her mind, *estúpido*.

Something's happened to George, she tells me— *¡Santa María!* You going out, take the dog for a walk, get the prescription filled, and vanishing away into thin air! *Por Dios*, we've been neglecting everything else on hand and nobody minding the store— *¡Oigame!* Just what the hell happened to you?"

Protheroe chuckled. "It's quite a story," he said. "You'll enjoy it, Lieutenant. You can take him right home—the doctor said a few days' rest and plenty of food, he'll be fine." He waved away Higgins' thanks, turning away to speak to the pilot.

"The car's just over past the gate, can you—" They had him by both arms.

"Sure, I'b fide," said Higgins. He was limping just a little. "This dabbed toe is all. Well, I'll tell you—all by owd dabbed fault. I got there just as they were getting out with the haul. Add haved you said it, Luis—the guy leaps toward trouble idstead of away, the bord cop! That's be. I wedt for by gud, I said, Hold it, add ode of theb fired at be add bissed, add I took after theb—thought, get the plate-nubber adyway. I caught up with Killeed—I foud out later it was Killeed—add grabbed hib, add he hit be with the butt of his gud, caught be off baladce, see—I got the hell of a crack od by head od the sidewalk, I guess I was out for a bidute or so. Adyway, I cobe to, he's got by gud add billfold, he's sayig, It's a cop, look, a real bad-hudter, a tod of law, he says, I always wadted get a cop all to byself, have sobe fud with, let's take hib, he says."

They put him into the Ferrari, Hackett perched in the jump seat behind. Mendoza slid behind the wheel. "We were afraid of that. And?"

"So," Higgins blew his nose "the other two dod't like the idea, but Killeed argued theb iddto it—they wadted to get away. Dext thig I kdow, I'b tryig fight two of 'eb id the back of the car. Killeed hit be agaid add they got be tied up with by owd tie add belt. I'b beig as obstructive as I cad, you udderstad, add the other ode, I fide out later is Starr, he says, for

186

God's sake of all crazy ideas, add Killeed says, we just give hib a little shot of morphide, keep hib quiet till we have tibe have sobe fud with the cop—"

"My God!" said Hackett.

"You bay well say so," said Higgins with feeling. "They did, add I suppose I should just be thadkful they did't give be ad overdose add put be out right thed. I guess I *was* out the better part of the dext twedty-four hours. Bost of that Bodday—I dod't rebeber adythig. Out like a light, I was. Dext thig I really rebeber, I was all tied up id the back of a car and they were arguig with sobe other guy."

"Knight," said Mendoza.

"Yes, it was after dark all right. I did't eved kdow what day it was. They'd stripped by clothes off—dowd to my shorts I was! Add thed we drove off—add drove, add drove—add that dabbed Killeed sat beside be tellig be all the thigs he was goig to do to be whed he had the tibe—"

"Yes, they'd been a little busy, making the deal," said Mendoza, "That would be Monday night. They still had the Caddy."

"I dod't kdow," said Higgins, refusing a cigarette from Hackett. "This dabbed code—add I was dabbed hugry *thed*—Killeed swillig beer there add the other two—well, I tell you, boys, about thed I was sayig to byself, This is it, George. Those bastards—pedigrees like that—"

"So were we, George," said Hackett. "So were we."

"I bet," said Higgins. "Add thed they decided to switch cars. The ode they had too hot. They rebebered be *thed*, the other two wadted to leave be right there, said it was crazy, ditch the cop for God's sake, every law-bad in seved states after 'eb for the cop— I tell you, Luis, I thought I'd had it. Bullet id the head, add off they go. But that Killeed—he said, sedse of hubor he got, he always wadted a cop all to hibself, as sood as they ladded sobe place he was goig to have fud with the cop—so they put be id the back of this statiod-wagod—

187

add they forgot all about be!" said Higgins. He sneezed indignantly.

"That would have been," said Mendoza, "some time on Tuesday."

"You cad't prove it by be," said Higgins. "I heard 'eb talkig add arguig, I dod't kdow whed but they gave be adother shot of morphide, I was out—add I dod't kdow if they stopped to sleep adywhere, but dext tibe I cabe to, they'd picked up the liquor sobe place add they were all gettig dicely oiled."

"Doing what comes naturally," said Hackett. "My God. My God, it's a mercy you weren't killed along with them—"

"Oh, are they dead? Good riddadce," said Higgins. They told him about that, rather disjointedly. "Dot surprisig," said Higgins. "By God, whed I thought what Bary bust be feelig —add all of you— Add thed they got lost. Id the boudtaids. They wadted to go to Redo—Killeed kept sayig he was goig to get back at sobe black-jack dealer there—but they got lost. Add they got to arguig, they were all tight as hell, tryig to read the bap—add they started to fight. Killeed add Trasker. They were rollig all over the seat, add they cabe iddto the back add fell od top of be. That's whed they rebebered be," said Higgins. "Add Trasker said 'This dabbed cop,' add Killeed was a goddabbed fool saddle theb with a cop, add he hauled be out add fired a shot at be add dext thig off they wedt. Tight as ticks. It's a wodder they did't crash the car right there."

"My God, talk about guardian angels," said Hackett.

"Even more of a wonder," said Mendoza, "that they managed to get another sixty miles or so away before they did kill themselves."

Higgins sneezed. "I badaged to get by wrists loose by rubbig the rope agaidst a tree," he said. "Add, dabb it, I rebebered the bit about boss growig od the dorth side of thigs, but how the hell did I kdow which directiod I wadted to go? Where the dearest civilized parts were? Dab it, I bight of beed od the bood! Dothig but trees add boudtaids, add sdow! I dever was a Boy Scout. I pulled dowd sobe pide-bradches, sleep udder sobehow, add whed the sud cabe out dext day, I got sobe warber. Wadderig aroud id that dabbed wilderdess— I dever kdew there was so buch ebpty ladd adywhere! Add I was starvig—add I kdew how you'd all be fussig add fubig— by God!"

"Well, we were," said Hackett. "We surely were, George."

"Add what Protheroe add I added up, we figure it bust've beed late Tuesday afterdood they left be up there. *I* could't say. I just waddered aroud, tryig to keep warb add lookig for sobe sigds of *people*— I saw a bear, add the ode skudk I saw I made tracks away frob—by God, I had visiods of by skeletod beig foud twedty years frob dow—till this bordig, all of a sudded I hear a botor—it was a Jeep—add rad iddto these two forest radgers—add was I glad to see theb!" Higgins sneezed. "I'b starvig—but the doctor said—"

And of course Higgins had a very rugged constitution, which had probably saved his life. "You'll take some time off," said Mendoza, as he drew up before the house on Silver Lake Boulevard.

"You're dab right I'll take sobe tibe off," said Higgins. "Do you kdow I've dropped eighteed pouds? Id four days?" He got out of the Ferrari. Mary and the kids erupted out of the house to greet him, the little Scotty barking hysterically. Limping, he went to them.

"Eighteen pounds!" said Hackett. "My God, I wish they'd kidnapped me!"

13

Mᴇɴᴅᴏᴢᴀ and Hackett went back to the office to pass the tale of Higgins' adventures to the other men.

"Eighteen pounds?" said Sergeant Lake incredulously. *"Eighteen pounds!* My God, I wish—"

"Don't steal Hackett's line," said Mendoza.

Piggott wandered in last of all, saying that Jesse Nash hadn't showed. The night men could stake it out; hopefully, he'd come back some time. And then they all went home.

When Mendoza steered the Ferrari into the big garage, he found Máiri MacTaggart's little gray Chevy sitting beside Alison's Facel-Vega; and when he came into the kitchen Máiri was busy over something on the stove, her usual sturdy bustling self. Alison was supervising the twins' supper at the kitchen table; he bent to kiss her.

"Didna I say so?" said Mrs. MacTaggart. "I knew the man was safe all the time. Such a nice woman, the Lord wouldna be so cruel."

"Well, I wouldn't say exactly safe," said Mendoza. "He was damned lucky, that I will say." He grinned at Alison. "Just wait till you hear the saga."

And the twins were both shouting at once. "Daddy read *el cuento* before bed—" Johnny. *"El Gato* all by himself—" *"No Gato—"* Terry—*"El Leopardo,* Daddy!"

"I had heard," said Alison, "about this stage. When they

190

want the same story over and over. But it's maddening all the same. And really, Luis—this language thing, we've got to do something to get them straightened out." And she added automatically to the twins, "¡Bastante! Quiet down, you two!—finish your suppers and we'll see."

Mrs. MacTaggart was carefully pouring Mendoza a jigger of rye; El Señor arrived from nowhere on the counter top and demanded his share in the raucous voice he'd inherited from his Siamese father. "Guidness to mercy!" said Máiri. "That cat!"

Belatedly discovering that master was home, Cedric ambled in from the hall and offered a polite paw. "Livestock!" said Mendoza, taking the glass. "Come into the living room and I'll tell you about George."

Hackett went home, to his brown-haired Angel and Mark and Sheila, and said, "Wait till you hear about George. My God, talk about guardian angels."

"I'm dying to—hear, I mean," said Angel. "All Alison knew was that he was safe. What happened?"

But Mark was being a jet bomber again and Sheila demanding attention, and it wasn't until they sat down to dinner that he could begin to tell her.

The Pallisers not yet having produced any noisy offspring to interfere with their privacy, Palliser told Roberta about it as he helped her get dinner on the table. "A miracle," he said, "but—after we knew he was O.K.—funny too, the way the Lieutenant said he was so mad, that unpredictable trio just forgetting about him." He laughed. "And Hackett saying he wished they'd kidnapped him—"

"Whyever for?" asked Roberta.

"Higgins dropped eighteen pounds," said Palliser; and she began to laugh too.

Friday, and Hackett's day off.

Reports waited on Mendoza's desk from Schenke and Galeano. First, a new one overnight: man's body found in Pershing Square. Evidently again the mugger using the unnecessary violence. I.D. on him but nothing else. An initial report signed by Schenke.

Jesse Nash had showed at the Maple Leaf Hotel and been duly tagged by Galeano. Just as he brought him in, the new call had come, so they had just stashed him in the facility on Alameda and left him for the day crew. Mendoza told Palliser and Grace to handle that; they might get an admission out of him.

Palliser said, "O.K., but that Trenton—"

"Trenton?"

"He just showed on the edge of the Deforrest-Parker thing —brought up in the same orphanage with Parker, ran into her by chance the day before the killings. Hackett asked me to see him—he's got a little pedigree from Ventura—and, I don't know, I don't much like him. I couldn't tell you why. He's got no record of violence, he looks as if he's trying to stay straight, and maybe it's natural he should be leery of cops, but —" He hunched his shoulders. "Just a feeling."

"And as I've told you before," said Mendoza seriously, "never ignore your feelings, John. Is that so? Well, I may take a look at him." Palliser passed over the address, the teletype from Ventura; he and Grace started for the jail, talking about Higgins' adventure.

Landers and Piggott were on the new one: one Byron Halsey, mugged and beaten and dead in Pershing Square. No shape to that sort of thing, unless by chance the lab should turn up something. The call yesterday afternoon had been a suicide; Landers had already turned in a report on that.

Lily Clevenger. Mendoza sighed. Hardly anything had been done on that at all. There had been front-page stories on it: she'd been somebody, if not exactly a star. Doubtless the demands from reporters for further details, of the desk sergeant in the lobby; he didn't know, he'd been too busy worrying about George. The inquest had been held yesterday; he wondered who had covered it, if anybody. Sometimes things came along a little hot and heavy.

However, some work ought to be done on Lily Clevenger now. The husband had been good: calling in only once, Lake said, to ask if they'd found out any more about it. The funeral tomorrow.

Gas stations. Hackett had left his list on Mendoza's desk; but now Mendoza got out the County Guide and pored over map forty-four: his beat, Central, that he knew so well. They didn't, did they, know where she might have been when she noticed the nearly empty tank. They could reason, somewhere near downtown because of where the body was left. Was that valid? Well, X probably wouldn't, even late at night, have wanted to haul a naked dead body around too long.

Gas stations. Where Lily might have picked up the grease somebody had tried to wash from her body. Mendoza shut the County Guide and stood up. He tucked the publicity shot of Lily he'd got from Clevenger into his breast pocket. The idiot boy and the lost horse—

He took the Pasadena freeway up to where Central's beat ended, just before Avenue Twenty-six, got off it and onto San Fernando, went around a block and got back on it headed downtown at Avenue Twenty-six. The first off-ramp he came to was at North Hill, just this side of New Chinatown; he thought that was a little too far off. Look back this far if need be, but for now he took the next off-ramp which brought him, roughly, to Temple and Figueroa near the Civic Center. The first station he came to was an independent; he drove in and asked questions. The proprietor said he stayed open to eleven on Saturday nights only. "Business don't warrant it, week days," he said. Mendoza rejoined the

Pasadena freeway and journeyed on to the next off-ramp at Third. There was a station half a block away; he drove in, asked questions. It was open to eleven five days a week, which was no use to him at all. He went on down Third and came to another a block away.

That one was open to midnight five days a week. "Who's your night attendant?" asked Mendoza, hauling out the badge.

"Oh. Oh—police business?" the youngish station manager was curious. "What's it about? Bernie? You're not sayin' *Bernie's* done anything?"

"I don't know," said Mendoza. "He's your night man? Here alone? Tell me about him—what's his name?"

"*Bernie!*" said the manager, astonished. "Well, for God's sake, Bernie wouldn't— Well, his name's Bernie Wolf. I hired him because I'm sorry for him, but nobody need be, you got to hand it to him, he's a good worker, reliable. He's got a disability pension from the Navy—he lost a leg in the Second World War— I guess he's about fifty-nine, sixty—yeah, he's alone at the station, but—"

Mendoza thanked him and drove out. It was possible, of course, but he didn't really see a sixty-year-old with one leg doing that job on Lily Clevenger. There was a station across the street, half a block back; she'd have had to turn across traffic into it, but it was the first she'd have passed and at that time of night— He turned out across traffic and went back to it. It was a smartly designed chain station, and a uniformed attendant came out promptly to him. He asked questions. It was open to midnight seven days a week. The night attendant on week nights? That would be Tommy. Tommy Manfred. Well, actually he was here right now, doing a lube job on his own car—

Mendoza regarded Tommy with interest. He was about twenty-four, tall and thin, with a weak chin, and introduced to a police officer with some questions for him, he looked nervous. "What you want with me?"

"I don't know," said Mendoza. He brought out the photograph. "Ever see her in here?"

"My hands are dirty." He just looked at it. "No, sir. She—I saw this picture in the newspaper. She got murdered, didn't she? No, I never saw her in here, never. I'm only on at night. No, sir."

Well, he was a name to put on a list, if they had to dig for it. Mendoza thanked him, got back on the freeway, and went on to the Sxith Street off-ramp. Half a block down was another chain station. The station manager came out and Mendoza asked questions. It was open to midnight seven nights a week. The night-attendant— The station manager was curious. "If you're thinking he, well, did anything, you're on the wrong track. I was lucky to get him—he's just been here about six weeks." The manager was a rather handsome fellow in his forties, tall and rugged. "My God, most of the guys, you just can't count on 'em—lazy, or don't show up on time, claim they're mechanics when they don't know beans. Jim, I'm lucky to get him. He's just out of the Army, did a ten-year hitch, so he's responsible. He's on from three to midnight, I spell him five to six. You want to talk to him, he lives just around the corner—got a room in a house on Seventh Place."

"I might do just that," said Mendoza. He did. He found Jim Lederer just leaving the quiet old house to have breakfast at a coffee-shop on Sixth. Lederer was about thirty, an upstanding fellow with good shoulders, frank blue eyes under thick dark brows, and a cap of dark hair. He looked at the photograph and said no, he'd never seen her at the station. "I'd have remembered," he said thoughtfully.

Mendoza sought the Ferrari again, got back on the freeway and went on to the next off-ramp at Eighth. Here, almost at once, he came on two rival chain stations on opposite corners, and tried the righthand one first.

It was open to midnight five nights a week. The night attendant? The station manager's own brother, Bud Talmadge, and if the police thought Bud had been up to anything— Mendoza soothed him, got the address and tried the opposite station. Here, as it happened, by default of the regular night man, the proprietor himself had been on duty four nights last week including Tuesday, and denied all knowledge of Lily Clevenger. He'd have remembered a girl like that, he said. Mendoza added his name, Fred Parkinson, to his list and got back on the freeway. And of course the next, and last, off-ramp was at the butterfly exchange itself, down there where all the freeways came together, and getting off the Pasadena freeway he found himself on Venice Boulevard, facing another chain station across the street. He pulled across traffic into it.

It was open five nights a week, a neatly-dressed young Negro told him. Night attendant? One Bill Dosser. Bill was all right, reliable and steady. Had a wife and two kids. Worked another job, days—moonlighted here. Which, of course, said nothing.

Mendoza went back to the office to think about it.

"I don't know how the hell you dropped on me," said Jesse Nash mournfully to Palliser and Grace. "How did you? Damn it, I like livin' nice at a nice clean place like that hotel, when I can—and now you stash me in jail, damn it! What count you got on me, anyways?"

"What count have you been up to?" asked Palliser. "You must have pulled more than one job to be living in a place like the Maple Leaf, Nash. Five bucks a day."

"It's a nice place," he said. He was a middle-sized man with a weak face and shifting eyes. "I never pulled nothing. I'm clean. I haven't done nothing since I got out."

"What are you living on?" asked Grace. "Got a job?" They knew he hadn't.

"I—well, I had some luck at cards and like that."

"Quite some luck," said Palliser. They were talking to him in an interrogation room at the new jail.

"Well, I did. Say, you guys are new to me. You new in Robbery?" Yes, he'd know most of the men in Goldberg's office.

"No," said Palliser. "We're Homicide, Nash."

"*Homicide*," said Nash. "*Hom*—— What the hell you want with me? I never got mixed up in nothing like that! You got the wrong—"

"Afraid not," said Grace gently. "You remember Robert Ardlow, Nash? Or did you ever know his name? A fellow you jumped, probably, over on Sixth about three weeks back. You left him in an empty house on Carondelet."

Enlightenment glinted in Nash's eyes, but he wasn't, of course, going to admit anything. "You can't prove no such thing."

"Oh, but we can," said Palliser. "You left your prints on his billfold, Nash. How much did you get off him?"

"Oh, hell," said Nash. "I did? Hell and damnation! Well, all *right.* Me and Danny, we needed some dough that night, both broke, see, and we just—well, he was dressed O.K. and looked like he might—we got him inna car, quick—Danny's car—and I know that place was empty, a dark street along there— And we only got three bucks off him, damn it! Three lousy bucks, and you send me up for maybe a one-to-three—"

"Little bit longer, Nash," said Grace. "He's dead."

"*Dead?* He— You're nuts," said Nash. "I hardly touched him with the knife—just to keep him quiet. I never—"

"Yes, but he was a bleeder," said Palliser. "You signed his death warrant, leaving him there bleeding even from one little cut, Nash." They had to explain that to him; he'd never heard of such a thing before.

When he got it through his head, he stared at them in horror. "I never meant kill nobody! I never meant—"

"The fact remains, you did," said Palliser.

But it would probably be a charge of involuntary manslaughter.

"So, what's Danny's other name?" asked Grace.

Landers and Piggott were out on a first cast on the new mugging, and getting nowhere. Byron Halsey had had a good job: he'd been supervisor of the maintenance crew at a twelve-storey office building on Wilshire. Halsey had paid a monthly fee to park his car in the big underground parking-lot under Pershing Square; and the car was still there, a '65 Ford sedan. His body had, in fact, been found just behind the little building at one corner of the square which housed the escalators to the three-tier parking-lot.

He'd have been leaving the building as usual about eleven P.M. the night before, said the personnel manager in the building. So it looked as if the mugger had caught him just as he came up there, to go down to his car, and dragged him around the building into convenient darkness.

Halsey had been a bachelor, lived in a single apartment on Normandie Avenue, close in to downtown. No known relatives. Nobody had any idea how much money he might have had on him.

"Sometimes," said Landers, when they knocked off for lunch, having looked at Halsey's apartment fruitlessly, "this is a discouraging job, Matt."

"I believe you," said Piggott. "On the other hand, Tom, you've got to think of the times when the Lord seems to take a direct hand. That Warthol thing—" He swallowed coffee and shook his head. "I still can't get over it. The purple cars— and out of the first batch Traffic spots at random, Goeltz— branded just like Cain with that iron."

But that was no help to them on this. Mendoza came in with Palliser and Grace and they told him about it. "Just nowhere to go," said Landers.

Mendoza told them they both knew better than that. "You go to Records. You collect the names of all known muggers with similar M.O.'s and you find them and lean on them."

They both groaned. "I was just trying not to think about it," said Landers. "What do you mean, similar M.O.'s? On a thing like this? The probably random mugging? It'll end up in Pending."

"Not until you've done some work on it," said Mendoza. "I called George. He's doing fine, with Mary making mustard footbaths and poultices and feeding him up."

"And if you ask me that was another miracle," said Piggott. Nobody denied it.

The postponed inquest on Wanda Deforrest and Anne Parker was held that afternoon. The expectable open verdict: Homicide had no evidence to offer against anybody. And damn it, thought Mendoza, they should have by now. When he got back to the office he called the lab.

Scarne told him they'd got nothing useful there at all. No prints identifiable except those of the two women. All the blood was Parker's apparently: she was Type O. The apartment had not been ransacked and there was money in Anne Parker's handbag. That, he had known.

Mindful of Palliser's small hunch, he went out to find Jerry Trenton. Trenton wasn't in his room and nobody knew where he might be; the landlady said nobody ever came to see him, he hadn't made friends with the other roomers; she thought he was looking for a job.

They had an A.P.B. out on Luke Abell, on Rhys.

And tomorrow was also a day. Mendoza went home.

Hackett came back on Saturday, and Rory Farrell sat at the switchboard in Lake's place. That was about all that was different on Saturday; except that Clevenger, Junior was calling in again, demanding to know what Homicide had found out, why they hadn't found out more, and implying they were all idiots. They seemed to be stymied, even at the routine, everywhere. Landers and Piggott were doggedly looking up the known muggers in Records, going out to find them, bringing them in to question when they could find them.

Palliser and Grace, pending the possible apprehension of Abell, should have been back on the Deforrest-Parker case, but there really wasn't anything else to do on that at all. They had talked to everybody who knew the women, there didn't seem to be any personal motive possible, and there was just nothing else to do on it.

At ten minutes to six on Saturday afternoon, Hackett came into Mendoza's office and said, "I think we throw Deforrest-Parker into Pending, Luis. It's dead." He felt his nose.

"I still want to see that Trenton."

"John's hunch." Hackett felt his nose again. "Damn it, you know I think I've picked up George's cold. Damnation. I haven't had a cold in two years. Angel keeps me packed with vitamins—"

Mendoza told him that as a cop, of all people, he should know better than to pick up things that didn't belong to him. The inside phone rang on his desk and he lifted it. "Homicide, Mendoza."

"We seem to have somebody down here you want, Luis," said Goldberg and sneezed. "Couple of squad-car men just spotted him purse-snatching on the street. The name rang a faint bell and I looked, and you've got an A.P.B. out on him. One Luke Abell."

"Well, don't tell me things are starting to move again," said Mendoza. "Somebody'll be down to get him, thanks, Saul."

"Don't mention it." Goldberg sneezed again and hung up.

"So John and Jase can do a little overtime," said Mendoza.

Resignedly Palliser and Grace called their respective homes and said they'd be late. Resignedly Roberta and Virginia said they'd keep dinners hot and expect their spouses when they saw them. Cops' wives get used to these things.

Luke Abell, brought up to the Homicide office for questioning, was sullen. Palliser and Grace looked at him and felt tired. He was big and mean and stupid as hell, and if he could think two minutes ahead, to the consequences of any act, that was probably the limit.

It took them ten minutes to explain to him who and what they were talking about. He didn't know Rhys's name: never had.

They had, of course, read him the little card about his civil rights, asked if he understood; he just stared. "You know," said Grace aside, "even if he says he does, any smart defense lawyer could convince a jury he isn't capable of it. I mean, just like the lady said, we do all come all sorts. This one is from under a rock some place. By his pedigree and everything else."

"Well, we've got to try, Jase," said Palliser.

It was the car, finally, that seemed to penetrate his mind. They convinced him, after about half an hour, that they knew he'd driven that car, had driven it the latest time it had been driven. Another man's car. With the man dead in the back seat.

"My God, we've been going around in such circles," said Grace, "I don't remember if Ballistics pinpointed the gun. Did they?" Palliser didn't know either; with this one, it wasn't immediately important.

"Where did you meet the man? Pick up the car?" asked Grace. "Come on, Luke. We know you did. A white Impala, Luke. You know cars?"

He grunted at them. "Tha' car. I needed a ride home was all. I was drunk 'n' I needed a ride down home. From up Hollywood. I been see somebody there—guy I know—'n' he dint have no car— I needed a ride."

Rhys the rabbit would not have picked up a hitchhiker.

Well, you didn't need to be a rabbit to have the sense not to do that. "Where, Luke?" asked Grace patiently.

"I was drunk. I don' remember. I din' know hardly wha' I was doin'. Oh, yeah. I waited inna lot. By tha' movie house. I was drunk—don' take nothin' off no white man—he din' have no call—I on'y ast him for a ride, 'at's all—'n' he call me dirty nigger, say get away— I was drunk, you can' blame me f'r—"

They shrugged at each other. Even that incoherent admission might be tossed out by the court. Diminished responsibility? They took him down to the jail on Alameda and booked him in, set up the machinery for the warrant, asked for a search warrant on his room—he'd had on him a scrawled address where he'd hired a room just today.

On Sunday morning they looked up the Ballistics report: it pinpointed an old Iver-Johnson, a .22, one of several models. When they had a look at Abell's room, there it was, an Iver-Johnson 57 target revolver, old and badly cared for. "A wonder the thing didn't blow up in his hand," said Palliser, looking at it.

At least that was off their minds; and, what with Myra Rhys, another little surprise it had been.

Landers and Piggott were still plodding ahead with the routine on the muggers on Monday. Hackett, coughing and feeling his nose, was by then positive he had taken Higgins' cold. "I shouldn't be here breathing germs all over everybody," he said.

"I never," said Mendoza, "pick up colds." To the reminder that he'd picked up measles from the twins awhile back he only grunted. "I just wonder, Art, if it wouldn't be a smart idea to check back on all these station attendants. By where Lily was found, these are the likeliest ones for about ninety percent sure. A rapist killer doesn't get started, bang, all at once as an adult. Something might show in their backgrounds to give us a lead."

"Sure. Peeping Tom, stealing panties off the clothesline," said Hackett inattentively.

"I think we do that." For once, Mendoza had taken Sunday off; the four days' fussing and fuming about George had tired him. He got up now, and the inside phone rang on his desk.

"I just thought you'd like to know," said Captain Fletcher, "that that Porsche you've been agitating about has just showed up." He recited the plate-number: Lily Clevenger's Porsche. "It was tagged by a squad-car, overparked, an hour ago. On Wilshire just this side of the freeway."

"*¡Parece mentira!*" said Mendoza. "*Aguarda un momento* —same general neighborhood, *and* just after I'd been poking around down there."

"There's some clothes in it," said Fletcher. "Ladies' clothes. Evening dress, underwear, high-heeled satin shoes, mink stole—"

"*¡Por Dios!*" Listen, you keep your paws off it! I want the lab on it—"

And he still hadn't found Jerry Trenton to talk to. Palliser's hunch. Maybe? A very small hunch? L.A.P.D. Homicide told tales about Mendoza's hunches, but he knew there was a rationality behind feelings: some people, empathic people, had the valid hunches. To the intelligent man Palliser, with the empathy for people, he could say, Never overlook your feelings.

But what with finding Lily's Porsche, and a couple of new things turning up—among them another stripped and beaten body in Pershing Square on Monday night, which had Landers and Piggott talking to themselves—he never got switched back onto that until Tuesday morning. When Landers came in and said, "Damn it, I think I've picked up that cold from Hackett. There's just a feeling in my nose. I haven't had a cold in years. And this *thing*—another middle-aged man, also a bachelor, a George Rose, projectionist at a movie-theatre on Hill, and damn it, he also parked his car in the lot under Pershing Square—"

"*Extraño*," said Mendoza. And suddenly, for no reason, thought of Palliser's hunch and Jerry Trenton. It was nine-thirty; he got up, told Landers he'd see a report and think about it later, and went out.

Deforrest-Parker. A long way round they had gone. It had looked first like the personal thing: a Lesbian angle maybe. Then, no. Something else. Whatever. Anne Parker the nice quiet girl, mothered by the chance-met widow in the apartment upstairs. And really, the only thing at all out of the ordinary—and that not much—was that quite by chance, the day before, Anne Parker had run across an acquaintance from the home-town. Could it say anything? Unlikely.

He parked the Ferrari illegally in a red zone on that tired old street, Bimini Place. He rang the bell of the rooming house. The woman opened the door, a thin woman, hair tied up in a pink turban scarf. Mendoza asked for Trenton. "I dunno if he's in," she said. "Left rear upstairs."

But Mendoza's eyes had moved to the stair behind her. A young man just coming down, and by Palliser's description, the teletype from Ventura, Jerry Trenton. A good-looking young man, wavy hair, straight features, and he was neatly dressed in brown slacks, an open-collared white shirt. He came to the entrance hall; Mendoza said, "Mr. Trenton?" and produced the badge.

His eyes flickered. "I told the other cop," he said on a slight gasp. "I don't know anything about it. How should I? Anne —I just happened to meet her that day, say hello. I didn't *know* her. All I'm trying to do is play it straight—make a chance for myself—you have to keep—"

And in that split second, Mendoza knew: whatever the circumstance, the details, the little hunch had been valid. Another surprise.

He said softly, "Yes, Jerry? You don't know anything about it?"

"No, I don't. I told the other one— I didn't even know where she lived, I—"

"She was listed in the phone-book."

"I—no," he said. "I don't know anything about it—or about that other woman—with the gun— I never was there, I told the—"

"Then how did you know the other woman had a gun?" asked Mendoza conversationally. The ownership of the Hi-Standard hadn't been given to the press.

Trenton stared at him and his eyes moved. He said, "I was —just trying—to get back, do things straight— I never have any luck—"

"I think you'd better come back to my office and answer some questions, Jerry," said Mendoza gently.

And Trenton put both hands to his face and said in something like a sob, "*I never meant such a thing—I never meant—*"

14

HE DIDN'T make any trouble for Mendoza; he followed him
out docilely, the landlady staring after them. At the car he
said dully, "I knew I ought to come and tell. I only wanted to
stay straight. And it was—an accident." He rode down to
headquarters in silence and Mendoza didn't speak to him.

Palliser and Grace were off; Hackett was in, and Landers
typing a report. Mendoza jerked his head at Hackett, who
followed them down to an interrogation room. "Mr. Gerald
Trenton," said Mendoza for Hackett's benefit, and precisely
recited the rigmarole about civil rights. "Do you understand
that?" Trenton just nodded.

"I don't care about a lawyer," he said. "That's all right. I
just—hope a judge would understand—how it happened." He
looked at Mendoza. "You were right, I did look up her address. Anne's. She worked at that place, I didn't know but
what she might, you know, persuade them to hire me. I've
been straight, I want to stay—but it's hard to get a job, when
you haven't any experience except at washing dishes in a restaurant, and—and a record."

"So you went to see her about that? Why did you carry a
gun?" asked Mendoza. "You did, didn't you? A Ruger Single
Six?"

"That's what maybe nobody'd believe. Yes, sir, I did. I'd—
I'd had that gun since before I—decided to go straight. A pal

206

of mine kept it for me when I was at the sheriff's farm. And I had it on me—that night—because I was going to pawn it," said Trenton miserably. "Only by the time I decided, the pawn-shop was closed, it was after nine. So then I looked up Anne Parker's address and went there. She was nice—she was a nice girl, she asked me in, and she said she was sorry, she couldn't get them to give me a job there, she was just a steno. And then—and then—it *surprised* me so," said Trenton suddenly. "I just hope you believe me. It came to me all of a sudden that maybe she'd buy the gun off me—these days, a lot of women keep guns, all the burglaries—and I could show her how to use it if she didn't know." He was talking eagerly now, anxious to explain how it had happened. "I took out the gun, and I started to ask her if she'd like to buy it—I never thought she'd—but she started screaming, she jumped up and started throwing things at me, she knocked the coffee-table over—I was so *surprised*—it came to me afterward, when I brought the gun out I guess she thought I was going to hold her up or something—I never meant— She threw a vase at me and cut my head, I was just standing there—it all happened so fast, and then—oh, my God," and he buried his face in his hands.

"Just take it easy," said Hackett. "Then what?"

"I—it was all so *fast*. It all seemed to happen at once. Her screaming, thinking I was maybe—I couldn't've made her listen, to explain. I'm just standing there, I had the gun in my hand, sure, but furthest thing from my mind was—was— And this other woman comes running in, a big woman, and she had a gun and she was yelling too, and she fired right at me—I saw her aim the gun at me, I just, kind of, threw up my arm like, and—and the Ruger went off and— I wasn't aiming it! I didn't mean to fire it. It just— And then she came at me, the big woman, she hit me with the gun-butt, a big strong woman, I—I just wanted get away, and I only hit her once, shoved her off me really, not like hitting—and she fell—I guess she hit her head on the wall, the window-sill, I don't know." He was silent, and repeated, "I don't know. It all happened so fast, I was so surprised and—and scared, I guess. It was like—a kind of nightmare. And then all of a sudden everything quiet, and there's Anne lying there, I guess she's dead —her head—before God, the gun went off in my hand, that other woman shooting at me! And Anne— All I can think is, get away." He looked up at Mendoza. He said, "If she'd just —given me time—all I wanted to ask her, I want to sell this gun, maybe you'd buy it off me. But she—started screaming—"

Mendoza and Hackett looked at each other. They had listened to a lot of sob-stories, over the years, and they could separate the false from the real. It came to Mendoza suddenly that they'd been thinking vaguely of the Deforrest woman as beaten to death: actually what the autopsy had said was, depressed skull-fracture. No open wound; no mark left on wall or window-sill for the lab. And enough people had been killed by random bullets before now.

Trenton looked at them. "You going to call it murder? I know it's not much use to swear to you—"

"We'll think about that later," said Mendoza. "It might not be as bad as you think, Trenton. I think you're leveling with us. We'll have to book you in."

"All right," he said in a dragging voice. "I know. I was just trying to stay straight—and this had to— All right."

But when they talked it over later Hackett said, "That's very likely just the way it did happen, isn't it?"

"*De veras*. We can wonder if Anne Parker had heard from some mutual acquaintance about his pedigree, and when he brought out the gun leaped to the conclusion. And Deforrest upstairs—yes, the she-bear and her cub—leaping to the same conclusion. Women living alone, conscious of the crime rise." Mendoza brushed his moustache. "I think it's very likely that's exactly the way it happened, Art. I think I'll have a talk with the D.A.'s office. Trenton seems pretty determined on keeping straight. We might get it reduced to involuntary manslaughter." He laughed. "And on general principles, I do not approve of reduced charges in homicide cases, but here I think we could say that the victims—mmh—at least helped to trigger off the homicides. Lesson for all of us," he added sarcastically, "about not leaping to conclusions."

The lab report on the Porsche came up about noon. It didn't say much to help them. There were no liftable latent prints anywhere on the car, a lot of smudges was all. Which said that possibly somebody had been careful. The clothes had been neatly folded and stacked in the tiny rear compartment of the car: blue nylon and chiffon evening dress, nylon lingerie, stockings, satin slippers. Nothing else in the Porsche but a current copy of *Vogue*. Kleenex in the glove compartment, maps, miscellany. The lab had vacuumed the car and would analyze the results, but for the moment that was about it.

Mendoza swore. Somebody—the X on Lily Clevenger—had had the Porsche for nearly a week. Why? A very hot car once she'd been identified. Had X hoped she never would be, that he could somehow keep the car? Then, after Mendoza had asked questions at all those gas stations, the Porsche abandoned. That said, didn't it, that one of those stations must tie in? One of those night attendants?

Both the Clevengers had been calling daily demanding to know what Homicide was doing about Lily.

Late on Tuesday afternoon they had a new call, and Landers went out on it, while Piggott resignedly typed up yet another follow-up report on the muggers out of Records. No lead at all had showed up on Halsey and Rose. They were assuming provisionally that the same X was responsible for Byron Halsey and George Rose, but they might be wrong even there.

The new one was at the Greyhound Bus Station at Sixth

and Los Angeles Streets, and Landers looked at it with frustration and annoyance. A dead man in the gents' rest room, a neatly-dressed middle-aged man lying on the floor there with a butcher knife in his chest. Plenty of I.D. in an alligator billfold; he'd been a William K. Moberly of an address on Edgemont in Hollywood. Five ten-dollar bills in the billfold. And that was all.

The ticket seller didn't recognize him. Nobody else in the place recognized him.

Landers swore and called in for a mobile lab unit.

Just after the call from the Greyhound station came in, there was a call from a squad-car on Bixel Street. Glasser was out on something else; Hackett went over to see what it was.

It wasn't, for Homicide, anything much: another senior citizen getting tired and taking the quick way out. In this case, the gas. The Fire Department was there, the building had been evacuated temporarily, and it was awhile before Hackett was let in. When he was, he found it depressing: an old man dead in bed, the note left propped on the bureau. A grammatical note in a neat hand: when they came to look, they found among other things a notebook full of press-cuttings. J. Presly Freeman, it seemed, had been an actor of some prominence in days gone by, but the water had rolled under the bridge, he'd had two operations for cancer and he was broke, and his principles prohibited him from applying for welfare. Finis.

Hackett went back to the office and told Mendoza about that. "And more power to him. Damn it, Luis, I feel like hell. I've got that cold all right. My throat's raw, and I've been sneezing— I'm going home."

He went home and called the house on Silver Lake Boulevard while Angel mixed up a hot drink of lemon and whiskey. "How's George?"

"Oh, he's fine," said Mary warmly. "Just fine. He's got his

voice back, and he's eating like a horse and feeling almost like himself again."

"Well, bully for him," said Hackett. "Let me talk to him. . . . I just thought you'd like to know," he said to Higgins, "that adding insult to injury doesn't cover it by a damn sight. After making all of us worry ourselves into ulcers over you— vanishing into thin air—for four days, you show up again and generously pass your damn cold on. Probably to the whole office. I've got it for certain, and Tom thinks he has too. Damn you."

"Have you?" said Higgins. "Well, I'm sorry, Art, but you'd better blame Luis. And your own curiosity."

"What the hell do—"

"He will drive that hot sports number with barely room for one passenger. And you were so anxious to hear about my adventures you would come along. Me breathing germs all over you. Has he got it?"

"Not yet," said Hackett hopefully. "I'm keeping my fingers crossed."

On Wednesday the results of the checks on those station attendants started coming in, and it was all negative. Not one of them showed up in L.A.'s records, and further queries had been directed at the F.B.I. Mendoza fidgeted around waiting for some results on that; as Art said, the rapist-killer didn't get that way all of a sudden, there was almost always a list of lesser sex offenses preceding.

There was no sign of Hackett by nine o'clock, when Mendoza called the house in Highland Park. "Well, he wouldn't be any use to you, Luis," said Angel amusedly. "He's lost his voice. But completely. That was quite a cold George brought back from Nevada. I've got Art on fruit juices and various other things, and I don't suppose he'll be in the rest of the week. Who else has got it?"

"I never take colds," said Mendoza. "Landers, I think. Give

him my sympathy, but if we mention adding insult to injury—"

"That's what Art said before he lost his voice," said Angel.

By noon on Tuesday Landers had been certain he had that damn cold. His throat felt scratchy, and he was sneezing and blowing his nose. "Lemonade with whiskey," said Piggott. "Medicinal purposes only—it's the best thing."

"I don't think I've got any lemons," said Landers, feeling sorry for himself. As a bachelor he didn't ordinarily mind getting the scratch meals for himself; but when a man was sick he needed somebody to take care of him. He wasn't hungry, and left half his lunch. "Damn it," he said, "you know we'll never catch up to this mugger, Matt. It might have been any one of them out of records we've talked to already. Not one damned lead—"

There was also Mr. Moberly, in the bus station with the knife in him; no leads there either. He hadn't lived at the Edgemont Avenue apartment long; nobody knew what his job was, or if he had had any relatives, or why anybody wanted to stick a knife in him.

"Satan going up and down," said Piggott. "But we have to keep on at the uphill job, Tom. The good guys against the bad guys." Tomorrow night was choir practise and he'd see that nice girl Prudence Russell.

"I guess," said Landers dispiritedly. At least tomorrow was his day off.

"Damn it," said Mendoza that Wednesday noon, to Palliser and Grace over lunch, "that's got to be a valid lead! Everything says so. The idiot boy and the lost horse— I went and looked. Considering where the body was left, it happened in the downtown area somewhere—*¿cómo no?* All right. There were six stations that looked likelier to me than any others— stations open to midnight—nearest the off-ramps roughly downtown that Lily might have taken, noticing the tank was nearly empty. I look at those night attendants—a couple looked likelier than the others—I check back on them. And what shows? *¡Nada, absolutamente!*" He swallowed rye angrily.

"So you missed the right station," said Palliser.

"*Estúpido*. No. I refuse to believe she stopped as far off as New Chinatown—or a mile past the freeway exchange—with the body at Figueroa and Olympic, near as makes no difference. We know now it *was* a gas station." They did. Taking its own sweet time as it usually did, the lab had finally come up with a thorough analysis of the residue of grease present on Lily Clevenger's body: it had contained dirty motor oil, like that drained from an engine during a change of oil, gasoline, cement particles, axle-grease and a faint trace of transmission fluid. The evening dress bore a few similar stains, as did the slippers. Lily had, in fact, probably been undressed and raped on the pavement at some gas station.

"And just after I've been asking questions at all those stations, the Porsche is abandoned. Tell me that's not significant!" said Mendoza. "Hidden in somebody's garage up to then—at least after we had the plate-number on the hot list. Probably since the murder, because X wouldn't know when that was. Or Traffic'd have spotted it. And I get this—this nothing from the check. These spotless innocent souls. Not only are none of them in records, that Bernie Wolf has three decorations for bravery from the Navy. *¡Por Dios!*"

"Not in our records," said Grace soothingly. "Maybe in somebody's. The Feds will tell you."

"That Moberly is another funny one," said Palliser. "I was talking to Landers, he said the man might have dropped from Mars—not a lead on him anywhere, nobody's got his prints, nobody knows him. And by the way, Landers has definitely got the cold, he said he probably wouldn't be in tomorrow. Or the rest of the week, likely."

"Which is something else," said Mendoza. "Insult to injury, George bringing home the cold." He was telling himself defiantly that he felt quite all right: the faint scratchiness in his throat was just from too much smoking, that was all. "Wait for the F.B.I., sure—but I take no bets. *Pares o nones.* The way things have been going lately—"

He went back to his office and got out the deck of cards and began to practise crooked deals. He remembered suddenly about ten minutes later that somebody—the station manager—had said that one of those night attendants had just got out of the Army. Which one? Lederer. He had looked clean and clear, but—being thorough, Mendoza told Lake to shoot a query to Army Intelligence. *¡Qué demonios!* he thought. Probably be told the fellow had won the Medal of Honor.

All that had to be significant—or did it? Sometimes coincidence took a hand. The surprises they'd had just lately—

Landers called in at two o'clock on Wednesday. He could only speak in a hoarse whisper, and he said not to expect to see him the rest of the week. Lake was sympathetic. No, he said, he hadn't any symptoms yet; but look on the bright side, if he did get it he might lose a few pounds. Landers sneezed and hung up.

Mendoza was still shuffling the cards at his desk. Grace came in at two-thirty and said he'd just run across something queer, and he didn't think it meant anything but he'd like Mendoza's opinion.

"*¿Qué ocurre?*"

"Well, it can't mean anything," said Grace rather plaintively, his brown face pensive. "But they knew each other—Byron Halsey and George Rose. The two men mugged in Pershing Square. They were both bachelors, but they had friends of course and I just ran across a fellow Rose worked with who said he and Halsey were old friends, used to have dinner together at this cafeteria on Ninth Street, four or five times a week."

"*¿Pues, y qué?*" said Mendoza. "That is funny, Jase, but what the hell could it say?"

"I can't imagine," said Grace, and Palliser came in in a hurry, the long yellow sheet of a teletype in his hand.

"You really do have a crystal ball, don't you?" he said, looking at Mendoza. "The idiot boy and the lost horse, my God."

"What have I done now?"

"Hit a jackpot." Palliser handed over the teletype. "This just came through." Grace moved to read it over Mendoza's shoulder.

"*¡Válgame Dios!*" said Mendoza, reading it. "*¡De lo lindo!* But—I didn't call this shot, John. It was just a stray afterthought. I thought he was the unlikeliest, of the whole lot. I really did."

The teletype emanated from Army Intelligence. James Francis Lederer had just been discharged from the Army after ten years in, sure enough; but the last eight years he had spent serving a military sentence for a murder committed in Germany where he'd been stationed: the rape murder of a German girl, assaulted on a city street.

He had just reported on the job, at the chain station on Sixth Street, when Mendoza and Palliser arrived in Palliser's Rambler to pick him up. He looked so much the responsible, trustworthy citizen: tall and dark, good shoulders, frank gaze, neatly dressed.

When Mendoza approached him he looked a little surprised, not nervous. "Did you think we wouldn't ask the Army, Mr. Lederer?" said Mendoza. "Eventually? We're not that stupid, you know—we can reason from A to B to C. We had it figured she'd noticed the gas was low and got off the freeway to find a station open. It was really only a question of elimination before we found the station. You'll come in with us and answer some questions now."

Lederer let out a long sigh. "Yes," he said expressionlessly.

The station manager, serving a car pulled up to the pumps, was watching curiously, recognizing Mendoza; now, the hose attached and gas running, he came up wiping his hands on a paper towel. "What you want with Jim?" he asked. "I told you—"

"So you did," said Mendoza. "All you knew. What you didn't know was that he's just finished serving time for a military murder charge—and he's probably just done another right here in your station. All right, Lederer, let's go." He looked back at the other man, who wore an expression compounded of incredulity and horror. "I'm sorry, you'll have to find another reliable night attendant."

They stood over him and asked questions, Mendoza and Palliser and Grace, in an interrogation room at headquarters. He was very quiet; he didn't say much for a long time. Mendoza explained to him again, patiently, how they had reasoned out what had happened to Lily Clevenger. Now they knew his record, they could guess the rest.

"Come on, Jim," said Palliser, "tell us about it."

He looked up slowly and said in a mild voice, "That's not my name, you know. My name's Bill Storey. They wouldn't have let me in the Army, by my right name, and I thought the Army'd maybe be a good place to—to try to change. I said I'd never been fingerprinted before, when I joined, and I guess they don't check. So many men in the Army."

"You had a record as Storey?" asked Mendoza.

He nodded. "But I found out—it's not a thing you change. It's—something in a man. I don't know— I guess I've always been a loner— I'm not bad-looking either, but I guess that don't mean much. I've never—I'm no good at getting girls to like me, I don't know how. It—I didn't mean to do it. That time, or—or this time. I'm sorry about it."

"Too late, Jim," said Mendoza, and he nodded again.

"I know. I know. But she—was—so—beautiful. Wasn't she? Wasn't she? It was after half-past eleven she drove in. So beautiful. Smiling at me so nice. I started the pump going and while I was washing the windshield I couldn't help—looking at her, wanting—and I thought, it was late, there wouldn't be any other customers, there wasn't anybody around at all, and who'd know— It came to three-eighty-five, she give me a five, and just then I saw how to do. I went into the office, like I was getting her change, and I turned out all the station lights when I went in the door—switches just inside, and only three switches turns 'em all out. And I—she was surprised, just that minute I get the door open and—and pull her out. I—had—to— She was so beautiful. Acourse she fought me some, but I was stronger. We got—you know, your hands dirty all the time, work around the station—this big roll of paper towels on top o' the pump, I grabbed a handful to make like a gag, she shouldn't yell—"

"We can guess the rest but let's hear it all," said Mendoza as he fell silent.

They didn't. After a while he said, "It's like bein' drunk. A little. I just don't know what I'm doin'. Those times. After-wards, I— I was just—so—terrible sorry. A beautiful thing like that and I don't know how or why but she's dead—"

"You didn't mean to make her dead, Jim?" said Mendoza. "She'd have accused you, you know, if she wasn't."

"I never think of that," he said. "No. Right then. I never meant her to be dead, no. But she was. And I was sorry about that too—all over dirty grease from the cement where— I tried to get her clean, with the hose, I didn't like her bein' all dirty like that—and her clothes, I put them in the car—"

"She was wearing a ring," said Mendoza quietly. "A big diamond ring. What did you do with it?"

He reached slowly into his pocket and brought it out—Lily Clevenger's one-carat diamond solitaire engagement ring. "I took it—sort of as a memento," he said. "I guess. She was—the most beautiful—thing I ever saw. I didn't know where to put her. I wouldn't have left her—that dirty alley—but there was a police car come along just as I turned in there and I was afraid—it was late, no traffic—after it went by I just—just put her there and—drove away."

"In her Porsche."

"It's a nice car," he said. "I rented one, awhile back, in Germany. It handles nice. I wasn't thinking just so straight. I thought maybe you'd never find out who she was, never know she'd had a car. I could keep it. But when you came—" He looked at Mendoza.

"But we'd found out who she was before that, Jim. She was in all the newspapers. Didn't you—"

"I don't read too good," he said. "I don't bother look at the papers. I was awful sorry, but—times—it's just, I don't know what I'm doin', and that's a fact."

Mendoza saw the Clevengers, father and son, on Thursday. They looked at him with grieved and bitter eyes and few words; there wasn't much Mendoza could say to them either.

"Is he legally insane?" asked Lily's husband.

Mendoza shrugged. "For the doctors. I don't know. It's a thin line, Mr. Clevenger. If you want my opinion, he's not. But I think he'll probably end up in Atascadero." With the criminally insane.

"To get let out how soon?" said Clevenger.

"Not quite so easy from there. And he'd have to stand trial. I know how you feel—"

"Do you?" said Clevenger. "You haven't had your wife raped and murdered, Lieutenant."

And Mendoza's mind jumped back four and a half years to a rather eventful night, and his mouth went flat and he said,

"*Claro que no*. I got there just in time, if I smashed up a twenty-thousand-buck car to do it. Never mind, I know how you feel. Just be grateful we got him."

The Clevengers had nothing to say to that.

And Landers was still in bed in his bachelor apartment, nursing the cold. Hackett got his voice back on Thursday, Angel informed Alison, but was hardly fit to go back to the office. Maybe by Monday.

Mendoza went on firmly telling himself that he'd just been smoking too much. He wasn't hungry for lunch, which he was looking at rather distastefully when Palliser and Grace came up to join him.

"Damn it," said Palliser, "I think I've got the damned cold now."

"Use the will power," advised Grace. "And that continues to bug me, you know—the fact that Halsey and Rose knew each other. One of the waitresses at that cafeteria—"

"They don't have waitresses at cafeterias," said Palliser, coughing experimentally.

"Yes, they do. To collect the dishes and carry trays for people. Her name's Betty Fellows. She'd heard them talking, and she says they came from the same town. Red Bluff, up-state. But it can't be important, can it?"

"No," said Mendoza. "They both parked their cars under Pershing Square, so the mugger, lying in wait, pounced on them there."

"I suppose you're right," said Grace. "It was just a little surprise—"

Piggott said on Friday morning that his throat felt a little raw and he hoped he hadn't caught that cold. Piggott was not a swearing man, but his pause was suggestive.

Nothing else suggested any lead whatever on anything. Moberly, the man at the bus station, continued to pose a mystery. They now had another unidentified corpse, male, and Piggott said it was time to throw Halsey and Rose into Pending.

Mendoza went up to Federico's for lunch with Palliser and Grace, and even a drink raised no appetite in him. He felt hot, his throat was raw, and he had definitely picked up the cold. If not directly from Higgins, from somebody else he'd breathed the germs on.

"You feel all right?" asked Palliser. "I don't. I think I'd better stay home tomorrow."

Mendoza naturally said he felt quite all right; he was using the will power on it. And the routine that went on forever continued to go on, without much result. At five-twenty they had a call to a brawl in a bar out on Washington, at least one corpse by what the squad-car men said. Glasser and Grace went out on it.

Mendoza took down the wide-brimmed black Homburg and went out to the anteroom. "I'm going home, Jimmy," he said. "Providence—or whatever—isn't being kind to us."

"I think," said Lake, "I've picked up that cold. My throat—"

"¡Por Dios!" said Mendoza. "Half the office down with it eventually. And I just talked to George awhile ago, and he's feeling fine. ¡Naturalmente!"

He came in the back door of the house on Rayo Grande Avenue. His household looked just as usual and sounded just as usual. All four of the cats were weaving around Máiri MacTaggart's legs explaining that it was their usual dinner time and hadn't anybody remembered? Alison was supervising the twins' supper at the kitchen table. Cedric the accidentally acquired shaggy dog came politely to offer an enormous paw in greeting. "¡Bufón cortés!" said Mendoza, accepting it, and everybody looked up to notice he'd come home.

"You'll be wanting a dram before dinner," said Máiri, hurrying to pour it. El Señor understood English and leaped to the countertop eagerly.

"*Amador*—" Alison got up, and he kissed her.

"Daddy—Daddy read *el cuento* before bed— *El Gato!*" shouted Johnny.

"No *Gato—el elefante pequeño!*" shouted Terry.

And Mendoza said, "*El Padre* is a weak reed, *niños. Mi hermosa*, I've got that damn cold. *¡Condenación!* I feel like hell. My throat—and I'm not hungry, but a drink might—"

"*¡Pobrecito!*" said Alison in concern. "Some hot lemon and whiskey—you'd better go straight to bed. Now, you two, let your father alone—"

Mendoza sneezed. "Yes, I've got it all right. And really, *cara*, you talking about a vow to use the English only—"

"Well, something's got to be done," said Alison absently. "Terry—Johnny—*¡Bastante ya! ¡Caray!* Quiet! I'll get you some aspirin, *hermoso*. All George's fault, getting himself kidnapped—"

And Higgins would say to that, adding insult to injury with a vengeance.